Praise for *Not Me*

"A gripping mediation about the fluidity of identity."
—Baltimore *Sun*

"A compelling portrait of shame, guilt and redemption . . . One's sympathies are torn this way and that while reading this novel because Lavigne does the near-impossible: He manages to put a human face on someone who worked with the abhorred SS. . . . Vastly credible."
—*Rocky Mountain News*

"Goes against the grain—in a positive, literary manner . . . pushes us to deal with the humanity of one justifiably banished from our sympathies . . . by forcing us to not simply succumb to the allure of the reprobate, but to care."
—*San Francisco Chronicle*

"Lavigne carves a new portal into the depthless mystery of the Holocaust."
—*Booklist* (starred review)

"Captivating . . . highly recommended."
—*Library Journal*

"Crisply written and never less than engaging."
—*Kirkus Reviews*

"Always interesting . . . From the first page *Not Me* holds the reader's interest. . . . A novel that raises all kinds of moral and philosophical questions surrounding the Shoa."
—*New Jersey Jewish News*

"Suspenseful . . . In his examination of identity, Lavigne raises issues ranging from adoption to Zionism, euthanasia to ennui. . . . This remarkably original novel was no doubt written in anguish in order to process the Holocaust and share some thoughts—many of them very interesting and painfully honest."

—*The Jewish News Weekly of Northern California*

"Michael Lavigne has an immensely powerful story to tell of guilt and redemption. Beyond its riveting plot, *Not Me* is a novel about the loss and recovery of love. In this sense it reminded me of Dickens's *Great Expectations:* Heshel Rosenheim is as mysterious and haunting as Magwitch, and the lesson that his uncanny life imparts to his son, and to Lavigne's readers, is on a grand human scale, and unforgettable."

—JONATHAN WILSON, author of *A Palestine Affair*

"What a daring, even dangerous, act of the imagination this novel is! *Not Me* challenges one emotionally and intellectually. It's that rare phenomenon: a philosophical thriller that will draw you in and leave you arguing furiously with yourself after you're done."

—RON ROSENBAUM, author of *Explaining Hitler*

"A disturbing yet surprisingly tender read that grips the reader from page one and never lets go. Michael Lavigne tells his intriguing story with intelligence, sensitivity, and flashes of scintillating wit. What more could you ask from a novel?"

—AARON HAMBURGER, author of *Faith for Beginners*

"A disturbing and important meditation on the question of identity. But *Not Me* is more than that. It's a pleasure to read. The suspense is there on every page."

—ARNON GRUNBERG, author of
Blue Mondays and *Phantom Pain*

NOT ME

not me

a novel

MICHAEL LAVIGNE

RANDOM HOUSE TRADE PAPERBACKS

NEW YORK

This is a work of fiction. Though some characters, incidents and dialogues are based on the historical record, the work as a whole is a product of the author's imagination.

2007 Random House Trade Paperback Edition

Published in the United States by Random House Trade Paperbacks, an imprint of The Random House Publishing Group, a division of Random House, Inc., New York.

Originally published in hardcover in the United States by Random House, an imprint of The Random House Publishing Group, a division of Random House, Inc., in 2005.

ISBN 978-0-8129-7332-7

Library of Congress Cataloging-in-Publication Data

Lavigne, Michael.
Not me : a novel / Michael Lavigne.
p. cm.
ISBN 978-0-8129-7332-7
1. Alzheimer's disease—Patients—Fiction. 2. Holocaust, Jewish (1939–1945)—Fiction. 3. Parent and adult child—Fiction. 4. Terminally ill parents—Fiction. 5. Fathers and sons—Fiction. 6. Jewish families—Fiction. 7. Philanthropists—Fiction. 8. Jewish men—Fiction. 9. Comedians—Fiction. 10. Ex-Nazis—Fiction. I. Title.
PS3612.A94425N68 2005
813'.6—dc22 2004051496

Printed in the United States of America

www.thereaderscircle.com

8 9

For my father and Sam; and,
of course, for Gayle

Every question possesses a power
that does not lie in the answer.

—ELIE WIESEL

NOT ME

CHAPTER 1

The last person in the world I wanted to know about was my father. I did not want to know if he had lovers. I did not want to know if he took diuretics. I certainly did not want to know if he liked to masturbate, or if, even occasionally, he fantasized about teenage boys. It was of absolutely no interest to me if he cheated at bridge, or if his secret ambition was to become a ballet dancer, or if he had an obsession with women's shoes, or if he washed his body with lemon, or if he hit my mother (especially, God forbid, if she liked it). So when I was presented with twenty-four volumes of journals, each bound with a rubber band so old it was as brittle as the leather cover it held together, and was told, "These are your father's, take them," I was less than enthusiastic. Especially since it was my father who gave them to me.

"These are your father's," he said, "take them."

"Dad," I said, "*you* are my father."

He looked at me quizzically. His eyes were like aspic. Cloudy. Beneath which something obscure, unappetizing.

"Where's Karen?" he asked.

"Karen is dead," I reminded him.

"That's not true," he said. "She was just here. I was speaking to her. Take these."

With his feet, he pushed the box of journals toward my chair.

"All right," I said, "I'll take them. But I won't read them."

Then he turned away, and looked out the window.

"I'm waiting for Frau Hellman," he said.

"Okay, Dad," I said. I had no idea who Frau Hellman was. Maybe someone from his childhood, or maybe his name for the lady who washed him.

After a little while I realized he had forgotten I was in the room. The space between us seemed to grow as if I were standing on a dock, and he were sailing away on the *Queen Mary*. I say the *Queen Mary* because he once actually did sail away on her, and I really was left behind, waving. Still, it was unthinkable that I would have a troubled relationship with my father. If I was not the perfect son, he was certainly the perfect father.

I reminded myself of that as I sat there looking at him drooling, his head lolling back like a toddler's asleep in his car seat.

"He's doing just great, isn't he?" the station nurse said. "We just love him!"

I held out the box to her. "Where did he get these? They weren't in his room before."

"I don't know. I think someone brought them."

"Who brought them?"

"He has so many visitors."

"He does?"

"You know how popular he is!"

Actually, I didn't know he knew anybody. I thought everybody he knew was dead. I thanked Nurse Clara—her name was emblazoned on her ample, nurturing breast—and walked out into the brutal Florida heat. The car was only a few steps away, but I might as well have been crossing the Amazon River. By the time I got there, my shirt was soaked and my legs were sticking together. I turned on the air-conditioning in the Caddy, but had to wait outside for the temperature to drop—the car was an oven. In my arms was the box of journals. They weighed me down painfully. Finally I sank into the plush leather seat and let the frigid jets cool my face, my underarms. I tugged my shirt away from my body to let the air caress my stomach with its icy fingers. I sighed in relief. I put the shift in reverse, and pulled out of the spot. It's amazing how long a Caddy will last, particularly if you never drive it. Dad bought his in '78. I looked down at the odometer. It had twenty-two thousand miles on it. And I had to admit it was comfortable, bobbing down the road on those marshmallow shocks, riding on tires of Jell-O. Like the kiddy-car rides he used to take me on before I graduated to the bumper cars and roller coasters. I recalled how I used to be embarrassed being seen in it, especially when my dad drove twenty miles an hour in a forty-mile zone. But not anymore. His Caddy was now the coolest thing going, only he would never know it. As far as he was concerned we still had the 1952 Studebaker. If he kept regressing on schedule, in another couple of weeks he'd be curled up with a bottle in the back of his father's '23 Daimler.

I pulled out of the parking lot and turned onto Military Trail. All the roads in West Palm Beach County look the same. Six lanes. No curves. Fast food. And every few feet the entrance to some development. The Lakes. The Bonaventure. The Greens. Everything had a *The* in it. They liked the word *The*. They also liked the word *at*. The Villages *at* The Palms. The Fairways *at* The Willows. I turned left at The Turn *at* Lake Worth Avenue.

The box of journals was sitting there beside me, sort of the way Mom used to sit next to Dad, waiting for an accident to happen. But unlike her, they smelled bad—musty and moldy, decayed. Well, maybe she smelled that way now, too, I thought. But I shook that away. I didn't know why my mind let such thoughts sneak in. I hated when that happened. But it was just part of being a comic. You always think funny. For instance, the box they were in—I noticed it was a Cheez Whiz box. This made me laugh. This is what Father chose to contain his life's writings? I also noticed the logo was different than it is now. So it was a really old box. He'd been working at this a long, long time. Saving this stuff up, just for this moment. His patrimony. Since he had no money, maybe he thought I could get it published or something. Why would he think that? He ran a wallpaper store all his life. Who would want to read about that?

I was jolted suddenly, by someone honking the horn. I looked up and the guy passed me, making a fist. I glanced down at the speedometer. I was doing twenty in a forty-mile zone. For some reason this did not strike me as funny—and I stepped on the gas.

I pulled up to his building at The Ponds at Lakeshore and turned off the engine. There were only American cars in the lot, primarily Cadillacs and Buicks, and most of them had American flags on them. A gaggle of women were standing near the entrance. They were all small. How did they get so small? I wondered. They had to be less small once upon a time. Will Ella be that small one day? She's five-eight now—could she end up four-ten? I stepped out of the car, thinking I would just leave the journals in the front seat for a while, but I knew I couldn't. I would have to take them upstairs. But I thought: Wait. How come they weren't in the apartment in the first place? I didn't remember ever seeing them there. I didn't remember him ever speaking about them. I didn't remember him ever working on them, for that matter. Why would they suddenly appear at the nursing home? Why wouldn't he just say, there are journals in the closet at home—I want you to read them?

The box suddenly looked even more dangerous to me. Poisonous. Like a scorpion that had crawled into my sleeping bag. I went around the other side and picked it up. It had to have been stored in a basement or attic—it had that smell to it, like damp earth. I thought: shouldn't I remember *something* about this? How could he have written twenty-four volumes without my ever having noticed? Maybe they were someone else's journals. Maybe he only thought they were his. That was possible. Totally possible. Sometimes he thought I was some cousin or someone named Israel—so why not?

I walked past the little ladies, and they all said hello. I said hello back and got into the elevator. I heard someone say, that was Gladys's son. No, someone else said, that's Rose's.

They never mentioned the men. The men had no children. Only the women. And anyway, my mother's name was Lily.

The elevator smelled like an indoor swimming pool. It crawled slowly up the side of the building like a dying man clawing his way out of a hole. It was only four floors, but in San Francisco I'd already be at the top of the Transamerica Pyramid. At least it was air-conditioned. But then the door opened onto the hall—which was no hall, it was actually a kind of gangway stuck on the outside of the building like an exposed rib—and the heat hit me again. I could feel rivers of moisture forming on my arms where the box rubbed against them. As always, it was a struggle to open the door. Finally, though, I stepped inside, shut the heat behind me, and put the box down on the dining room table. I went to the refrigerator and made myself a seltzer.

Then I picked up the phone to call Ella, but then I didn't.

You call because you want to connect, but you don't connect, you can never connect, you can't wait to hang up, you hang up, you feel utterly alone—like you're stuck in the bottom of a swimming pool and can't hear anything except your own breathing. The thing is, you see, it's the words. It's just like a stand-up routine, or a sermon maybe. You work hard on the words, and you think the words say it, but actually it's the delivery, and the delivery is in your body, your eyes, the fact that someone is right there in front of you and even if you can't see them as individuals, it's that you smell them, you sense their bodies there, it's physical, it's visceral.

But then why do comedy albums work? And radio? Not to mention things that are written, like, say, the Talmud? My theory was hopeless, and I knew it.

Anyway what would I say to her?

She was oddly vexed that I'd come out here again. "If you'd pay as much attention to your son as you do your father . . ." she said when I first told her, but then she just let herself drift into silence. "By the time I get there he might not even recognize me," I'd tried to explain. But I doubted she heard me, since she'd already hung up.

I supposed I could tell her about the box. I could ask her if she remembered anyone named Frau Hellman. Then I could ask her what she thought I ought to do.

"I don't know," she would say. "I'm not sure." She didn't like to make decisions for me. At least not since the divorce.

If I told her I didn't think I wanted to read them, she would say, "That's fine." If I said I was going to read them, she'd say, "That's fine," too.

Really, when you think about it, you don't have to have actual conversations with people you know well.

Also if I called, what if Josh answered? I couldn't face him just then. I wasn't sure why. And why was my own father suddenly so desperate to talk to *me*—now when he didn't even know what year it was. I looked over at the Cheez Whiz box. All its little advertising slogans seemed more like curses and portents than inducements to slather some spread on a cracker.

I finished my seltzer, marveling at the tenacity of that generation of Jews to hold on to its old habits. How many places in the world could you still get seltzer delivered to your door?

I fixed myself a little sandwich and sat down at the dining room table. On the wall directly above my head was a tapestry of the Old City of Jerusalem—bright, tacky colors, somewhat abstract, and obviously made in Israel. In the living room just beyond, the walls seemed festooned with Judaica—fiddlers on roofs, flying goats, old, bearded men wrapped in prayer shawls, framed calligraphic paper cutouts of Hebrew letters. On the bookshelves were innumerable *tchotchkes*—cloisonné ashtrays in the shape of menorahs, ritual spice boxes, candlesticks, commemorative Israeli coins set off in black velvet, a sterling silver–covered Passover Haggadah (also made in Israel), and on the top shelf, standing like the guardian of all that is Jewish, the Hanukkah menorah—which in fact was surrounded by four lesser menorahs, all of which were given to my father in honor of some achievement for the Temple Men's Club, or the B'nai B'rith, or AIPAC. There were photos stuck among the books, too—of Mom on the Hadassah Executive, the Sisterhood, and the ladies from ORT. Of Dad shaking hands with Elie Wiesel. Of Dad shaking hands with Natan Sharansky. Of Dad shaking hands with Golda Meir. (That was his favorite—it hung on the wall in a big frame, right between my sixth-grade school portrait and Karen, two months old, naked on a blanket.)

I think it got worse once they moved down to Florida. In New Jersey it was more prints of famous paintings—Rembrandt, van Gogh, Picasso. The books on the shelves didn't seem so relentlessly Hebraic. A Stephen King novel or two. *Valley of the Dolls*. And all the things we kids brought home that had to be displayed:

drawings, ceramics, term papers, birthday cards. But even then, the Jewish paraphernalia seemed to swallow up everything like kudzu, and by the time I left for college, my parents' house could have been mistaken for the temple gift shop. It was funny, really. I used it as material for one of my best routines.

But now as I sat there regarding the Cheez Whiz box of leather-bound diaries, and hearing somewhere not too far away the laconic song of a bull alligator emerging from the canal that cut through the eighth fairway of The Ponds at Lakeshore golf course, and picking up the aroma from next door, or perhaps from the floor below, of brisket simmering in the Dutch oven, and noting as well that Mrs. Eagleberg, several doors down, had reached that point in the day when she spoke to her daughter in Chicago as if there were no telephone line connecting them, so loudly did she elucidate the machinations of her bowels and the tribulations of her swollen ankles—all these things filled me with a terrible longing.

They were gone. They were all gone. First it was my sister, Karen. Suddenly one day she had ovarian cancer. Everyone was screaming, Why wasn't it diagnosed? What was the matter with those doctors? And then they were blaming each other—my parents, I mean. Why did you always have to pick on her? Me? I never picked on her—you picked on her! She always had to be the best, you could never accept a B. It had to be an A. An A+. But that was you, my dear, not me. And so on and so forth. And all the while the operations, the chemo, the alternative treatments. The yoga. The fruit diet. Reflexology. I even tried the laugh treatment on her. I showed her funny movies. I told her funny jokes. Then she was gone.

After her it was my mother. And very quickly too, or so it seemed to us, even though a decade passed between them. I remember my father saying, "They were like peas in a pod." Mom just dropped dead playing mahjongg. At the pool. On a Wednesday morning. In her one-piece floral bathing suit, the kind with the little skirt on it, for modesty. Her hat slipped off and fell into the pool. It was a detail that everyone seemed to notice, and each of her mahjongg partners individually reported this to me, usually in a whisper, and usually with tears. *And Michael, her hat slipped off just at that moment, and fell in the water, and floated to the other side.* I would hold their hands and nod. It was so solemn, so filled with portent. I had no idea why.

And now it was my father. He had already been going for quite a while. Even before Mom died. But now, he had pretty much disappeared. Not every day. Not every moment. But mostly. And it wasn't just the Alzheimer's. He'd pretty much stopped eating a couple of weeks before. Nobody had to tell me what that meant. His hat had fallen off, and when it landed in the water he'd be gone for good.

All right, I said to myself, but in his voice—Heshel Rosenheim, you want I should read your diary, I'll read your goddamned diary.

CHAPTER 2

I have always known that my father was born in Germany and that he spent several unspeakable years in the concentration camps, and that after the war he met my mother in New York and they married after only a few months, having experienced love at first sight. But when I opened the first of the journals I was nevertheless surprised that it was written in German. I knew how much he hated that language, the very sound of it would make him cringe and cover his ears. Still, it was the language of his youth. He had come from an assimilated family, a family of intellectuals—my grandfather had taught philology and German literature—or perhaps it was something else—at a university—I think in Berlin, but possibly somewhere else—I was never clear on this—and my father grew up in a strictly German environment. He always told me how he did not speak Yiddish as a child, but learned it in the camps, where he also, as he put it, learned "the language of Shakespeare" from a friend of his—a device to keep their minds active—and so all his English was peppered with Yiddishisms. When he didn't want me to understand, he spoke to my mother in Yiddish. Jewish, he called it. But I knew for him it was also the language of suffering, which is why he studied and mastered Hebrew during his first years in America.

I would have lived in Israel, he said many times, nodding sadly, but your mother wouldn't go.

Instead they visited many times over the years. And gave money. Sometimes I could not understand why they gave so much and then would tell me that they couldn't afford to buy me a new bicycle, or send me to camp for the summer. I always had to go for two weeks. Everyone else went for four. I began to resent all this Jewish fervor. Though in later years it served me as an endless well to draw from.

Anyway, the first journal I picked up was in German, and I could see how naturally the writing flowed, how elegant, even, was the hand; an old-fashioned Teutonic script, like you see in war documents, in Nazi archives, and I have to say it sent a shudder down my spine. And yet I knew it was my father's handwriting, because I had seen him write this way when he helped me with my own studies in German. I had decided in college that I wanted to be a philosopher, so I took German. My idea was to read Kant and Hegel in the original. But as you can guess, that never happened. I barely could read Kant in English. And my German never got very far at all. I would never be able to read my father's journals.

He's crazy, I said to myself. He's lost it.

I put the journal back in the box and shoved it into the back of the guest room closet.

I started working on a new routine, about dating for people on Social Security. Some hours later, the phone rang.

"Dad, when are you coming home?" It was Josh.

"Well, I can't come home right now," I told him. "I have to take care of Grandpa. He's sick."

"I don't feel well either," he said.

"How's school?" I asked him.

I hated these conversations. They went nowhere, and only made the both of us miserable. But if I didn't call, he'd call. He wouldn't let more than a day go by. When the phone rang, I knew it had to be he.

But it was okay—I would make him laugh. I can be funny. Actually, most people think I'm hilarious. But here's the truth about comics: we're depressed, every last one of us. And in my case also obsessive, neurotic, paranoid, immature, and irresponsible. But depression is the universal. It is trite to say we comics hide behind our humor, or use it as a way to be popular, or to cover up insecurity—and all of that is probably true—but at the heart of every laugh is the inability to get out of bed in the morning, the impossibility of really appreciating anything. Everything must always be turned into something else—does anyone ever wonder why?

What the comic sees is the big nothing. What he sees is emptiness, vacuity, folly. And what is the ultimate folly? To look out into the vastness of the universe and somehow conclude that your life means something, in fact, that anything means anything at all.

So I made Josh laugh by telling him how Grandpa kept talking about Frau Hellman.

"Maybe he just wants some mayonnaise," Josh said.

He cracked me up.

"Yah," he went on in a goofy Nazi accent he picked up from my Mel Brooks albums, "und ven you see her, be sure to tell her to brink der Miracle Vip!"

And he's only twelve, I thought.

"Promise me you'll never go into comedy," I said.

"I want to be a doctor," he reminded me. "You know that."

I didn't ask him about his mother, though God knows I wanted to. The one time we had a conversation about her he told me she was dating. That was not a good conversation.

Perhaps it will not surprise you that I had not slept with a woman in three years. Which is virtually impossible to accomplish in San Francisco, as there are so few straight men. All my single friends were going out with twenty-five-year-olds. Good-looking twenty-five-year-olds. But I couldn't do it. I wanted to do it. I even tried to do it, sort of. But I couldn't. In a city full of Victorian mansions, I was the only real Victorian. So, when I took Josh home those evenings I picked him up from school, I hung around Ella's house as long as I could. I never made a pass at her, but I just couldn't seem to leave. She would always be polite, but eventually even I couldn't avoid getting the message, and then I'd have to go home. I lived for the moments when she would ask me to stay for dinner. I'd say no. Josh would tug at my sleeve and drag me to the table. That was a taste of heaven.

The next day I went to see Dad as usual. It was in the morning and it was still cool, and they had him sitting on the screened-in porch with a bunch of other old coots. There was a lot of spittle everywhere. And odd noises.

"Dad."

"Do I know you? Harry? I thought you were in Buenos Aires."

"It's me. Michael."

"You should see the look on your face. I was only kidding. I'm not that gone yet. Maybe tomorrow."

"I knew you were kidding," I said.

He smiled. "Did you maybe bring a cigar?"

"Yes."

I gave it to him. He carefully opened the cellophane, lovingly sniffed the tobacco.

"You wouldn't happen to have a match, would you?"

"Sorry," I said.

"Then what's the point?" he said.

"You know you can't."

"What? It's going to kill me? For Christ's sake."

But he didn't make a big megillah of it. He just ran the cigar along his lips, tasting it, and then stuck it in his mouth.

"I'll chew," he said.

"That's fine," I replied.

"How's Ella?" he asked me.

I reminded him we've been divorced for three years.

"We should have her for Seder. Discuss it with your mother."

This time he wasn't faking. In and out. That's what it was like. Sleeping, waking. He's dreaming, I realized, that's all. His eyes were like glazed doughnuts again.

In a little while he said, "Your father gave you something to read. Did you read it?"

"No," I said, "it's in German."

"I despise German," he said. "Who would write in German now?"

"You did."

He did not seem to hear me. He opened the *Miami Herald* and slipped on his reading glasses. He looked so much like my father. Sitting in his favorite chair in the living room, the TV blasting, chewing on his cigar, reading the newspaper, shaking his head at the idiocies of whoever had been elected, going on about a news item no one else had read yet. I sat down beside him and put my hand on his knee. He didn't look up.

"Yes," he said, "it's good to be a Jew."

I was somewhat taken aback. "Why'd you say that?" I had to ask.

"*Deutsch ist die sprache des Todes,*" he said with a wry smile, as if he were repeating something he had just read on the Op Ed page, only in the *Düsseldorf Times*.

And for him nothing could have been more true. German was, and would always be, the language of death.

"Dad? Do you know who I am?" I said.

"Don't be a nudnik. Of course I know you."

"You gave me something to read, do you remember?"

He looked at me suspiciously, but I could see he did remember.

"It's in German. Why?"

He continued to look at me, his eyes trying to go cloudy, but something holding them in check.

"I can't read German," I said.

"Oh!" he said, grabbing my shoulder with one of his big, bony hands. "Don't be such a pessimist. Always shortchanging yourself. Always thinking you're not good enough. It's all there in black and white."

"I don't know German, Dad."

"Of course you do!"

"But I don't."

He smiled patiently, and then it was his turn to pat me on the knee.

"Talk to your mother about it," he said, and with that he went back to reading the paper, and in a minute he had fallen asleep.

My relationship to German was not so clear.

It was obvious that I chose to study it out of a perverse desire to stand up to my father. He had a very strong personality, and his constant carping about Germans and anti-Semitism, and the failure of German culture and the communal guilt of the German people (and the Poles, and the Ukrainians, and the Lithuanians, and don't forget the French—those anti-Semitic bastards—and the Americans who closed their shores, and the goddamned British who tried to abort the birth of Israel), finally all seemed ludicrous to me. Germany was not only about Hitler. What about Beethoven and Bach, Goethe and Schiller, Kant and Wittgenstein?

"All for nothing," he said.

But how long could he carry the war with him? And why should my generation suffer the same tunnel vision? I didn't tell him I was taking German until a whole semester had passed. But when I came home to New Jersey for the Christmas holiday, he had my grade report stuck on the refrigerator with a blue-and-white magnet in the shape of the State of Israel.

Neither of us said anything till dinner.

"Your grades are good!" he said at last. Mom gave him a look. But it did not dissuade anybody. "I noticed you have begun your study of languages."

"Yes," I said. I put down my fork.

"That's good. That's good," he said. "The study of language opens the mind. You get to see how other cultures think."

"Well, that's what I want. I want to learn how people think."

He took a long, slow bite of pot roast, and swallowed with excessive delight, as if it were the most delicious pot roast Mom had ever made. Then he took a long, slow sip of wine, swooshing it around in his mouth, as if the Gallo Hearty Burgundy was Château Lafite.

"And you picked a most excellent language," he went on. "The language of Hegel. And Nietzsche. *Man and Superman.* I mean *Übermensch, ja?*"

"Heshel . . . ," my mother tried to intervene, but we all knew it was hopeless.

Karen looked up happily from her mashed potatoes.

"No, no, my dear," he said with unctuous civility, "I think it's wonderful. Wonderful!"

"Dad," I said, "it's just a *language*."

"Well, then," he said, "perhaps you'd like to read *this*!" And he pulled out a large, gray volume from under his chair, and slammed it on the dining room table right in front of me. It was volume one of the original German transcripts of the International Military Tribunal at Nuremberg. He had all forty-two volumes.

"So, you do still read German," I said.

That's when he stormed out of the room, and out of the house, too. We heard the back door slam, and then the screen. "That wasn't nice," my mother said.

"What wasn't?"

"That last remark."

"Well, he wasn't nice to me."

"He's your father," she said. She looked over at Karen. "And close your mouth when you chew!" she said. That was the end of the matter.

But I knew I couldn't leave it at that. He didn't speak to me for the entire three weeks of vacation (and I was just a freshman—it still mattered to me, I still thought of the house as my house, too), and when I went back to NYU, he did not go to the bus with me. This upset me much more than I let on, even to myself.

I would not abandon my German, just on principle. But I had to make up with Dad. My solution was to ask him for help.

I started with a phone call. Dad, I said, I don't understand the *ge*'s. You know . . . *gemeinschaft*, *gezeichnet* . . . what's with the *ge*'s? He hung up on me. I called him back. Dad, I've got this test coming up, and I don't understand all the cases. I actually don't even know what a case is—I'm going to fail! He hung up again.

Ten minutes later the phone rang. What kind of test? I told him what kind of test. He told me what a case was and hung up. A few days later I called again. How come the *S*'s look like *F*'s? How come so much stuff is capitalized in the middle of a sentence and it's not a name or anything. Soon I was coming home on weekends, loaded with work. I had to write an essay, I told him, on my favorite foods. I spread out my papers on the kitchen table and appeared to be struggling. I noticed him going to the refrigerator a lot, and I could sense him looking over his shoulder at me. Then he was standing next to me, looking over *my* shoulder. Then he had drawn up a chair and was pointing with his finger at my crude mistakes, and thumbing through the dictionary to show me the right words. And finally we were discussing the essay itself, and how best to express, in German, my love for Grunning's chocolate fudge swirl ice cream. At the very end of that day my father even mumbled something about the beauty and intricacy of German grammar. This scene was repeated in suburban New Jersey almost every weekend for two years, the father and the son, the notebooks and the textbooks, the pencils and pens, the glasses of soda or beer, the bowl of chips, the plate of sandwiches, the mother coming at last to chase us away and set the table for dinner. It was the one thing, in my whole life, I did solely with my father. It was something like an affair, really. By the second year we were conversing in German about everything. In fact, it was in that language that I first told him about Ella.

I gave it up because I didn't want to come home on weekends anymore. I had a girl. I was in love. Plus I had given up on philosophy, and switched over to psych. And also, I now recalled, I was so proficient at it, I really didn't need to take the kind of college courses they offered. I could read just about anything in German, so long as I had a dictionary nearby.

Huh! I thought, that afternoon driving back from the nursing home, maybe he's right. Maybe I can read those journals.

Funny how I had forgotten how much I knew. It was almost as if I wanted to blot out those days, and deny how close to him I had been.

I went back to the apartment determined to read them. And yet when I went into the closet to retrieve them, I felt too tired and hungry. I told myself I'd do it tomorrow, when I had more energy.

CHAPTER 3

I have to preface what happened next by explaining that my father, Heshel Rosenheim, was one of the kindest, most warm-hearted and generous people on the face of the earth. I do not say these things lightly or sanctimoniously. He was a genuinely good guy. He won awards from just about everyone: from the B'nai B'rith, from the Anti-Defamation League, from the Simon Wiesenthal Center, from the Zionist Organization of America, from AIPAC, from the Jewish Federation, the American Jewish Committee, the Jewish Community Relations Council, from Hadassah Hospital on Mount Scopus, from the Holocaust Museum in Dallas, and the ones in Los Angeles and New York, too, from Yad Vashem in Jerusalem, from the Jewish Oral History Project, from Israel Bonds, from the Federation of Jewish Men's Clubs (Con-

Schopenhauer or Heidegger, there emerged through his native tongue an imprint at least of who my father might have been. More boyish, more brash, more easy with a joke, more likely to slap me on the back. It was like unearthing a relic of what he must have been before. *Before.* With survivors there is always a before. And it is always some halcyon, half-imagined paradise—painted in the rich and shining colors of youth. The before is always remembered with a sigh. I had known quite a few survivors in my own childhood—my father belonged to several groups, and later worked on projects to document the Holocaust—and they all had the before. When they spoke of it, their eyes softened as the vision of the mother or father, the baby brother, the sweet-smelling challah, the white tablecloths, the favorite toy came into view, rising from their broken hearts like fragrant smoke. They would smile, they would coo, even. And then, they would sigh, and the veil would fall and they would once again become the *after*. But my father was the kind who never talked about any of it. Never spoke of the before. Never compared it to the after. Never spoke of the during. In fact, as far as I was concerned, my father had no existence before he met and married my mother. In our family it was well known that he had declined to testify at Eichmann's trial. It's true, my mother would say, they called, they asked, but he said no. Yet I remember him watching the trial on television. He could not take his eyes away. He seemed to study Eichmann as if trying to find in the movement of his head, or some mole on his cheek, the secret of how such a mild-mannered nebbish could be the conduit of so much evil. But through it all, my father never said a word, never discussed it at the dinner table, never even shook his head in disgust. The very sight of the man must have crushed his vocal cords, as in a nightmare, when you open your mouth to scream, and cannot make a sound.

As I sat there, now, years later, in Florida, I knew that once I opened these journals all that had been hidden would be revealed.

He had written it for my eyes only, in our secret language, the language of his youth and perhaps of his truest self—his before.

The Cheez Whiz box now sat on the floor next to Dad's La-Z-Boy chair in which I had plopped myself. This throne of old age and weakening mind stood in a corner of what they called the Florida room—what we used to call in New Jersey the sun parlor—a little enclosed addition just off the living room, with floor-to-ceiling windows through which I could see the morning's first golfers make their way down the green that ran alongside my parents' building. Across from the La-Z-Boy was the TV, which in his last years was turned on much more than in the past, though I doubt he was really following. Books on Jewish themes were everywhere, many of them with bookmarks in them, indicating he had not finished reading them, had lost interest, couldn't remember what he had just read. A shofar, covered with dust, was stuck between Ben-Gurion's *Israel: A Personal History* and Moshe Dayan's *Diary of the Sinai Campaign*. If he had been so single-minded in business, I thought . . . but he wasn't, and that was really that.

Each of the journals was dated in large penned script on the cover. I set them out on the floor until I found the oldest one, dated June 1978. I knew immediately why he had begun to write. That was my before, too.

I put the other volumes back in the box, arranged my paperback *Cassell's English-German Dictionary* on the table beside me, reclined the La-Z-Boy into a comfortable position, and opened the dry, powdery, cheap leather cover of Journal #1.

I already guessed how it would begin.

We buried Karen today, in the plot I had purchased for myself and Lily. She was 18 years old. 18 years old. Who buys a plot for an 18 year old? Lulled. I was lulled into thinking everything would be all right. I thought, oh yes! we do have a future! But oh! How I have cursed this family!!!!

As soon as I read these words, the scene came rushing back to me. Speeding home from NYU to find my mother at Karen's hospital bedside, weeping, too late. She was gone. So was my father. He wasn't there. I held my mother as best I could. It was awkward, somehow, to do it. It was a reversal of roles, a role I had yet to learn, one that gave me no pleasure, and only distanced me from my own feelings. I had always protected my sister as a kid. She hung out with us older guys, even dated some of my friends in my last year of high school. She was only two years behind us, and she was beautiful and smart and funny. We smoked a little dope together, too. If you want to know the truth, she was funnier than me. I mean, I could make people laugh—but she could just cross her eyes and everyone would crack up. When she died, I think it made me funnier. I stole her style. Not on purpose. It just came over me, and every so often I'd notice—hey, that's how Karen would do it.

I recalled now that my father had disappeared from the scene, emerging only late that night from the attic where he had gone to be alone with his collection of stamps—he collected Israeli stamps—and quietly made his way downstairs to drink a cup of tea. A lot of people had shown up that day, but they were all gone now. Mom was asleep with a Miltown the doctor had given her. I was sitting in the sun parlor, wondering what was next, and I saw him steal down the stairs in the darkness and put on the kettle without turning on the kitchen light. It was really at that moment that I knew everything had changed, that I had not been dreaming all this, that Karen would never be coming home, and that I had lost something irretrievable, something even beyond the loss of my sister. In fact, now that I thought about it, I recalled that we didn't stop the lessons because of Ella, or because I changed majors. It was because there was no one to come home to. I remembered trying to start them up again a few weeks after the funeral. He just looked at me with a mixture of pity and contempt, patted my shoulder and said, not today. Maybe next week. But next week never seemed to come. And then I stopped trying. And then, only then, did I switch my major to psych.

From that moment on my father seemed to slip further away from me, drowning himself, as I saw it, in good works for the Jews. For my part, I began to have a physical reaction against Jews and anything Jewish. I quit Hillel, I ate bread on Passover, I had bacon in my refrigerator, and if it weren't for the fact that I was in love with a Jewish girl, I would have gone out of my way to date Gentiles. I even put up a Christmas tree my senior year, but when I brought one home that first year to Ella's, she actually threw it out the window. It was only one of those little desktop acrylic things with all the ornaments already attached and it made hardly a sound as it landed in the snow, but well into spring and summer you could still find tinsel here and there in the courtyard, stuck between cracks in the pavement, or hanging from the droopy arm of a crocus.

Sure, I'd go home for the High Holidays, for the Jewish New Year and the Day of Atonement—the Days of Awe—of *Awe,* my father would intone pointedly. When I was little he would look down at me and say, "You know what 'awe' is? It's the feeling you get when your mother walks in the room carrying a brisket!"—and then he'd laugh and scruff up my hair with his knuckles. But when I returned to that synagogue, either alone or later with Ella and once or twice even with Josh—a synagogue I had known all my life (I knew every detail of the stained-glass windows, every name on the memorial plaques; I knew that the Abramses sat to our right, and the Glassmans to our left)—I writhed in discomfort, especially when they came to the part where they recited every possible sin a person could do—*just in case,* as my father would say; just in case what? And the thing was, you knew you *had* committed almost every single one of them. *For the sin we have sinned with impure thoughts. For the sin we have sinned by wanton looks. For the sin we have sinned by telling lies.* And here was my favorite: *For the sin we have sinned by folly of the mouth.* That was my vocation, for gosh sakes. That's what I was going to do for a living. I was guilty! Guilty! *For the sin we have sinned by stealing someone else's material. For the sin we have sinned by screwing up the timing.* And worse: *For the sin we have sinned by following Ella after she left the library to see if she was still sleeping with Larry Pressman!* And there I was, beating my chest with the rest of them, hating every minute of it, unable to stop. I would touch the fringes of my tallis and adjust my skullcap and wonder, who is this person I am pretending to be?

On some level I found the whole thing funny. I used a lot of it in my early stand-up routines, which I did first at a little club for NYU students, and then at open mikes around the city. My life at that time apparently was hilarious. I began to have success. The only people who didn't find me all that amusing were my parents. But what could be funny to them? After you lose a child, what's funny?

I went back to reading my father's journal, though with renewed trepidation. I reminded myself that I didn't want to know what his secrets were. And I certainly didn't want to revisit certain events in my own life. I hadn't thought seriously about my sister in years. Karen equaled: "*You have any brothers or sisters?*" "*Yes, but my sister died when I was twenty.*" Karen was just a name, a time marker in *my* story, a closed case, an answer at a cocktail party. "*Oh, I'm sorry,*" they'd say. But reading even just the first paragraphs of my father's diary—or whatever this was going to turn out to be—had created turmoil inside my heart. She had risen from the dead, as if, as they say, at the end of days God breathes life into the bones of the righteous, and they walk the earth once more. That's what it was beginning to feel like. The end of days.

Dad did not write very much more about Karen though. Apparently she was not the real subject matter, or maybe it was just too painful for him.

I now know, he wrote, *that I can run away no longer. Like Jonah, trying to escape the will of God, I have caused the storm to rise, and like him, must be thrown overboard, lest all around me die on my account. One cannot hide from God's wrath, no more than from His grace. He will find you! And all your works are naught! Is my great love for the Jewish People not enough? Of course not enough! Never enough! Just vanity! Why should He care for my feeble gestures? Why should He care about my feelings? They count for nothing in His eyes, and rightly so.*

I had to put it down. This was ridiculous. It didn't sound quite as bad in German as it does in English, because German tends to be high flown and fanciful, but my God! All that biblical crap. All that hair pulling. All that rending of clothes. Jonah? Please! I mean, I understood he was upset because of Karen, and even somewhat hysterical, sure, of course, but twenty-four volumes of this?

I skipped down several paragraphs until I saw my own name. What would he have said to me? I wondered. We who never talked about it—about Karen—about his life in the camps—about anything except the fact that he didn't want me to go into show business and the fact that I was a *shonda*—a shame—for denying my Jewish heritage. I remember telling him, being born something is just an accident, but how you live your life is your choice. And I don't choose to be Jewish! I had said that in my mother's presence I now recalled, and even then I was ashamed, because her face grew red, yet she said nothing, and did not allow herself to cry. My father as usual stormed out of the room and called me a Nazi. When I looked over to my mother, she had her back to me, clearing off the table, but I could see that her hands were shaking. I went off and watched TV.

But here, in the day of crisis, he had written to *me*.

And so now, my Michael, my firstborn, my young hero with the sharp tongue, my beloved son, my hope, the time has come to tell my story. You will assume that I have thought about this for a long time—but you must be assured that it is not because of you that I have withheld—not because of anything about you, not even because I wanted to protect you. Rather, I have tried so desperately to reinvent myself, to cast off the past like a rotten coat, to never, ever even think of it, lest God hear my thoughts and somehow punish me again. That was cowardice, I admit it. But over time, it became something else—love. I am a Jew, first and foremost. I embrace it with all my heart and soul. I yearn for all that is Jewish in the world to rise from the depths and purify the air around us—to spring clean our souls! That is the power of the Jewish life—cleansing and hopeful and joyous. So why go back in time to another world, a dark and gruesome world, a world of hatred and pain?

But God will not let me alone. I am punished for my sins through my beautiful and innocent daughter. And if I do not now confess, will you be next?

Whatever you learn of me, from this day forth, remember, man is nothing but a vessel of God's will—even so—he must bear the responsibility of his actions, as if they were his own.

He put a mark under these paragraphs, like this =========, and I realized that he was done writing for that day.

After that there were several blank pages, a page or two with some scribblings that had been violently crossed out and obliterated, and finally what looked like a title page.

It read, simply,

A Story

And when I turned the page, I was surprised to see not the continuation of the diary, or journal, but what appeared to be the first paragraphs of a novel.

CHAPTER 4

Heinrich Mueller joined the SS in 1939, largely because his cousin, SS-Obersturmführer Hans Mueller, of Special Unit 4, had returned from the front, that is, from Poland, and told him he was a fool if he let himself be drafted into the regular army.

"And anyway," Hans had said, "everyone thinks you're head of the Gestapo already."

He was referring of course to Heinrich Müller, the chief of the Gestapo, because of the similarity between their names. But Heinrich did not wish to be a policeman. So he signed up with the Waffen-SS, thinking he would be a war hero. Instead, he was trained as an accountant, and attached to the Budget and Construction Office, but not in Berlin. He was given his silver death's-head for his cap, had his rank raised to second lieutenant, and was sent to do the books in Bergen-Belsen. He was well suited for the work. He liked numbers. He also enjoyed the study of language. He spent his spare time reading English, and found, much to his amusement, that he had also picked up a great deal of the Jewish dialect as well, simply from interacting with the few inmates he had impressed into service as bookkeepers, and with whom he found himself conversing almost as if it were a normal day at the office. In fact, he took special pleasure in aping their ways and amusing his friends in the officers' club—the self-deprecating shuffle, the unpleasant singsong cadence, the curiously convoluted logic. Still, he would never have considered this knowledge of Jewish worthwhile, for he could not regard it as a language. It was just a bastardized mixture of tongues. Just a joke to amuse his friends.

Two years later, he found himself transferred to the East, namely to the Majdanek Concentration Camp, near Lublin. The job was similar, but more depressing. By comparison, Bergen was a spa. For here the smell of burning flesh was constant, and in the blocks themselves the stench of excrement and rot overwhelming. It made him hate the Jew even more. He was lucky though. He rarely had to leave the relative comfort of the SS compound, which was far across the highway. And in any case, his responsibilities were for Camp B, the labor camp, and not the other operation, to which he decided he had no connection at all. He worked in his office, taking his meals in town. Lublin was but walking distance, except on very cold nights. It was not that he agreed or disagreed. He saw its necessity. And frankly, he was too busy to worry about it. There was so much to account for: clothing, jewelry, artifacts, furs. Plus the cost of new construction, of food, of supplies, which were, by the way, very hard to get, and even harder to keep track of. However, he could tell you exactly how to derive the utmost profit from a human being, given the cost of his ration and general upkeep, and taking into account his initial age, health, height, weight, and national origin.

In 1945 Heinrich Mueller found himself back in Bergen-Belsen when Majdanek was abandoned under pressure of the Soviet advance. It was there, in Bergen-Belsen, in April of that year, that he was liberated by the British.

This occurred in the following way. Heinrich, sensing the end was near—it was not a difficult calculation, after all—starved himself for three weeks. When the day approached and many of the Germans fled, only, he assumed, to be caught and hanged, he instead shaved his head, exchanged his uniform for the rags—which he carefully deloused—of a dead prisoner, rolled himself in the mud, and waited. While he was lying there in a trench, surrounded by—but not touching—dead bodies, he had noticed that many of the prisoners had been tattooed with numbers. They had not done this at Majdanek, but he saw no reason not to ice the cake. At night, he slipped back into the officers' compound, and with a needle dipped in ink, he tattooed a number into his forearm. He had copied the number from a corpse that had been lying next to him. Then he hurried back to the trench.

When the troops arrived, he crawled out from among the dead bodies, and was saved. They fed him a little Spam.

=========

They asked him who he was. He held out his arm.

No, they said, your name.

He looked at them with the blank stare of the walking dead. A young soldier walked up to him and took his hands. It's all right, he said in Yiddish. I'm Jewish, too. What's your name?

He realized with panic that he hadn't thought of any name. They looked at each other for what seemed to him an eternity.

Heshel Rosenheim, he suddenly said.

It was the name of one of the Jewish bookkeepers from whom he had gleaned so many Yiddish words. It was the first name that popped into his head.

=========

He did not know if the real Heshel Rosenheim was alive or dead, but it really didn't matter—unless of course he ran into him. But other than Rosenheim and a few of his other Kapos, *there was almost no one who could recognize him. For one thing there were sixty thousand prisoners here, and most of them had just arrived from somewhere else, spirited away from death camps farther east. He was in a position to know this, after all. He was the bean counter. So, he reasoned, he could be from anywhere. Who would question him? He thought about things now, about how things work out. For years he secretly despised himself for doing so little for the Fatherland, stuck in that office doing calculations. Yes, yes, he knew how important his task was—still, he had only been a* bürohengst*—a pencil pusher. But now, he realized with a kind of joy, he had actually been fortunate! And indeed he was pleased with himself. Pleased that he had had the foresight to stay away from the main camps, pleased that he had so little to do with—well—anything. For one thing, he wasn't the type to go out and shoot people. And he almost never frequented the brothel. The filthy Jewish women held little interest for him. And thus there were few prisoners, if any, who might recognize him. And those who could—why they were almost certainly dead. As for Rosenheim, surely he was dead too. No one could survive that long. Such a thing would have been economically unfeasible.*

In any case, his main worry right now was to avoid the typhus that had spread throughout the camp. He kept to himself. He drank only from the army water tanks. And he watched carefully for every opportunity to help himself, staying as close as he could to the British soldiers. But something happened in those first two days that struck him as hilarious. The stupid British in their zeal to help these insects, these roaches, plied them with rations. The greedy Jews stuffed themselves with food, and soon were convulsed in the dirt, screaming their guts out, puking and shitting at the same time, and in an hour or so they were dead. They had eaten themselves to death.

But Rosenheim—for that is the name he now knew himself by—had starved only a few weeks, not a few years. His bowels had not yet shriveled to the size of a pencil lead. Nevertheless, he ate carefully, and sparingly. The British merely thought he was simply too far gone to care about food.

They sent him to a hospital in Lübeck, and from there to a D.P. camp near Geringshof, in the American Zone.

Not surprisingly, he recovered his health more quickly than most.

=========

I literally jumped up from the La-Z-Boy, as if suddenly it was on fire. I couldn't stop my hands from shaking, yet I could not put the journal down. It was glued to my fingers, like when you touch something really cold, like an ice cube or a metal pole that sticks to your skin—and it burns like hell, but you can't let go. It seemed like it was leeching the blood right out of me, because I was completely dizzy, light-headed, I thought I might faint, and my heart was racing, and everything in the room was spinning. What in God's name is he talking about? I cried. What, what, *what*? It was like pressure inside me rising, like a wave of vomit. *What?* I cried. *What?*

Finally I threw the volume down on the side table. My hands felt so dirty. When I looked at them, I saw they were coated with a slimy film of orange-brown dust from the deteriorating leather.

Then I thought: I could not have been reading it right. After all, my German was rusty—to say the least. But I knew that except for the few words I had to skip over, I'd read with amazing accuracy and speed—Oh, I got it right, all right. I got it right.

Was my father not my father? Was he someone named Heinrich Mueller? *A Nazi war criminal?* No! These thoughts were too impossible. Nothing, nothing in his life, in his bearing, in his speech, in his work, could ever point to this. He was a man of light, not darkness. No. It had to be something else.

Certainly the writing could imply that he was not the Nazi at all, but his victim. Yes, he could have been twice over the victim of Heinrich Mueller! First as a concentration camp slave, and then having lost his identity to him. He had been used, without his knowledge, of course, as a cover for this Heinrich Mueller, to avoid prosecution, to shield him from justice! Surely, the pages to follow would show how he discovered this subterfuge, and how he revealed it to the world, and how he led the police to this . . . this . . . (I struggled for the word)—*pencil pusher*! Or . . . or . . . was it all just . . . a story . . . a novel . . . a work of imagination . . . the result of some sort of twisted, inverted logic of self-abuse . . . some sort of working out of my father's guilt in which he turned himself into the villain of his own story, the mastermind of his own degradation—a monster—because . . . because he could not bear to be a survivor—or worse—because he *had* done something horrible, something monstrous, in order to survive.

I had heard of *Kapos,* of course. The prisoners who were like trustees—who guarded the other prisoners, beat them, lorded over them, taskmasters of their own people. Or the Jewish *Sondercommandos* who worked the crematoriums, shoving bodies into ovens, yanking gold from teeth, stoking the hellish fires for an extra ration of bread—to live another week, another month, perhaps even another year. Was that his lot? Was he one of those?

I could not imagine anything remotely like it.

I felt faint and had to sit down. But I did not want to sit again in my father's chair. I stumbled toward the kitchen, which, even then, was still to me my mother's world. The world of cooking, and having a cup of tea, a nice chat, a little piece of something just to tide you over. I sat down at the little Formica table, so small it really sat only two, and I yearned for my mother—something, I had to confess, I had not done at all since her death—not because I didn't love her, but because it strangely seemed as if she were still alive. How often had I seen her in the years since college anyway? Practically never. Once a year, maybe. And on the phone—how often did I call? And when she would finally call me, what did I have to say? So the fact that she was dead did not really register. It was as if she was merely on the other coast, and I'd see her when I'd see her, and I'd talk to her when I'd talk to her. And now I wanted more than anything in the world to talk to her, to ask her. I needed to know what she knew.

I tried to conjure up her voice, but there was only silence and the hum of the refrigerator. So I sat there by myself trying to calm down.

All I could think about was that the table was so *small*. This made me intensely sad, and I didn't know why. And then I recalled that when I first came to visit them here, ten years before, the three of us could not sit at this table together, even for a cup of coffee. And it was then that I understood: as far as they were concerned, I existed in some other realm. From now on, it was just the two of them. Like before I was even born. And that's why we had breakfast in the dining room. And lunch and dinner in the dining room. And the cups of tea, the nice chats, the little somethings just to tide me over? Perhaps they didn't happen at all.

I now remembered her saying, "Thank God for Ella! You could get a Nobel Prize, and I'd be the last to hear it."

Yes, I was silent in those days. And she was silent now.

In any case, I reasoned, whatever she knew, she knew then, she knew my whole life, and never said a word. Why would she have spoken now, even if she could?

I would have to go to him.

But I was really pretty much out of control.

I drove the Caddy at sixty miles an hour, careening around all the old people driving their big cars, zipping past the Einstein's Bagels, the Checker's Burgers, the Captain's Table, the Denny's, their parking lots full of Jews with nothing to hide.

I kept saying to myself, I'll just ask him, that's all. I'll just ask him.

But he was in one of his good-bye states. When I entered the room, he asked me if I was there to fix the television.

"I'm here to talk to you," I said.

"Are you the repairman?"

"No, I'm not the repairman, goddamn it."

"The television," he said. "I can't get Jackie Gleason."

"Dad!" I cried. "Please! Talk to me!"

"I want *The Honeymooners*." Tears welled up in his eyes and he began to sob. "It's Saturday night!"

The Honeymooners had not been on Saturday nights for forty years. He seemed inconsolable.

"I'll fix the television," I said.

"You'll fix the television?"

"Yes," I said.

That made him weep even more.

Suddenly I threw my arms around him. I was trying not to falter, for I felt quite faint. I took a deep breath—to calm myself, I suppose—and up came the familiar, even intoxicating, scent of tobacco and hair tonic and the slight rancidness of age. My father! I held him tight. But I had the terrible feeling I no longer knew who it was I was holding in my arms.

"All right," I said to Nurse Clara, "I need to know who brought that box of journals to my father."

"Why are you taking that tone with me?" she replied. She had huge breasts and a chirpy southern accent. Her tinted hair was cropped short, and she wore a large black crucifix around her neck. She was used to dealing with abusive patients, and I could tell she wasn't going to take it from me either, but I didn't care. I just went ahead and raised my voice.

"Just tell me who brought the goddamned box!"

"If you keep taking that tone, I'm going to have to ask you to leave," she said.

Normally I would have been contrite, or made a joke, or simply backed down. I was a big backer-downer. But at the moment I was beside myself. Frankly, I thought that quite understandable.

"Now you listen to me," I said. "Someone has given my father something that is very damaging, very destructive, and I need to know who it was. This is my father I'm talking about!"

Now she backed off a little.

"What are you talking about? Drugs?"

"Not drugs! Books!"

"I know this is a very stressful time for you," she said. "And I'll try to find out who brought the box." But I didn't like her tone.

"And who are all these visitors you say he has?"

"This isn't a prison, you know," she replied. "We don't make people sign in, and I haven't a clue who most of them are. Maybe if you spent more time here yourself, you'd meet them."

She smiled at me, but her eyes were almost as blank as my father's. Then she made a show of going back to her work.

I was fuming. I was shaking, even. In fact, I realized I hadn't stopped shaking from the time I'd finished reading that chapter until this very moment. I went back in and sat with my dad. He was mesmerized by the TV. A total zombie. He didn't even know I was there.

But nobody else came in to visit him either, and in a couple of hours I couldn't take any more, so I decided to go home.

Nurse Clara looked up at me. I could tell she watched until I was safely out the door.

Later that night the phone rang. It was my son, Josh.

"Why aren't you calling?" he asked. I could hear his throat catch. "Why am I the one calling you?"

CHAPTER 5

I was standing there in the Florida room, looking at all the journals laid out on the floor. I knew I should stop reading right then. I should put them away in their Cheez Whiz box, and throw the whole lot of it back in the closet.

Probably he was just making the whole thing up anyway. He'd been a *Kapo* or something like that, that's all. So what? I mean, let's face it, every time you look at a survivor you think, how did *he* make it through? What did *she* do to slip through the jaws of death? He was ashamed, that's all. I could live with that. I could forgive. After all, I told myself, think of what he went through. And probably—knowing him—it wasn't even as bad as he made it out to be. Okay, maybe he betrayed someone in some small way, maybe he stole someone's bread, maybe, maybe, he did pull gold out of the mouths of dead people, perhaps he did shove them into the fires—but they were already dead—he didn't kill them! Or maybe he was the one who told the children not to worry, it was just a game—something like that. Something that made not one bit of difference in the ultimate outcome of things. Who of us, really, in truth, ever affects the ultimate outcome of things?

I bent down and picked up Journal #1 and shoved it in my pocket.

I must have really been crazed by then, because I took the book, jumped in the Caddy, and drove over to Starbucks. I ordered a coffee. I stood there like everything was normal and waited till they called it out, *Grande double decaf latte!* I said thank you. Perfectly normal. I slipped the cardboard heat shield over the paper cup. I added two envelopes of Sweet'N Low. I found a table near someone who was writing on her laptop. She looked like one of those people who is trying to write a novel. Feeling the journal in my jacket pocket, I cried to myself, Why does everybody think they have to write?

I found myself dialing Ella.

She sounded asleep.

"Hello?" she mumbled. I could feel the bedsheets in her voice, I could smell the morning rising off her body, I could feel my ear nuzzle against her back, I could taste her red hair through the mouthpiece.

Oh, Ella! The comfort of those days flooded over me like chocolate, sweet and pleasantly bitter.

"Who is this?"—muddled, her voice was chalky. I suddenly realized it was only five in the morning in San Francisco.

I hung up.

I saw that my hand was still shaking.

Why couldn't I let go? It was three years already.

"I hate being poor!" she had told me, as if that was a good reason for leaving the father of your child. "And I hate that you always joke about everything. We can never have a serious conversation. You never listen!"

"I'm ready to listen," I said. "Just let me get my steno pad." (Oh God, how I regret that now.)

"And I hate that you're on the road all the time. And I hate when you come home, because you disrupt everything. And I hate that you don't seem to care. You just don't seem to care about anything."

Nothing could have been further from the truth. I did care. It just didn't look that way because I'm funny. And funny people can't seem to control themselves. They can't just drop the curtain and end the show. It's a curse, believe me. But that didn't mean I didn't love her. It didn't mean I didn't care about her or Josh, our lives together. I just genuinely thought it was grand to live in a rundown bungalow, put a couple of lawn chairs out on the AstroTurf, rest our drinks on the backs of our plastic flamingo drink caddies, and invite the neighbors in to have a look at our collection of velvet paintings. It wasn't even a joke to me. I thought it was cool. (So, by the way, did a lot of my comedian pals, but that didn't seem to have much currency with Ella.)

"I want to live like a normal person," she told me.

Back at Starbucks, the cell phone rang.

"Did you just call?"

"Who is this?" I said. (I couldn't help myself.)

"You know perfectly well who this is. Do you know what time it is?"

"Why do you think I would call *you*?"

"Oh, please," she said.

I heard her flush the toilet. I could imagine her slipping up her panties, dropping her nightgown over her bare legs, rinsing her fingers in the tap water. Her hair would be a rat's nest sitting atop her head like a crown of thorns. She had a lovely, long, slender body and a mass of ruby pubic hair, and lovely, long, slender fingers, too. And she was pretty. Genuinely pretty. In the summer she had freckles.

That's what I saw as I heard her scold me in that old familiar way.

"Did something happen?" she said. "Your father? He's okay, isn't he? Michael, are you there?"

She had psychic sonar, that one, like a fruit bat. I could never get away with anything. But I always lied anyway.

"I just miss you," I finally said.

"So he's okay?"

"Yeah," I said, "he's fine. Do you miss me too?" I asked.

She of course ignored me. "You should call Josh more," she said—it was her usual rap. "He frets."

"I know," I said. "I know."

"He needs you, believe it or not."

Josh, bless his heart, was always my in.

"I was thinking, Ella," I went on. "I mean, things are better for me now. I'm doing pretty well. There is a very, very good chance they are going to pick up that pilot I was working on. Very good chance. Probably eighty percent chance. And I've been getting a lot of work in Vegas. Almost headlining."

"Michael," she said.

"I was thinking maybe we should get back together again. For Josh."

"Josh is just fine."

"Not just for Josh," I hurriedly amended. "Not merely for Josh."

It was like the proverbial dike breaking. "I love you, Ella," I cried.

"I love you too," she said, but I could tell she didn't mean it in the same way.

"So why don't we?" I said.

She sighed.

"Think about it," I said.

"All right," she replied. There were a few seconds of silence, then she decided to finish up. "Tell your father hello for me. You know how I feel about him."

When I flipped shut the cell phone, I noticed that woman was still typing away furiously. I reached for my father's journal and set it on the table. I could hear the hiss of the espresso machine like the airbrakes of some cosmic Greyhound bus opening its doors, waiting for me to get on—trip to nowhere—and then the barista calling, *Grande soy macchiato!*

=========

The D.P. camp at Geringshof was controlled by the Zionists. There was a woman there by the name of Moskovitz, an Austrian Jew who'd been in Auschwitz. In some ways she was an attractive woman. Thick hair cascading from her kerchief in satin ringlets, and her eyes, when she was aroused with an interesting notion, sparkled like rubbed coal. One day she grabbed Heshel by the hand and said, "Rosenheim. Come. Something you should see." She led him past the front gate, and they strolled down the dirt path to a field. Perhaps she wants to copulate with me, he thought. She was a strong, fleshy woman now, and he had not enjoyed a female in many, many months. And since he was not alone in being uncircumcised—many assimilated German Jews had avoided that particular barbarism, as he thought of it, in the years before the war—he wasn't worried on that score. As they walked along he remarked on the weather, and rather gallantly picked a wildflower for her. She took it, and twirled it about in her fingers, but in a moment they had arrived where she wanted to arrive, and he saw that romance was not what had brought the sparkle to her eye.

Before him stretched several large patches of garden, a machine shop, some hastily constructed farm buildings, and two neat rows of tents. Groups of men and women were planting in one field, while in another, others were bent over young green shoots of lettuces or squash—he had no idea which—weeding with trowels and hoes. They cannot help but be slaves, he thought.

"Kibbutz Buchenwald!" announced Moskovitz. "Good name, isn't it? They thought they would kill us all there. But you see, even that name gives us hope!" She squatted down and drew some earth into her hand, smelling it with deep satisfaction, and then tossing it back with distaste. "But this is only preparation," she said. "The earth in this place is profane. There is nothing here for us." She smiled up at him. "We will get strong, and we will go to Palestine where we can live as human beings. Come," she said, "you can join us."

"Why me?" he said.

"We've been watching you," she said, "like a lost sheep. Speaking to no one. Hiding in corners, watching, listening, as if you still have something to fear. No attempt to find family or friends. You've lost everyone, including yourself." She was still squatting, but now she brushed the dust from her hands and pointed outward, to the workers in the field. "We have a new family now."

Rosenheim was stunned. His ruse had been even more successful than he could have possibly imagined. Clinging to his corner, taking his meals alone, keeping his own counsel (as he now realized they said of him), he had studied the fatalistic shrug, the supercilious lifting of eyebrows, the long-winded jokes they thought were funny, the endless flood of caustic commentary, all the little gestures that reeked of Jew. Without moving a muscle he mimicked them. He had lived among them so long! He could intuit their every thought, their every mood, their every excuse for remaining alive. But when she held out her hand to him so he might lift her up, he could not help himself: he hesitated out of a kind of revulsion.

"It's all right," she said, helping herself up. "You don't have to be afraid anymore."

She put her arm around him, and every particle and cell in his body cringed. Yet he walked along with her toward the group that had stopped their work and were resting on their hoes, watching them.

=========

They handed him Herzl's The Jewish State.

Then they gave him Ahad Ha-am and Pinkser. The pamphlets of Ben-Gurion and Jabotinsky.

They put him in Ulpan, where he spoke nothing but Hebrew twenty-four hours a day. He no longer planted potatoes. He planted tapuchim adamim. *He dug with a* ya-eh, *not a shovel, and he ate with his* hevrah*—his comrades—and let his voice ring with theirs in revolutionary song, and stood and wept with the rest of them when they chanted the* Hatikvah, *and kicked his feet as high as they when they danced the* hora. *He knew what they were doing. They were stamping on the graves of the Aryan race.*

It was madness.

But the trials began in November, and of forty-five staff members from Dachau, thirty-seven were quickly sentenced to death. And then the trials of the great German leaders began. That plodded along, but he knew it would end in the same way.

So he danced the hora, *and he read his lessons in Hebrew and Yiddish, but under his breath he cursed them all in German.*

=========

The boat that took him to Palestine was the Dora Heliopolis. *It was intercepted by the British near Haifa and sent back to Cyprus. One month later, he was spirited onto another vessel, and this time he landed successfully off the coast of Netanya.*

He sloshed through the waves onto the shore in utter darkness, led only by the sound of the man in front of him. Many fell on their faces and kissed the earth, their mouths filling with wet sand; he could not see them exactly, but the beach was crawling with creatures, and he did not suppose they were sea lions. He fell on his face and ate sand too.

He heard someone cry, "We are free! We are free!" And then someone tugged at his shirt, and hurried him on toward the waiting lorries.

Most of his group was taken to Kibbutz Afikim, but he was sent to Naor, a kibbutz above Ashdod on the Mediterranean Sea, on the road to Tel Aviv. The caravan split up, but he was happy to see, as a match was struck and cigarettes were lit, the woman Moskovitz seated across from him. He smiled perhaps for the first time since that day he had seen the prisoners die from overeating.

In Naor they grew oranges. Because of his age and health he was also quickly recruited into the Haganah.

"None of you know how to be soldiers," they told them, "but in this land we only have ourselves."

When they gave him a rifle, he behaved as if he did not know how to handle it, which was made easier by the fact that it was such an old weapon he was genuinely unfamiliar with its use.

But he could not as easily hide the fact that his SS training had turned him into an excellent shot—mainly because he could not resist the pleasure of hitting the target. So they gave him a better rifle and placed him in the watchtower, and he sat there many afternoons, and many evenings, smoking cigarettes and watching the blue-and-white Jewish flag play and flutter in the wind just above his head.

When they handed him his new weapon, the major said, "Whatever you were, you are no more. You are now a Jewish soldier."

Sometimes when he sat in the tower he imagined himself picking off the kibbutzniks one by one. Other times, Moskovitz might climb up and join him, bringing along pieces of dark bread spread with halvah and chocolate. They didn't talk very much, but he could see she was happy. The others meant nothing to him, but he liked Moskovitz. At least for now, however, he did not touch her.

But what irked him more than anything was that these Jews were so horribly disorganized. The army unit was without discipline, everyone was called by his first name, including the commander, and no one saluted anyone. As for the kibbutz, it might as well have been run by children.

If they go on this way, he thought, they'll be overrun by the Arabs as soon as the British leave. The thought gave him a certain amount of satisfaction, but it also frightened him. Before that happens, he decided, I must go over to the other side, resume my true identity, and quietly slip into a comfortable exile. Silently he plotted his escape.

In the meantime, though, their sloppiness just got the better of him. Finally he went before the kibbutz council, and begged them to change their ways.

"Well then," said this fellow, Avigdor, who was a sabra, and hence one of the worst offenders, "organize us!"

So the first thing he did was take over the books. He was appalled. Cross-outs, erasures, pages that didn't balance, money going out with no signatures, produce being sold for who knows how much? It was impossible! From now on, everything would be catalogued—every item, every penny, every nail that came into the kibbutz would be noted, indexed, accounted for—and the same for everything that went out. Only in this way could they ever hope to make a profit and turn this makeshift farm into a serious enterprise.

Pretty soon no one would purchase so much as a dish towel without first getting Heshel Rosenheim's okay. And if you wanted to know where something was—who had what where—it was again to Heshel you had to come. It was Heshel who knew how much the kibbutz spent on furnishing Ben-Eliezar's room and how much on Rifka and Dudi's—so when it came to making allotments, the council always deferred to Heshel. And when the disputes arose—why should Shuli get a radio, and not Hannah?—it was Heshel who mediated, and, to tell the truth, arbitrated. In a matter of months, his word was law.

"Jews!" he muttered to himself.

And he would write something else down in one of his books.

=========

I shoved the journal back into my pocket and got the hell out of Starbucks. My father was insane. None of this could have happened. Nazis don't end up running kibbutzim, and they don't join the Haganah. And even if they did, the thought of my father in the Haganah was ludicrous. He couldn't even ride a bike.

The writer lady looked up at me. Longingly, I thought. I wanted to scream at her. Her hair was long and undyed, a terrible, terrible mistake. It was obvious. Husband had left her for a younger woman. But what I hated most of all was that I could see she was making the assumption that we were from the same place—the township of dumped spouses. Wrong! I was telling her. I'm from the City of the Damned.

But as I got in the car I found myself staring at her through the big plate-glass windows of the coffee shop. She had immediately gone back to her furious typing. I couldn't take my eyes off her. I hated her. I hated her for writing. For telling her stupid story. Nobody wants to hear it! I silently screamed at her. I hadn't thought of drugs in a long time, but I thought of them then. I put the car in reverse and peeled out of the lot like a high school dropout at Shoney's Big Boy.

CHAPTER 6

It was afternoon, the heat of the day. I was sitting by the pool, the very pool by which my mother had died. When I laid myself down upon the chaise longue, I half expected to see her hat floating on the mouthwash-blue water, drifting toward the deep end where the diving board sat rusting and unused.

No one was about. The golf courses had emptied an hour or two ago, and the sunbathers and swimmers had moved inside the clubhouse to finish their games of bridge or work out on the stationary bicycles. Televisions were on. Naps were being taken. I sat alone under an umbrella, sweating.

That woman at Starbucks had had a strong effect on me—more than I had realized at the time, because I just couldn't stop thinking about her. I wasn't thinking about her sexually. It was more about the fact that somehow I was in the same club as she was, even though I was at least ten years younger than she. She must have been over fifty. And when she looked at me—well—I got the feeling that I looked *tasty* to her. I didn't want to be tasty to her. I wanted to be quite *impossible* for her.

I held Journal #2 in my burning palm. I laughed—maybe I needed to do what Dad did. Start my own set of journals. Ceremoniously hand them over to Josh at the point I become a semi-vegetable.

But hadn't I done more than my share to mess him up already?

I remembered we were driving down I-80 because I decided to take him up to the Mr. Fun Arcade, where they had all kinds of video games, go-kart racing, miniature golf. He really had wanted his friend Sam to come along. "We could have Sam and Evan and Ross," he begged. But I told him I wanted it to be just the two of us—father and son—something special. Reluctantly he acceded, but even as we walked to the car he was suggesting we could stop by Sam's—Just Sam, Dad! No one else!—and see if he was, as he put it, "available." Josh was eight years old. He spoke about Sam as if he were King Solomon. Sam says I don't have to worry about the reading tests—they don't really count. Sam eats his hamburger this way, with relish and avocado, and not with ketchup and tomato. Sam buys his clothes at Banana Republic, not at Penney's. He didn't quit begging me to stop at Sam's until we actually got over the Bay Bridge and even Josh had to concede it was too far to go back. Longingly he looked at the retreating San Francisco skyline as if he were being carted off to prison.

"It'll be fun," I said.

"No it won't," he replied.

I looked over at him. One part of me wanted to throw him out of the window, and the other part of me wanted to weep. I began to sense how foolish this junket was. I wanted to say something light and engaging, but I was gripped with the idea that anything

I might come up with would sound hopelessly stupid to him. He took out his Game Boy and started playing his millionth game of Tetris DX. I flipped on the radio. I put it on classical. He immediately changed it to rap.

But it was a beautiful, warm day once we got out of the city, with its malignant fog and depressing, gray air. Here the sun was shining brightly and the temperature jumped twenty degrees all the way to eighty, and we drove along merrily, at least I did. I loved leaving the fog and hitting the hot air. Each time it startled me, woke me to the wideness and strangeness of the world. I rolled down all the windows and let my hand play in the wind. And pretty soon even Josh couldn't resist the glorious sunshine and wide brown hills, the warm summer air and cloudless sky, and just like that he gave up being glum and started talking about baseball. On good days we did that. I actually knew almost nothing about baseball, but I was ever so clever at bouncing his questions back at him so he'd think I had the same statistics at my fingertips as he did. Do you think Barry Bonds is going to get out of his slump? he asked. I assured him he would, because hadn't he always in the past? And then I'd say, what's he batting anyway? Oh, yeah, right, but last year he was . . . what? Right. So there's no reason to suppose—and he's a switch hitter, isn't he? Oh duh, that's . . . uh . . . who? Santiago! Right! When he got tired of that, we'd do the same thing with rap music and Saturday morning cartoons. Even though he was still sitting with his feet up on the dashboard and his nose in his Game Boy, it seemed he had scooted closer to me, and I reached over and ruffled his hair.

When we got to Mr. Fun, which, for all its immeasurable appeal to grammar school boys, was a rather lackluster affair stuck just off the freeway in the middle of cow pastures and sheep farms, I presented him with a bagful of quarters, and he disappeared into the blaring labyrinth of the video arcade. It was a colossal waste of money, but I loved watching him. He swelled with the pleasure of being in control, and I with him. He knew exactly which machine to go to first, and how to behave with the other video-crazed kids, so that in seconds he was part of a group and was even invited to join in a round of air hockey. I hung back and watched from a safe distance. When the other kids finally wandered off, he challenged me to a game of Missile Command and fully and gleefully humiliated me. But I was proud that he could beat me fair and square. Unfortunately, he, too, was humiliated a few minutes later, because he was deemed too short to race the go-karts on his own. They said I had to drive for him. But when no one was looking we switched places. He just burst with joy. We're so happy together, I said to myself, so maybe it will all work out.

And later we had fun in the bumper cars and we took turns in the batting cages, where I stood close behind him and guided his swing and felt his sense of accomplishment as the ball went soaring out into the field—not very far, in the scheme of hit balls, but for me they were all home runs. We ate hot dogs and hamburgers with pickle relish (they didn't have avocado), and we drank orange sodas and munched on fries, and ate ice cream right after that, and at some point we even had cotton candy, and for the first time in his entire life I let him go into a public restroom by himself.

By the end of the day, his hands sticky with cotton candy and his mouth stuffed with Jelly Bellies, flushed and tired and a little sunburned, Josh didn't argue when it was time to go home. My arm around his shoulder, we strolled to the car.

"It was fun, Dad," he said.

A few minutes into our ride home, I thought it was time.

"Listen," I said, "I have something important to tell you."

And then I explained about his mother and me.

I watched his happy face freeze, then melt. His cheeks quivered and his little hands were pressed into tight balls.

"But what am I supposed to do now?" he cried.

"You don't have to do anything," I explained.

"Am I supposed to go back and forth between your houses?"

"Something like that. We'll work it out. It won't be so bad. It'll be kind of fun. We'll be bachelors."

"I'm not going to live with Mom?"

"No, no, you'll live with Mom. I meant when you're with me."

"And how often will that be?"

"I don't know yet. How often do you want to be with me?"

He looked at me hard. "How am I supposed to know that?" he said.

We rode on a little longer. The sun was sinking in the sky, bringing down on us a blinding, desperate brightness.

"I'm really, really mad at you!" he suddenly exploded. "I'm really, really mad at you." And then he started crying, not like when he scraped himself, or when he was made to go to his room, or when he didn't get to stay up, or even when he was afraid to tell us his grade, or the time he got stuck climbing those rocks and couldn't go forward and couldn't go back and was just hanging on for dear life. It was some other cry I had never heard before, a cry so deep it was almost silent, so sharp it took all his breath away, and mine too.

The tears just poured out of his eyes.

"I know you're mad at me," I said. "You have every right to be mad at me. But we're friends, Josh. And we need each other. We're best friends. You're my best friend."

He looked up at me and shook his head.

"You're not my friend," he said. "You're my father."

I had to pull over a few miles down because he had to throw up. I held his head and felt his small body contracting and heaving under my hands. I gently rubbed his back as he seemed to go limp and almost sleepy. I took off my shirt and wiped his face. I hugged him and eased him back into the car. The little puddle of vomit stared up at me from the asphalt, and I tossed my shirt into the bushes.

When I came round and slid in behind the wheel, he was already asleep. I thought of the intimacy that had just passed between us, and I shuddered with dread.

But really and truly I wasn't a bad father. We were always laughing, all three of us. Always having fun. Lots of times we did skits together. I would set up the video camera on the tripod, and then think of a premise and give Ella and Josh characters and we'd do improv. It was great. I had dozens of those tapes. After the divorce, I used to look at them all the time. She didn't want them. She gave them all to me. I must admit, that hurt my feelings.

I thought of these things while I stretched out on the chaise. My mind had a tendency to wander like that. I tried to remember what had started that train of thought—something about the woman with the long undyed hair. Something about the longing in her eyes and the angry way she typed.

I thought: there were lots of good things about me as a husband! And Ella liked a lot of things about me, too—because she told me so. Maybe I should make a catalog of all these things. I should list every single thing she liked about me, and present it to her. A kind of ledger of the good me.

I started mentally jotting them down:

Excellent pancakes
Good foot massage
Fun at parties
Professional-sounding telephone voice

Able to fix electrical things
Ambidextrous tongue

This was good, I thought, a good start! I could quantify my worth as her husband. I could help her see the logic of getting back together. I could present an irrefutable case.

Loyal to a fault (did NOT fool around even after you stopped having sex with me)
Flosses

Oddly, I soon began to fall asleep again, even though I had just gotten up from a nap. My mind wandered along this pathway until it grew dull and stupid, but for a while I had been really taken with this idea of quantification, with the idea that the universe was actually made up of little pluses and minuses that you could sum up and write down in a ledger. Sure, we like to think of everything as a mystery, from human relationships to ecology to cosmic forces; it's comforting to believe all experience is indecipherable, ineluctable—whatever word you want to call it—but we're wrong. Yes, we're wrong, and for a few seconds there I got it. I knew my little epiphany would get fuzzy and then wear off completely in just a few minutes—but to feel that there really is this checklist of good and bad, right and wrong, existence and nonexistence, fact and error, life and death—what joy! It was so heartening to think I could actually understand something. Right there, poolside, where my mother had fallen onto the mahjongg tiles and knocked the iced tea off the table, a spirit of love pervaded, not sorrow. The hat floating across the water did in fact mean something. It meant straw hats float! It meant that if I got into the water and lay on my back and allowed the water to own me, why, I'd float right across to the other side too. I loved this list thing! I loved saying, *See! Ella! This is who I am!* Unfortunately, I didn't have a pencil or paper with me, and I knew I'd forget most of my best attributes if I didn't hurry back to my father's apartment to write them down, but I just couldn't muster the energy to get up. It was too hot. The sweet, calm water lapping against the side of the pool had lulled me into a lazy state of mind. Maybe it was the sun beating down on my head, or the fact that I hadn't eaten all afternoon, but for the first time in a long while I felt hope. And that was striking. So striking. Because until that moment I had not realized how hopeless I had become.

I looked around. It was a nice pool house. I felt good about it. Palm trees. Tropical flowers. The lovely sound of a lone Lincoln Town Car puckapucking down the soft, newly paved asphalt drive. I had a list now. I had a case. There was love in the world after all. Everything grew dim and pleasant as I drifted toward sleep.

But I felt something in my hand and looked down. It was, of course, Journal #2, and I woke, just like that.

I should have tossed that goddamned diary into the pool and flown back to San Francisco that very day. But I didn't. It was Dad's . . . whatever it was. And I couldn't abandon him. I just couldn't.

=========

They called him the "Yekkeh," the German. By which, by the way, they meant a German Jew, and not a German at all. It was a term of affectionate opprobrium deriving from his anal retentiveness, as the Jewish Doktor Freud would have called it, his compulsion to put everything in order, his need for cleanliness, and his fear that the slightest disarray opened the door to the ravages of chaos. As far as Heshel was concerned, he found this nickname an amusing irony. As long as they thought of him as German, he could be German. It was as if he had drawn a disguise over himself by drawing himself as he really was. "Yekkeh." The kibbutzniks seemed like children to him. Pets. He found that he somehow wished to protect them against themselves, as one protects sheep from wandering blindly into quicksand, or horses from running frantically into the burning barn.

He would do what he could to help, and then he would leave forever.

In the meantime, they liked to have movies on Saturday nights. Naor was only an hour from Tel Aviv, but to the kibbutzniks that seemed a million miles away, so once or twice a month they set up the projector in the Bet Am and watched old films and outdated newsreels. Heshel did not like the newsreels. They frequently focused on the Nuremberg Trials. He watched as Nazi after Nazi was condemned to die. Occasionally he even saw a familiar face sitting in the docks. He forced himself to sit there, and even cheer, but it terrified him. On this particular evening, the newsreel began by showing warehouses full of pocket watches, coats, suitcases, pens, handbags, and the inevitable shoes. It showed footage of happy Germans during the war, receiving relief packages of clothing and hats, of children clutching refurbished dolls and teddy bears, of a line of grateful old men being fitted for eyeglasses. Then it showed one of the American prosecutors waving a document in his hand and pointing an accusing finger at the prisoners in the dock. A moment later the film cut to a close-up of the document, laid out so it could be read, the letters, each as big as a man's torso, filling the screen from top to bottom. The camera slowly panned down the page. It was in German, but of course Heshel could read it easily, and anyway, the narrator explained what it was.

REPORT BY SS-STURMBANNFÜHRER WIPPERN, CONCERNING VALUE OF MONEY, PRECIOUS METALS, OTHER VALUABLES, AND TEXTILES OF JEWS

17	Gold Fountain Pens	RM 1,900
4	Platinum Watches	RM 1,200
2,894	Gold Gentlemen's Pocket Watches	RM 1,427,000
7,313	Ladies' Gold Wristwatches	RM 1,828,250
6,245	Gentlemen's Wristwatches	RM 62,450
13,455	Gentlemen's Pocket Watches	RM 269,100
51,370	Watches to Be Repaired	RM 258,850
22,324	Spectacles	RM 66,972
11,675	Gold Rings with Diamonds	RM 11,675,000
1,399	Pairs Gold Earrings w/ Brilliants	RM 349,750
7,000	Fountain Pens	RM 70,000
1,000	Automatic Pencils	RM 3,000
350	Razors	RM 875
3,240	Pocket Books	RM 4,860
1,500	Scissors	RM 750
2,544	Alarm Clocks to Be Repaired	RM 7,662
160	Alarm Clocks, Working	RM 960
477	Sunglasses	RM 238
41	Silver Cigarette Cases	RM 1,230
230	Thermometers	RM 690
462	Boxcars of Rags	RM 323,400
253	Boxcars of Feathers for Bedding	RM 2,510,000
317	Boxcars of Clothes and Linens	RM 10,461,000

The total, the narrator concluded, after adding many other items plus cash and precious metals, came to one hundred million, forty-seven thousand, nine hundred eighty-three reichsmarks and ninety-one pfennig, and was signed by Wippern, SS-Sturmbannführer, and dated Lublin, 27 February 1943. The narrator went on to say that this itemization of goods came from a single concentration camp, and covered a period of only three months, and that by December of that year, another two thousand boxcars of loot was sent to SS warehouses from this single source, including 132,000 wristwatches, 39,000 pens, 28,000 scissors and 230,000 razor blades. Himmler himself ordered that 15,000 of the ladies' wristwatches be given as Christmas presents to ethnic Germans who lived in occupied Soviet territory, whereas pure silk underwear was to be delivered directly to the Reich Ministry of Economics.

There was complete silence in the hall, but Heshel Rosenheim grew faint. Moskovitz looked over and saw that he was swaying in his chair, gasping for breath.

She took his hand to console him. She understood: it was too unbearable to contemplate the people beneath those numbers, the wrists without the wristwatches, the spectacles without the faces, the rings without the fingers. She stroked his hand and touched his cheek with an almost otherworldly delicacy. You are here now, she seemed to tell him, all that is over. Never again will we put ourselves into someone else's hands. They may kill us, the Arabs, the British, right here where we stand, but not without a fight. We may die, but like men, and we will never again subject ourselves to the whims either of their goodwill or their hatred. No, she seemed to say, no one will ever again control our destiny. She was like a rock of gentleness. He saw all of this in her eyes as he pulled himself together and nodded to her that he was all right again.

But you see, he recognized something in that document that she would never have guessed: his own handiwork. For he himself had written it at Majdanek. He himself had estimated the number of looted articles, assigned value to the various categories, managed the numerous calculations. In fact, he had regarded this very inventory as one of his greatest accomplishments at Majdanek. And then Major Wippern had stolen the credit for himself.

Back in 1943, he was distraught, furious. But now, as the neatly typed words burned through the movie screen, and the voice of the announcer filled the theater with outrage, Heshel thought once again: How fortunate I have been! As if God himself had intervened on his behalf! Back in those days, he merely thought that he had been too afraid to complain. But maybe it had been God's hand that turned him into a coward. In any case, he had revenged himself on Wippern by miscalculating the shipments and exaggerating the quality of goods, which then—with letters demanding a refund—were frequently sent back as unusable—mainly because of bloodstains, bullet holes, and the failure to remove the yellow Jewish star which officials of the Winter Relief Agency found "disturbing," complaining that no one would want to wear them. On top of all this, Lieutenant Mueller had figured out how to steal just enough in the way of watches and stockings to keep himself in cognac and cigars and to finance the occasional lost weekend, but he abruptly ended this practice when a number of fellow officers over at Auschwitz were summarily hanged for pilfering and "sabotage."

And now, as he sat there in the kibbutz communal hall that served as theater, meeting room, dining room, and schoolroom, it all came back to him—the rows of tables piled high with eyeglasses, combs, and brassieres, the Kapos *busily sorting and counting, the warehouses filled with leather, fur, goose feathers, the smell of human fat rising in dark, moist clouds above the gray encampment—and trying to shake the image from his brain, he looked over at Moskovitz. What he saw in her eyes was pity.*

He got up, even though the feature had not yet started, and rushed from the room.

=========

The sun had moved somewhat toward the west, and I could now hear voices. People were beginning to move back outside. Soon the card players and aquamaids would be poolside. I did not want to be around people. I gathered my stuff and shuffled along on my flip-flops in the direction of my father's building. Near the entrance I ran into the ladies' club.

"It's Golda's boy," one of them said.

A pursed smile corroded my face. "I'm Lily's," I said.

They looked confused. But of course. Lily had been dead eight years.

"Heshel," I said. "I'm Heshel's boy."

Then they gathered round me happily and started asking me how was *Hesheleh,* how was my own family doing back in—where? San Francisco? Morris and I were in San Francisco! Fisherman's Warf! Did you know you look like a movie star?—which one does he look like, Bessie?—and when do you think he'll be coming home, your father?

When I told them I thought he wasn't, they all nodded knowingly, and one of them took my hand, and another said, "It's good you're here. You're a good son. We all should have such a son," and another offered, "You know, I've got a chicken in the oven."

But I thanked them and made my way to the elevator.

"He's a wonderful man, your father," I heard one of them call after me.

And then another one sighed, "Ach, it's terrible to be so old!"

And one said to another, "I think his name is David."

"No, no, no," said a third, "Sophie's is David. Heshel's is Barry."

As the door closed, locking me into the stinking, moldy elevator, I gave up the idea of presenting Ella with my list.

CHAPTER 7

I needed a plan. I was not generally a person who made plans. Once upon a time I did, but that was long ago, and since none of them ever amounted to anything, I now distrusted all plans. But I had to find out who brought those journals. That was the key to the whole thing. That person, and that person alone, knew the truth.

I decided to watch and wait.

I drove over to the nursing home, pulled into a spot facing the building, and turned off the engine. You could do that in the early evening, when the temperature dropped into the eighties. I positioned myself so I could look directly into his room, which was on the first floor. It was only a two-story building anyway. If someone entered his room, I'd pounce. That was my strategy.

At first, no one came. But then I saw a shadowy figure slip past the window. Tall, dark, somewhat elegant in gesture, he bent down over my father's bed. I swung open the car door and sprinted across the lot, pushed my way through the main entrance, ran down the hall, and literally jumped into the room.

A huge black man was lifting my father in his arms and helping him into the wheelchair. He looked up, startled; then smiled.

"Oh look, Heshel! It's your son come to help with dinner!"

"Lamar," I said.

"See, Heshel!" he screamed good-naturedly in my father's ear, the way orderlies who work with old people do, and pointed at me. It was dinnertime. I watched as Lamar tucked a small blanket around my father's legs.

Lamar had a kindly face, but he was very strong, and my father was docile in his hands. He was efficient, gentle, and at the same time imposing and even intimidating. The tasks at the Lake Gardens were divided along rather rigid racial lines. The nurses by and large were white, but Christian. The orderlies were almost entirely black, like Lamar, except for Rodrigo, who was Puerto Rican. The cooks were invariably Filipino, and the cleanup staff was Mexican. The receptionist and the manager were Jewish, and the owners were a corporation in Texas. It was remarkable to me how well everyone got along, and how, sadly, things never change.

I watched as Lamar wheeled my father out.

"Lamar," I said, "did you see a box of books in here?"

"Books? No, I don't think I did."

"It was a Cheez Whiz box," I said.

He looked at me somewhat sideways. "I don't think I did," he repeated. "Is something missing?"

"No, Lamar. Nothing to worry about. Nothing is missing."

"I wasn't worried none," he said, and moved my father down the corridor toward the dining room.

=

Eventually I followed them into the dining hall, which also served as the assembly room for bingo night, and the theater for movies, and the cabaret when the out-of-work comedians came to *tummel*. I often came at dinnertime. It was a strange but affecting bond between us. He liked when I helped him eat, and even though part of me found it gross, wiping half-chewed peas or dollops of custard from his chin, I felt happy to do it. Happy is perhaps not the right word. But it was all we had.

My father had reached that stage of life when it was almost impossible for him to bring a fork into his mouth. Instead, he had to lean his whole body forward, meeting it somewhere just above the bowl of tapioca. He preferred that I feed him. And then there was always the possibility that I would bring him a pastrami sandwich from The Charm. He liked it with Russian dressing and coleslaw, like an East Coast Sloppy Joe. It occurred to me, as I watched him and Lamar disappear down the corridor, that maybe I should drive over to The Charm and get him a sandwich. But I was not in the mood to bring him a sandwich. I was in the mood to kick his teeth in. Only, of course, he didn't have any teeth. That was the other thing about Alzheimer's. They forget to put in their teeth.

"You got me a sandwich?" he said.

"I didn't have time," I said back.

He looked a little annoyed, but he was gracious and attempted to butter his roll. I had found him at his usual table in the corner. He sat by himself. Like I tried to tell the nurse—he had no friends anymore.

I watched him fumble with the roll. I didn't move to help him.

"Who's Frau Hellman?" I said.

His eyes suddenly grew frightened. "Who?" he said.

"Frau Hellman. You mentioned her the other day."

He seemed to have already forgotten about the roll even though it was still in his hand, because he turned to me and said, "What did I do with my sandwich?"

I could see I was going to get nothing out of him. Even so, I pressed on.

"Was she, like, from the concentration camp?"

He looked at me sharply. "The what?"

"Here," I said, "eat your fish." I cut off a little piece of fish stick and offered it to him on the end of his fork.

He took a bite and said, "You know we never, ever talk about that. Your mother wouldn't like it."

"Why not?" I said as casually as I could.

"I don't want this fish," he muttered.

"Which concentration camp were you in?" I asked. I affected a nonchalant tone of voice.

I was surprised when he said, "Many. First here, then there."

"Majdanek?"

"A graveyard," he said.

"And you were there?"

"Where?"

"Majdanek."

He stared down at his plate. He seemed to turn into stone, except for the rapid blinking of his eyes, as if he were on the verge of falling asleep. His head fell onto his chest. Desperately, I decided on a frontal attack.

"Your journals," I began.

"What?"

"The journals you gave me."

"What journals?"

"You gave me a box of journals."

Suddenly he shook his head violently. His arms jumped from his sides like two groupers convulsing in a net.

"Dad!" I grabbed him by the shoulders. "I need the truth."

He looked up at me, but his eyes were full of uncertainty. He searched my face for a clue, as if he were struggling to figure out exactly who I was.

"Is ever'thing all right?" It was Lamar.

"I think he's having a fit," I said.

"Humm." He nodded. "I be taking over then." He wiped the spittle from my father's chin, and spun his wheelchair away from the table so that he could not see me. "Do you want your dinner?" he asked him. "If you're not good, then no dinner." He said this so gently he could not have meant it.

But after a few minutes it became obvious my father didn't want his dinner after all, and Lamar took him back to his room, his body leaping around in the chair and his arms still flailing about like someone had plugged him into an electrical socket.

I watched them go, sitting awhile in front of my father's plate of fish sticks. It was terrible, seeing him that way, as if my questions had already put him in the electric chair. It was terrible, but I have to be honest. When Lamar wheeled him, kicking and gyrating, from the dining hall, I actually heard myself say, "Die, you son of a bitch, die!" I guess I didn't say it aloud, because nobody turned to look at me. But *I* heard it, and I might have been as dead as the fish on that plate, for all the compassion I had in me in that moment.

That's when I got up and started wandering through the halls of the Lake Gardens nursing home. I could not have said exactly why I was doing what I was doing—indeed I had a strange sense of déjà vu, almost as if I were recalling a dream while I was still in the dream—but there was a sort of dark clarity running through me as I set about my task. I passed the nurse's station, taking note of its layout and where each of the nurses sat, and where the monitors were, and who tended to stay put, and who felt compelled to respond to the constant call buttons. I smiled at them and they nodded back. Then I ambled on down the hall, past my father's room which had its door shut anyway, and checked out some of the areas I had not seen before. It never occurred to me to really *look* at Lake Gardens before. There was a maintenance closet, a small employees' lounge with a few humming vending machines and a coffee urn, an equipment room where they kept the portable EKG machines and other—rather run-down and outdated—electrical devices, and then there was the dispensary where they kept all the medications. I lurked about this room for a minute or two just to see how it worked. Soon a nurse came up, slipped her key in the door, and disappeared within. In a little while, carts filled with sleeping pills, heart remedies, blood thinners, and stool softeners were wheeled out and pushed down the corridor, stopping at each room with their little gifts of salvation in a paper cup.

Beyond the dispensary was the end of the hall, a dark space leading to a stairwell no one ever seemed to use. I walked all the way down, turned around, and walked back. By that time, I could see that my father's door was open, but I didn't go in. I'd decided I'd had enough. I wanted home. It had gotten dark by now, and drenchingly humid. I stepped out into the parking lot and a herd of mosquitoes instantly materialized on my arms and neck, like pigs around a trough.

=========

This simple thing to have done was to slip out of the kibbutz and walk to Egypt, to Gaza. Once there, go to the first army post or police station, tell them . . . that's where the plan fell apart. Tell them what? He had no papers other than his kibbutz papers and those forged for him by the Yishuv. They stated that he was born in Petach Tikva, which as far as he knew was somewhere in the north of Palestine. But even if he managed to find some British or German documents, his arm bore the tattoo of Auschwitz—which of course also made it impossible for him to have been from Petach Tikva. Sometimes he thought he might have been saved by his SS tattoo, but he didn't have one. He'd been glad of that immediately after the war, but now it seemed a shame. His only hope was to find someone to vouch for him—some other German. And that did not seem likely.

Then he thought about stowing away on a ship for South America, or even the United States, sliding down the anchor chain with the rats, and swimming to safety. But how would he live? He was not afraid of starving. But he was terrified of closed quarters, of being locked away in some container filled with oranges or dates, with no air, no light, no way out. And the possibility of getting caught. Of being jailed, and then hanged, or of summarily being tossed overboard. His mind raced with possibilities. He did not wish to be a coward, but he had to admit that he was one.

One evening, Heshel walked alone among the orange trees along the eastern edge of the settlement. Beyond them, they had just begun the experiment of planting bananas, and there were sunflowers and cotton as well, but here in the orange groves there was a sense of quiet and security. The harvest was over, yet the rains had not yet come—it was that week or two in October when the air was as still as a sleeping child, sweet smelling and pure, and a kind of Sabbath settled into the groves, a time apart. Heshel Rosenheim was wearing the blue work shirt that they had given him, and the loose-fitting blue work pants as well—he did not favor shorts—but his sleeves were rolled up all the way to his biceps and his collar was flared open in the style they all affected. He reached up to gather a few leaves, and in the light of the moon he saw how muscular his arm had become, how thick and callused his fingers—for it must be said that even though he did the books, he still was required to plow the fields, to milk the cows, to scythe the alfalfa, to chop the vegetables when his turn came in the kitchen. And he did not mind, in fact. During harvest that first year, waking at four in the morning, making his way in the dark to the groves or the fields, following a few steps behind the others, climbing the ladders, filling his sack with ripe fruit, noticing out of the corner of his eye the sun beginning its journey into the Palestinian sky—the Yishuv, they called it—the settlement—he felt alive and unafraid. He did not believe anyone would harm him, as long as he stood with his head in the trees.

But on this lovely, cloudless evening, the moon also illuminated the number carved into his arm. It seemed phosphorescent, like the glow of bacteria on an old piece of ham. He recalled the desperation of that hour, of crawling out of the mountain of corpses—they were not people to him then, or now—they simply were the stink of war, the fallen—more like piles of fish than anything else—and he remembered how he made his way in darkness to the SS command. It was not the darkness of tonight, but an utter darkness he recalled, a dream darkness, yet his eyes were like torches lighting his way. With such a singular state of mind, nothing could have stopped him. How had he become that machine of survival? He could not say, even now. Yet he recalled how, hiding under the desk, with no light but what the lamppost cast through the grimy windows, he stabbed himself over and over with the sharpened nib of steel—the very nib he had used to record the kilos of human hair to be made into pillows, the thousands of wedding bands to be melted into gold ingots—this he used to press the ink deep into his starved and strawlike flesh, tears running from his eyes, but feeling no pain. It was all there, written in his arm.

He kneeled at the base of the tree, holding it up to his eyes.

Whose number is this?

Who died so he might live? Another Avigdor? A Mira? A Sophie? A Yitzhak?

What brought him to this place? Who did this to him?

He took out his pocketknife and began to jab at his arm, scraping at the tattoo like one would a piece of toast, to get off the burnt. Clean it up! Make it right again! Like a madman he drew the knife over his skin, chopping and scraping, peeling his flesh into a bloody pulp.

"Stop!"

He felt a hand grasp his wrist.

"No, no," he tried to say.

But Moskovitz held him firmly, wrestled the knife from his fingers, and threw it to the ground. Then she put her arms around him, swaying, squeezing him so tightly he could barely breathe, as if she could suffocate the demon within him.

"None of that matters anymore!" she cried to him, her lips moving upon the nape of his neck. "It's all in the past."

She held his face between her two thick hands.

"This is what matters," she said, and she kissed him upon his mouth, opening her own with hunger and praise. He was overwhelmed by this kiss, by the softness of her lips and the yearning of her tongue, and he fell back against the tree trunk and fainted.

=========

Moskovitz had a first name. It was Fradl. When he spoke this name in the silence of the orange grove it melted upon his tongue. Fradl.

He had wanted her to reek, to stink of foreignness. He had wanted the touch of her flesh to burn him, to make his own skin crawl with revulsion. He had wanted her mouth to repulse him with the taste of vomit. He had wanted to have to run into the darkness, overcome with nausea, doubled over, puking at the very thought of her naked thighs.

But none of this had happened.

Instead, when he opened his eyes and saw her face glowing above him like a bright moon, he uttered her name. And when she kissed him again, she did not taste of offal or garlic or rot, or any of that—but of flowers and fruit, of wine in fact, seductive and slightly sweet, like the first bite of dark chocolate, at once familiar and exotic—and impossible to not want more. When she touched him, first on the face, and then sliding her heavy fingers beneath his shirt, it was with such delicacy and yearning it made him tremble. For the slightest instant, he recalled the touch of his mother—yet it was not a mother's touch, not at all. And before he knew it, he was touching her in the same way, only harder, and more hungrily.

Comforted, aroused, terrified, he made love to her beneath the orange trees, and heard himself say her name over and over, and over again.

=========

"Fradl," he said again.

Their legs were entwined, and her head rested cozily upon his shoulder. He stroked her hair and watched the stars move lazily across the heavens. Her hand still caressed his chest beneath his opened shirt. She laughed and said she would have to sew the buttons back on. She remarked that she had never heard him say her name before.

"I'm glad you finally called me that," she laughed, "because I'm changing it to Yael."

"Really?" he said.

"Sure. And my family name, too. I'm going to be Yael Bat Tsedek."

They all changed their European names to some made-up Hebrew concoction. But suddenly he didn't want her to. She was part of that time, not this. This was the link between them, even though she could not possibly know of what that link truly consisted.

"You should get circumcised," she said.

=========

He had learned enough Hebrew to understand that Bat Tsedek meant "daughter of the righteous," but he did not know about Yael.

"She's in the Bible," she told him, "a warrior. She murdered the enemy of Israel as he slept. He came to her for protection, but she killed him anyway. So be careful." She found this highly amusing. Her laughter was quiet though, as if she did not wish to injure the serenity of the trees.

"Shall I call you Yael, then?" he asked.

"No. You must always call me Fradl," she replied softly. "In that way some piece of my past will always give me joy."

She reached for his arm. It was still bloody and raw where he had tried to obliterate the tattoo. She kissed his wound, and then closed her eyes.

"You should get rid of the ghetto name as well," she said sleepily.

"They used to call me Heinrich."

"You mean in school?"

"Yes."

"Won't do," she said, and before he could reply, she fell asleep.

He lay there trying to make out the constellations he had learned as a boy. They looked a little different in this part of the world, but he was good at it, and he discerned Pegasus and then Aquarius and Pisces, and then got caught up in the Milky Way, and in the odd idea that he was looking at his own universe as it rotated around him, while he could do nothing but sit still and watch.

Why had he done this thing? Was the hollowness within him so vast he could stuff his belly with anything at all, like a beggar rooting through mountains of garbage for a morsel to eat, or the Jews of Bergen-Belsen, so parched with thirst, they greedily drank water polluted with human waste? Is that why he took this woman?

He must be very careful, he thought as he lay there, not to fall in love. Not even to like her very much.

Still, when he felt her breast rise up against him as she inched even closer in the sweet embrace of sleep, he allowed himself to breathe in the scent of her hair, and place a kiss upon her tender Jewish nose.

=========

When the phone rang that night, I let it ring. I knew it was Josh. I wanted to talk to him more than anything, to allow his sweet, green voice to heal me, just the sound of it—but how could I speak to him? What could I say? I felt like my entire life was pasted over with lies, and I could not lie to him, not anymore. I could not ask him about his homework. I could not joke with him about Frau Hellman. The little willpower I had left was just enough to protect him from me, even though I knew it must have hurt him.

An hour later, when he called again, I let it ring some more.

I showed up at Lake Gardens at eight the next morning. Somehow it was already sweltering. The sky was thick with dull gray clouds, but I knew it wouldn't rain. The water would just hang in the air like shreds of hair, gluing itself to my skin and making me itch without any hope of scratching. Down on the lawn, a few women were pushing their husbands in wheelchairs along the asphalt path. They moved so slowly they seemed to be standing still. As I walked toward the entrance, a coconut fell onto the grass with a great and terrifying thud. Had I been a few steps to the right, it would have killed me.

I hated Florida.

I found Dad in a mostly comatose state, rocking his torso back and forth, and occasionally mumbling something I couldn't make out.

"Hey, Dad," I said. "It's me."

"Israel?" he said.

"No, Dad, me."

Me. That was a word that was beginning to have no meaning either. Is it a name? Or a declaration of some sort? A complaint?

I sat down beside him. I waited a few minutes to see if he would come out of it, but he just slipped farther and farther into negative space. I took the moment to look at his chart. He was on Exelon—a cognitive drug—twice a day. There were a few other things I'd never heard of. I wrote them down on the little pad I used to sketch out my comedy routines. I fiddled with the Levolors—open, close, open, close—and absently drew the curtain round his bed. With the blinds closed as well, I got the strange, not unpleasant feeling I was deep under the sea, in a diving bell, for it was so quiet and cut off from the life around us. Then I pushed open the curtain and the bustle of the nursing home came pouring in, full of the usual misery and defeat.

He hadn't noticed any of it.

After a while, I turned on the television, and, right on cue, Dad opened his eyes, and we both watched *Good Morning America*.

CHAPTER 8

I had been up reading all the night before, so it's not surprising I fell asleep sometime during *Regis and Kelly,* and when I opened my eyes the noon news was on. I wasn't quite sure where I was. I never followed the news anymore, so I had a hard time understanding what they were talking about. I guess it happened after Ella moved out with Josh. As I sat there looking blankly at the TV screen, I remembered why.

Ella was running around packing things. Stuffing Josh's toys into boxes. Putting school books into paper bags. I told her she could have the house, that I would go. But she didn't want it. I thought it was because of all the memories, a house filled with sadness, that sort of thing.

"How could you ever think I would want to keep Josh in a dump like this?" she said.

But she said all kinds of crazy, unhinged things then. She was upset. I tried to make it easier for her. I told her, "Okay, okay, then take whatever you want. Anything. I don't care." But she didn't want anything. Not even the kitchen stuff.

"It's all crap," she said.

I remember trying so hard not to take it personally. "But I thought you liked it here."

"Michael, I did it for you," she said, shaking her head. "Oh, what's the use?"

"Well take the television at least," I begged her.

"I don't want your fucking television," she said.

"But it's a Sony!" I cried.

When they drove away in the Honda, I was standing in the doorway holding the TV in my arms. Suddenly I threw it as hard as I could, right at them, but it only landed a few feet away on the lawn. It didn't even break. It just sort of bounced on the AstroTurf.

I watched them disappear over the crest of the hill. Our block had become so ugly. There were no trees and hardly any grass. Some people had asphalt painted green. Others had gravel or a combination of mulch and redwood chips. And I was the one with the AstroTurf. It used to make me laugh. But now I felt sick. I closed the door and went inside.

When I came out the next morning, the television was gone. There was a dent in the AstroTurf where it had landed. The dent never went away. It was still there when I left the house, and I included it in my note to the landlord, about the wear and tear I didn't feel responsible to pay for. *Slight disfigurement in AstroTurf* is how I put it.

The days and weeks after they left were pretty horrendous.

One day I noticed that the *Chronicle* was piling up on the front steps. There were maybe five, six weeks of newspapers. I called and canceled my subscription, and then I loaded all the newspapers in paper bags and put them out for recycling. It was the first time I ever recycled. I always celebrated that event as "recycling day." The day I started my life over as something else. If anyone could call what I did for the next three years living.

Anyway, that was it with the news. So when I awoke in my father's room in the nursing home and heard them talking about taxes and politics and drilling for oil, it was like Greek to me—no, not Greek, because I knew Greek—like Armenian. Something like that. No, it was even worse than that. It was listening to words you were supposed to understand, but couldn't. Like in a dream. And then I realized it was exactly what my father must be feeling—surrounded by meaninglessness in this all-too-familiar world. What could he make of it? I was suddenly overcome with this feeling—of empathy—what else could it have been? And so I turned to my father to take his hand.

But when I looked over, I saw that he was gone.

I ran out of the room and right into Nurse Clara. I bounced off her large bosom, like she was a trampoline. It felt good, I had to confess, and I felt a little aroused. But she looked at me with scorn.

"Where's my father?" I said.

"Calm down," she said. "He's in the rec room."

I was confused. Rec room? *My* father? Playing pinochle? Foosball? I didn't even know there was a rec room.

Nurse Clara fingered her big black cross and smiled. "Follow me," she said.

We emerged into a large, bright room with Ping-Pong tables

and shuffleboard on one side, and a visiting area and card tables on the other. There were some chess boards set up, too, but no one was playing.

My father was on the couch, waving at me. He had a big happy smile on his face.

"Michael!" he called, "Michael!"

"He seems so alert," I said to Nurse Clara.

"Oh," she said, "he's always this way when he's had visitors."

His hair was combed. His goatee was brushed. He was holding a cigar.

"Who came to see him?" I demanded.

Nurse Clara waved amiably at my dad. She obviously thought he was cute. "I don't know," she said. "The usual."

"The usual? Who are these people?"

"You were asleep," she said. "They didn't want to wake you."

"But who are they?"

"How would I know?" she said. "Ask your father."

Her answers glowed with reasonableness. And then she heard herself being paged, patted me on the shoulder, and walked away.

I came up to my father. I had to admit he looked terrific. Not only were his teeth in, but no food particles adhered to his goatee, he had dressed in real clothes, and he was reading the *Miami Herald*. I couldn't help feeling terrifically happy just then, as if nothing we had been going through mattered one bit. He looked great. He looked strong. Is this how he looked to Moskovitz? A name, by the way, I tried to blot from my mind. Of all the things I had read in those journals, this making love under the orange trees was perhaps the most troubling.

"Hey, Mikey!" he said.

"Hey, Dad, what's up?"

"Fucking Republicans!" he said. "The rich get richer! Disgusting." He jabbed at the article he had been reading with his well-trimmed index finger.

"Yeah, well, you donated to the Republicans, too," I reminded him.

"Republican *Jews,*" he corrected me.

I could never follow the logic of that, but now was not the time to try. Dad was back!

"Nurse Clara tells me you had visitors," I said.

"Oh yes!" he said. "And I got my nails done."

He held out his hand, showing his neatly cut and polished nails. He had always liked to have his nails done—beautifully rounded, glazed in clear polish. Mark of a gentleman, he always said.

"You got a visit from a manicurist?"

"Don't be silly," he said. "Just friends."

"What friends?"

"What difference does it make? Friends!"

I looked at him. He was beaming. He had color in his cheeks. His eyes were twinkling. He chomped down on his cigar.

Everything, everything was on my mind. The journals. The invisible friends. The whole history of our lives. But what could I do?

"It's such a beautiful day," I said. "Would you like to go for a walk when it cools down?"

"Sounds good," he said.

"In the meantime," I went on, "I could drive you to the mall."

"Oh," he said, "that would be excellent. I could pick up a few things."

What he would need to pick up, only God knew. But I was so delighted with his sudden good health I didn't care. And in a few minutes we were stuffed in the Caddy on our way to Boynton Beach Mall.

=

South Florida is Mall Country. Huge ships of commerce floating on landfill, shimmering turquoise and coral like the insides of swimming pools, and equally inviting. Everyone goes to the mall. The only other option in Palm Beach is Worth Avenue, which is way too expensive for anyone on a fixed income, although I knew my parents used to go there, stroll down the avenue and gaze at the windows of Cartier and Chopard, or feel the fine leather at Myers Luggage, or admire the hats at Peter Beaton. My mother would make Dad try on stuff, but he'd never buy anything, though I know for sure he bought *her* something once at Georgio's of Palm Beach—a cashmere sweater that she cherished as much as any piece of jewelry she owned. But mostly they went to the mall. And they didn't feel one bit denied, either. The mall was like a treasure chest for them, a huge, walk-in closet of endless possibility. And they'd always run into friends there, too. Frequently the women would do the actual shopping, while the men would perambulate the long arcades, smoking cigars (before that was outlawed) and arguing condo politics, or divvying up responsibilities for whatever fund-raising drive was on that month. Other times they'd all go walking together, men and women, no one buying much of anything, just passing the time pleasantly, enjoying the air-conditioning.

But in the car I was trying to put together my picture of the Nazi from Bergen-Belsen with the cigar-smoking *landsman* strolling the mall and waxing poetic about his last trip to Israel. I found myself gripping the steering wheel, because otherwise I thought I might scream. I glanced down. My knuckles were white.

"You got a match, maybe?" he asked as we made our way down Congress Avenue.

I looked over at him. The last thing he needed was to smoke. But I said, "Use the lighter. I think it still works."

"Of course it works, it's a Cadillac!"

He winked and pushed the lighter in. In a moment he was happily sucking smoke into his lungs, filling the car with its masculine perfume. I admit I liked the smell. How could I not? Every room in our house in New Jersey had been filled with it. Our cars were like traveling ashtrays. His clothes, his skin, his hair, all reeked of cigar.

"Want one?" he said, pulling a dark stogie from his shirt pocket.

I don't know why, but I accepted it, tore the cellophane with my teeth and bit off the tip. He held the red-hot lighter towards me. I was amazed at how steady his hand was, not to mention the look in his eye. Was I dreaming? Had I flown back in time and found him young again?

I pressed the end of the cigar onto the hot coils and puffed.

"Turn it," he instructed me.

I did as he told me, lighting it evenly.

"I don't know, Mikey," he said after a minute. "I really want to go home."

"I know you do," I said.

"I don't want to die there."

"I know," I said.

We turned into the parking lot, and I drove around looking for a handicapped spot. As usual they were mostly taken, but finally I found one. I helped him out of the car, and then watched as he stood there in the burning sun, staring at the huge pastel edifice as if it were Mount Rushmore.

"Been a while since you've been out," I said.

He laughed.

"When you're my age," he replied, flicking his cigar, "it really doesn't matter where you are."

=

We were passing The Sock Shop when I tossed this one off: "So, you were in Palestine after the war, right?"

He didn't answer me right away, and then he said, "Let's go to the cigar store. It's down here somewhere."

"In '47 or '48. Before the State."

Still he said nothing.

"You were there, right?"

He saw the Mr. Humidor up ahead, and quickened his pace. We were now speeding along just above a crawl.

"That wasn't me," he said.

"I'm sorry?"

"You're mistaken," he said. "That wasn't me."

"But I was reading that you were in Palestine."

"No," he said, entering the store, "I wasn't. That was someone else."

I watched him descend upon the rows of cigars like Attila at the gates of Chalon, but unlike Attila, Dad emerged victorious, cradling an armful of dark brown smokes. He would probably die before he could consume even half of them. He laid them on the counter like an offering to the gods.

"Do you have money?" he said to me.

I gave the man my Visa card. I asked my father if he really needed so many cigars.

"When again am I going to come here?" he said.

"What are you talking about. We can come here whenever."

"Mikey!" He smiled, grabbing a bunch of my cheek between his fingers. "Don't kid a kidder."

I still had his journal in my jacket pocket. I could have, I should have, taken it out then and confronted him. But the salesman gave me the credit card slip to sign, and I let the moment pass. Anyway I was in a state of shock. The bill came to two hundred and twenty-two dollars and sixty-seven cents.

CHAPTER 9

He seemed so happy, sitting there with his bag of cigars. He had told me a couple of times on the drive back that he wanted to go home, so I made the turn onto Lake Worth Avenue and headed over to The Ponds at Lakeshore. It was on the way to the nursing home anyway. I wanted to surprise him. We rounded the golf course and pulled up to Building 3. I angled the Caddy into his assigned spot.

"Come on," I said. "Let's go inside."

I opened his door, helped him out. He stood there, looking around, taking it all in.

I guided him along the pavement to the entryway, and then helped him into the elevator. It wheezed up the side of the building and deposited us on the third floor, where we made our way along the ramp toward his apartment.

I knew, of course, that when we went in he'd see all the journals spread out on the floor—and then he'd have to come clean. We'd have to have that conversation. My heart was pounding, but I said nothing, and just watched him shuffle down the gangway.

Finally we stood at the door. The little buzzer with the number 304 imprinted under it. The little ceramic plaque with the name Rosenheim surrounded by pink roses. On the door frame to the right, the mezuzah, fashioned of green glass (in Israel, of course), waiting to be kissed.

I gave him the keys.

"Go ahead," I said.

He looked at me, suspicion entering his eyes like a dark green light. Suddenly he dropped the keys as if they were befouling his hands.

"Where are we?" he said. "I want to go home."

"But we are home," I told him.

"I want to go home!" he cried. "I want to go home! I want to go home!"

I picked up the keys and put them in my pocket.

"Okay," I said. "We'll go home."

Later, when he was asleep back at the nursing home, I took out the journal and, feeling more miserable than ever, forced myself to read.

=========

From this point on Rosenheim avoided Moskovitz.

=========

He avoided the scent of her breath. He avoided the sound of her husky laughter. He avoided the sight of her ringlets leaping from the pins that held her hair during work hours. He avoided her shadow at sunset. He avoided the memory of her breast in his hand. He avoided the taste of her collarbone.

When he sensed her presence, which was almost always, he walked the other way.

But he always ran into her. Everywhere he was, she was.

In the first days after the orchard, she was not careful at all, always wanting to walk with him, rub against him, talk to him about anything, chatter of love. She was completely without guile or shame.

At first, Heshel Rosenheim merely stiffened when she slipped her hand into his. But then began the cross words, the pursed lips, the icy looks. Crestfallen, she moved away. She could have written it off as a bad mood, but when it happened over and over, and then over again, she obviously got the message. Out of the corner of his eye, he noticed her always staring at him—from across the room, or as he passed her in the milking station, or looking up at him as he sat in the watchtower smoking his cigarettes. He never looked back at her. And each time, the bright hope and anticipation that lit her face faded into confusion and shame.

More and more he wanted to escape.

He even thought of turning himself in. In some ways, it would be better than this. At least then he would know who he was.

Still, at night, he would awake sweating, knowing he had been dreaming of her. It was the sex, he told himself.

=========

He decided to make contact with some local Arabs, but it was difficult. Hostilities were already breaking out—riots in Jerusalem and attacks in the North. Yet in those days many of the Jews and Arabs were still friends. He could wander off the kibbutz one afternoon and find himself in the little Arab village just to the southeast; he might be invited by the headman to have tea or coffee; he might accept, sit down upon the carpet, and offer in return some sort of aid to them. Money perhaps. Cigarettes. And then he might say he felt as strongly as they did that this land was theirs, not the Jews'. Why should the Arabs have to pay for what happened in Europe? In fact, he would say, he wanted to travel east, to Transjordan, to offer his services to the Arab Legion, and then he would tell them: I am not even a Jew. Yes! he would say to their startled ears, I am a German. A soldier. Your natural ally. Your friend. My knowledge of soldiering can help your cause. Perhaps we might work together . . . perhaps you might know someone who knows someone . . . to spirit me out of the country before any of the Jews even notice I'm gone?

It did not seem a likely plan.

Still, on a cool November evening he put on his flannel jacket and went out for a walk. The kibbutz was on high alert, and guards were walking the perimeters, their rifles at ready. A Bren gun had been set in the watchtower, on a slight rise, looking down upon the plains of Ashdod. He passed a sentry and waved. It was that Dutch Jew who had somehow survived Mauthausen. Amos, he called himself. Who knows what his real name was. Hans? Cornelius? Nys? He was not much with a gun, Heshel knew, and like all the Dutch, rather flat-footed in his conversation.

"You making a walk?" the Dutchman said. His Hebrew was not very good either.

"Yes, just down towards the village."

"Oh!" he said. "Not such good idea."

"I'll be fine, I'll be fine," replied Heshel Rosenheim. "They're friendly there. Remember how we helped them during the harvest? Nothing to worry about."

He knew Amos could barely understand him anyway, so he chatted on, speaking quickly and colloquially, and when the look in the Dutchman's eye seemed thoroughly befuddled, Heshel cried "Shalom!" and walked down onto the road toward Al Qalil. The sky was clouding over, and he could feel the first bluster of a cold front swinging in from the sea. A wind from Europe, perhaps bringing a storm. He was thinking, what wind brought me here? How could he ever get back? Maybe he should just give himself up, after all. He had heard that German prisoners of war in Egypt were already being released, and were joining the Egyptian army as mercenaries. But he reminded himself he was not an ordinary soldier. He was a war criminal. Not that he had ever actually done *anything. What was he, after all, but a bookkeeper? Just like on the kibbutz. He had merely kept things in order. Which is not actually an action. He merely entered items into a book of accounts. That's all.*

The clouds, white against the black sky, floated in front of the moon. Same as God! he said to himself. He was thinking of the Jewish New Year and their Day of Atonement. He's just a bookkeeper too! Even though Naor was not a religious kibbutz, they still celebrated the High Holidays, all gathering in the main hall, mouthing their absurd prayers—On Rosh Hashanah it is written, *they sang,* on Yom Kippur it is sealed! *The Book of Life. That's what they call it. God opens His book of life and death, and in you go, for good or ill. What else is that, but bookkeeping? And no matter what happens, does anyone blame God? Forty million die, and here they are, still praying!*

He could see the lights of the village just down the hill. He was walking now on the dirt path that cut through the mostly open terrain—some sandy desert with patches of scrub, with few outcroppings of rock or trees, but as the road descended toward Al Qalil, a ridge jutted out of the sands to his right, where frequently on clear nights he would come to study the stars.

He began to practice what he would say when he got to the village. He knew many of the men there by sight, but not by name. He had been there only a few times, and only rarely did the Arabs come up to Naor. It was a firm rule that only kibbutz members did kibbutz work. No hired hands. Yet there were some on the kibbutz who went down often, who had close, even tender relations with them, and he had tried very casually to glean as much as he could from them—who got along well with the Jews, who resented them, who wanted to live in peace, who did not. He knew he had to be clever in what he said, and to whom. His worst fear was that they would betray him to the Jews.

As he descended past the ridge, the smell of hearth fires came up to greet him, and the sound of goat bells. It was peaceful and charming, and he had to say there was an irresistible quality to the landscape. Still, he would be glad when he was done with it. He could see a few people moving about in their stone houses, and the first notes of Egyptian music from someone's radio began to reach his ears. He had some packages of American cigarettes with him which he had managed to get recently on a trip up to Tel Aviv, and he touched his breast pocket to make sure they were secure.

It was at just that moment that he thought he saw a flash, and felt something smash against him with such crushing force it thrust him down into the sand like a rag doll. Instantly he heard a loud, terrifying noise. He tried to get away but he was unable to move. It was if a boulder had landed on his chest. He was starting to go black when he realized that shooting was going on all around him.

=========

The attack on Naor was repelled very quickly. It was just a little foray of Arab irregulars, bent on terror. The elders of the little Arab town were horrified and organized a peace mission to the kibbutz. They brought gifts of cheese and milk.

Heshel Rosenheim was the first and only casualty from either side. He received the contingent of elders in his bed in the kibbutz infirmary. He thanked them. They assured him of their desire to live side by side with their Jewish brothers. When they left, he turned over in bed and found himself weeping.

Later he drank the milk and ate the cheese. Everyone came to visit him, except Moskovitz. He grew depressed. He seemed to be languishing.

And it was from his hospital bed, some days later, that he heard all the singing and dancing out on the lawn. The U.N. had voted for partition. The dream of two thousand years had come to pass. Soon there would be a Jewish state.

=========

It was late when I got myself ready to leave. We'd gone into dinner, and I'd sat with him. He didn't speak much. Nobody else had come to visit him. I was exhausted. When they put him in the bed and he nodded off, I thought of examining his body for bullet wounds. I had never noticed any scars on him, but then again, when had I seen him naked? Even on the beach he wore one of those sleeveless undershirts—Italian tuxedos, we used to call them. Not that we went to the beach all that often. Most of our vacations were "educational." Frequently that meant going to places like Washington, D.C., or Gettysburg. A lot of museums. Very little seashore. They did send us to camp, but it was Jewish camp, where we ate kosher and had to pray every morning, even though no one was religious, including the counselors. And when Mom and Dad came out for parents' day, my father would never do any of the activities. Never take off his shirt and play volleyball, for instance. He preferred to sit and comment.

Tonight, the collar of his pajama top was buttoned as always. It was one of his idiosyncrasies that he had managed to impart to his loyal keepers. But on this evening, as the sun finally relented and sank behind the palm trees and into the swamps to the west, I reached out and loosened his collar, and opened the next button down, too. I didn't see a thing. His skin was wrinkled and mottled and darkened in spots, but there were no scars.

I can't say I was exactly relieved. But it was enough for me not to look further. I pulled the sheet over him and tiptoed out.

The vestibule was quiet. Most of the inmates of death row—that's what it was, after all—were tucked in their beds, too. Televisions could be heard softly moaning behind closed doors, and a few last husbands and wives wandered about, delaying as long as possible the drive back to their empty homes. Nurse Clara was not on duty. I was hoping she would be there. I found a certain comfort in her strong will, the size of her bosom, and the strange prowess of her cross.

It was another nurse who stopped me.

"Oh, are you Mr. Rosenheim's son?"

I told her I was.

"This came for your father." She handed me a letter. It was addressed simply to "Rosenheim."

"Thanks," I said.

I casually stuffed the envelope in my pocket.

"Have a good night," she said. "See you tomorrow."

I calmly strolled through the door. But once outside, I ran to the car like a man who just robbed a convenience store.

I slammed the car door shut and without thinking revved the engine and pumped the air-conditioning onto my face and arms. Even though the sun was gone, the car seat still stuck to me like melted gummy bears. My heart was pounding. As I peeled out of the lot, bugs smashed onto the windshield, leaving disgusting globs of white mucus directly in my line of vision.

The letter in my pocket seemed to grow larger and heavier until it threatened to crush my chest. I couldn't wait. I had to read it. I spotted the Starbucks and pulled into the parking lot.

Hunched over like a criminal, I stealthily slipped the envelope out of my pocket and set it before me on the table. *Rosenheim.*

I studied the name.

I had actually thought of changing it. Well, I had changed it, hadn't I? My stage name was Mickey Rose. So for most of the world that's who I was. A guy with a cartoon name. A Shecky Greene kind of name. Like I was a *tummler* in the Borscht Belt. I remember making up that name. I was eleven years old. I was in my bedroom. My life was in ruins. Everybody at school hated me. I was the fat kid. The spaz. I couldn't play baseball, and I was afraid to play football. My father wouldn't let me join the Boy Scouts because it was *goyisha* and it met in the Presbyterian church, never mind that half the kids in it were Jewish. When I walked past a bunch of girls, they always snickered. Other kids threw things at me. The bullies stole my homework, scrawled obscenities in my locker. I was one of those kids who saw those ads in the back of comic books—*Learn to play the piano and be the life of the party*—and took them seriously. At home I was a god, but at school I was an insect. I began to resent my parents for loving me. I began to see their adoration as a form of stupidity. I often stayed home sick. I watched TV a lot. I did magic. Card tricks. I put on shows with my little sister. One day I brought my magic tricks to school for talent day. I dreaded my turn, but finally I had to stand in front of the class. Looking out, I saw the faces of the enemy. Panicked, I started with my best trick, the interlocking rings. But something happened. In the middle of the trick, I forgot how to do it. I banged the two rings together and they wouldn't join together. I banged and banged. The class burst into laughter. I said some elaborate hocus-pocus and tried squeezing them together. Nothing. The class howled. I twisted them right and left, but nothing worked. I just couldn't remember how to do it. Finally, I looked up at them, almost in tears. But their faces had changed. They weren't the faces of the enemy. They were wide-eyed and happy. They thought I was doing this on purpose! I said some more hocus-pocus, and stomped on the rings with my feet. They screamed with laughter, and the more I twisted and banged and stomped and couldn't get the rings to interlock, the funnier they thought it was—no, the funnier they thought *I* was—*they loved me!*

Finally I just put the rings on my head and took a bow. The class exploded with applause. Mrs. Schwartz nodded at me. There was a smile even on her face. Mrs. Schwartz. Smiling. In my entire fifth grade, I had never seen her teeth. It was as if God had reached down from the sky and touched my shoulder. I returned to my seat no longer the class outcast. I was now the class clown. I was flush with victory. I had wrestled with the angel—only in my case it was three aluminum rings—and my name was changed from Jacob to Israel.

Thus it was that evening, alone in my room, Mickey Rose was born.

And by now just about everyone called me Mickey. Mickey Rose. In Vegas, I was Mickey Rose. In Tahoe, I was Mickey Rose. When the babes wasted their time hitting on me in the comedy clubs, it was Mickey Rose. All my comedian friends called me Mickey Rose. Really, it was only Ella who called me Michael anymore. And my father, of course. And as for Rosenheim, well, Josh was a Rosenheim. And my driver's license was a Rosenheim. And I got airplane tickets as a Rosenheim. But was *I* a Rosenheim? And now I was wondering, were any of us Rosenheims?

I picked up the envelope and sniffed it. Nothing. I don't know what I was expecting, anyway.

I slid my finger under the flap, but hesitated to tear it open. I sensed someone close to me. Slight hint of perfume, or perhaps skin lotion. I looked up. It was the typing lady, the one I had seen here before. My first thought was that she was following me.

She also hesitated, and then smiled.

"I know you," she said.

"You do?"

"Yes. You're the comedian. I saw you at the Mirage. You were doing this thing with a puppet. The rabbit with the filthy mouth. It was hilarious."

I was speechless. My finger was still hooked under the flap of the unopened envelope.

"It was you, wasn't it? I can't remember who you were opening for."

"I wasn't opening," I finally said. "I was just the lounge act."

"Right, right!" she said.

She stood there and looked at me for rather a long time.

"I don't remember your name," she then said.

Now it was my turn to stare at her in silence. It seemed I had to make a choice here.

"Mickey Rose," I said.

"Right, right!" she agreed, as if I had passed a test. "Can I sit down?"

"Excuse me?"

"I was just wondering if I could sit down. You're the only person under eighty I've seen around here. I'm visiting my mom. You, too?"

My finger was still embedded under the flap of the envelope. It seemed suspended in time, liminally poised at the gateway to my destiny, while above me loomed some sort of Fury or Circe sent by the Fates to impede my progress, only she was a middle-aged hippie woman who pounded out diatribes on her laptop. Why, I wondered, didn't she just dye her hair? And the Japanese fabrics, the Native American jewelry, the purse that looked like an Afghan rug?

But what could I do? I nodded and she sat down, resting her chin upon her upturned hand and studying me as if I were a lab specimen. I put the envelope back in my pocket.

"My name is April," she said. Her eyes were quite blue, I noticed. And her nails were, too, though the smile that she now offered radiated perfectly brilliant white teeth.

I tried to think of something to say. "I've seen you typing," I offered.

"Oh, that, yes. It's impossible to work at my mother's. She's always talking to me. But I've got deadlines."

"Ah," I said. I knew she wanted me to ask her what kind of deadlines.

"I'm editing an anthology," she continued. "The introduction is already past due."

"Really?" I said.

She laughed, revealing an unexpected girlish quality. "I see I'm fascinating you," she said. "Are you from New York, too?"

She seemed genuinely disappointed that I was not, but then she picked up on the fact that I lived in San Francisco, and started dissing it in a fairly amusing way—in just the same tones she might use to kvetch about New York. It was her way of connecting, of trying to say she might actually consider going to bed with me if I could muster the slightest bit of manly intentionality. She was lonely, I was lonely, it all made sense. And so even though all I really wanted was for her to go away and let me read my letter, I did not send her away. I had at my fingertips a million strategies for sexual avoidance, and yet nothing escaped my lips except a bit of foam from my cappuccino.

I watched her flirt with me. It was like watching a fish in the tank at a Chinese restaurant.

This struck me as funny, and I laughed. She thought I was laughing at her jokes, so she redoubled her efforts. She said that the problem with San Francisco was that all the women looked like Donna Reed, and so did all the men.

This, by the way, was not a funny joke. It was so unfunny, in fact, that I felt I had to do something. I started in with my Florida shtick—Fountain of Youth, Two Old Jews Meet on Miami Beach —that sort of thing, got her going, and then transitioned into Little Old Lady jokes, Cuban Cigar jokes, and then the coup de grâce—something I had been working on—Hospice Humor!—the lighter side of death and dying. I was cracking her up. She was the perfect audience—like Ella used to be. By the time I was through with her, I'd say five words and she'd be on the floor. I'd mug and she'd spit up her coffee. And when I finally slowed it down—because, frankly, I was running out of steam—I looked at her. She looked nice, to tell you the truth, wiping the tears from her eyes. And we fell into that dumb silence that often occurs between the last joke and the first kiss.

"I guess writing comedy is kind of like writing poetry," she said.

"Is it?"

"You look for the holes in things. Then you go for the kill."

I smiled at that, because I knew what she meant, and it felt really good to know what someone meant for a change.

"Are you a poet?" I asked her.

"I am. But perhaps not as good a poet as you are a comic." The way she leaned into me reminded me of a cat rubbing up against a table leg.

All around us they had put the chairs up on the tables, and the attendants were waiting with their mops.

"We've got to get out of here," I said.

"I'd invite you to my place for a nightcap," April laughed, "but my mother's home."

Well, there it was. Now was the moment to suavely suggest we go to my place. But I could feel that letter in my pocket, like acid, burning through to my skin.

And anyway, what about Ella?

I said good night and drove myself home to The Ponds at Lakeshore.

At home, I opened the letter, read it, and ran to the bathroom just in time to throw up.

CHAPTER 11

Dear Mr. Rosenheim:
I hope this letter finds you well. I have enclosed the following photocopied document at the request of your agents in this matter, which I hope you find in good order. I shall have it delivered by messenger to your father's current place of residence, as instructed.

Best regards,

Harold W. Kaufman
Librarian
Holocaust Archives
Los Angeles, CA

PAGE 23, MEMORIAL BOOK, THE TOWN OF DURNIK, LITHUANIA

Rabinowitz,	Moshe	Treblinka
Rabinowitz,	Esther	Treblinka
Rabinowitz,	Feisle	Treblinka
Rabinowitz,	Yitzhak	Dachau
Rachmann,	Velvel	Woods outside Lititz
Rachmann,	Haim	Dachau
Rachmann,	Sissele	Unknown
Rachmann,	Layla	Unknown
Rachmann,	Pinchas	Auschwitz
Rachmann,	Deborah	Birkenau
Rebbenich,	Lev	Bergen-Belsen (?)
Reich,	Artur	Unknown
Reich,	Leah	Ravensbrück
Reisman,	Dora	Auschwitz
Reisman,	Israel	Auschwitz
Reisman,	Bassa	Auschwitz
Reisman,	Rachel	Auschwitz
Reisman,	Gittl	Auschwitz
Roffman,	Rifka	Majdenic
Roffman,	Yosef	Majdenic
Roman,	Golda	Treblinka
Roman,	Hayim	Unknown
Roman,	Mordechai	Unknown
Rosenheim,	Malka	Majdanek
Rosenheim,	Hinda	Majdanek
Rosenheim,	Yehudit	Majdanek
Rosenheim,	Mimi	Majdanek
Rosenheim,	Dov	Unknown
Rosenheim,	Moshe	Auschwitz (?)
Rosenheim,	Yehudah	Majdanek

Rosenheim	Abraham	Majdanek	
Rosenheim	Heshel	Majdanek	✓
Rosebaum	Dovid	Sobibor	
Rosebaum	Faivl	Belzek	
Rosebaum	Natan	Belzek	
Rudolf	Judah	Unknown	
Rudolf	Masha	Unknown	
Rudolf	Dinah	Unknown	

=========

In the fall of 1947, Heshel Rosenheim was twenty-seven years old. The world around him had suddenly changed yet again. A war of terror and small actions had begun in earnest in expectation of the departure of the British. Throughout the Arab world, Jews were being attacked, their neighborhoods pillaged. Beirut, Cairo, Alexandria, Aleppo. There was a massacre in Aden. It seemed the world was repeating itself, but for some reason this did not give solace to young Heshel Rosenheim. A bus was attacked on its way to Jerusalem. Jews were singled out and killed. In December, there were Arab riots in Jerusalem. In the same month, a group of Jewish settlements in the Negev called the Etzion Block were surrounded and cut off. On the other side, Jewish Irgunists threw bombs at a crowd of Arabs at the bus station at the Damascus Gate. About the same time, fifteen Haganah soldiers were ambushed and killed by the Arab Legion. The Stern Gang then broke into an Arab home and killed five people.

In the meantime, Heshel lay in his bed, motionless and silent. Everyone left him alone. Not all wounds, they told each other, are physical.

One afternoon though, Tuli, the local Haganah commander, came by.

"They're forming a special Palmach unit," he told him. "To protect the Negev and the Etzion Block."

Heshel said nothing, just continued to stare out the window. Tuli looked out there, too. All he could see was the tractor shed.

"They want you," said the commander.

He would be sent to a secret camp and trained as Palmach—the elite strike force. He was strong, he was brave, he was smart, he had proved himself good with a weapon, and he had the clear head of a leader. Everyone knew this. Everyone looked up to him. This would be no time to shirk his duty or fall prey to dark thoughts.

"Enough with doing the books," Tuli said.

A week or so later, Heshel packed his few things in his small cotton duffel, and waited by the roadside for the lorry to take him away. Soon enough, he saw a small convoy approaching, casting up dust into the gray sky. The rain that had threatened so long was finally on its way. A new season was upon him in this strange land without seasons. He turned to look back at the kibbutz. He was surprised to see Moskovitz standing at the gate, the wind blowing her hair wildly, her skirt fluttering and flapping around the poles of her legs. But it was not Moskovitz, was it? Yael was her name now—Bat Tsedek—yes, she was a stranger to him! The wind raised her skirts and tore at her hair, but it didn't fool him: she was too solid to let any force of nature carry her away. He found his hand rising, unwilled, in a gesture of farewell. Oh! he yearned to run to her, he did! He wished to throw down the duffel and take her in his arms and kiss her wildly on the mouth, as wildly as the wind that now pelted her lips with dust. But his feet, of course, did not move. All he was allowed was the small movement of his arm, good-bye. Just then the lorry pulled up and a soldier leaned out the window—Rosenheim? Heshel hoisted his duffel onto the truck bed, unshouldered his rifle and threw that in as well, and finally lifted himself over the gate and jumped in. He turned, leaned out, and waved at her again. At last she waved back. Even before he was settled in, the caravan turned around and took off down the road. Looking back toward the kibbutz, he saw that she was still standing there, braving the wind and the first few drops of rain that would soon, he knew, become a torrent. All too quickly she became small, just a dot on the landscape, until at last she dropped her hand and ran back into the compound and out of all sight. He took a deep breath and settled onto the wood plank that served as a bench in the back of the truck. He nodded to the men and said hello. Then he turned his head outward once again, and the last thing he saw before they closed the flap to keep out the rain was the smoke rising from the little Arab village where his little hope of escape had evaporated in a burst of gunfire, and where now the women were preparing dinners of lamb and vegetables for their frightened families.

=========

He spent three weeks in camp, and emerged an officer. The man called Heshel Rosenheim was once again a lieutenant. Only this time his dream would come true. He would be on the front line, defending the homeland.

The thought made him laugh, especially when he took stock of himself in his new uniform. Gone were the elegant black tunic, the dazzling double S's, the smart cap with its intimidating death's-head insignia, the dashing epaulets, the elegant dagger. In their place worn-out khakis, open collars, a pair of baggy trousers, and a pair of short pants. As for boots, there were none, or none worth calling boots—just heavy brown shoes. He looked more like a factory worker than a soldier. But they did give him a little short-waisted jacket—the kind the American general

Eisenhower wore—and he liked that. There was also a helmet that looked very much like what the British wore in World War I, and he had a suspicion that that's exactly what it was.

Frequently he thought of taking his own life. But why bother? The end would come soon enough. It was perhaps not a coincidence that this training camp was just north of Megiddo, on the site of the biblical Armageddon.

And more and more he thought of Moskovitz.

=========

By now the land was turning green with new growth, but nobody noticed. In January, Kfar Szold, on the Syrian border, was attacked by the Arab Liberation Army. A huge explosion rocked Jerusalem, destroying the Jewish Palestinian Post *building. In the Negev, several kibbutzim were cut off. In the Etzion Block, a pitched battle was already under way. Lieutenant Rosenheim was given his orders. His company was loaded into open trucks in spite of the rain, and they headed south.*

They were to bring desperately needed supplies to the remote outpost of Revivim, and then break off the main convoy and swing toward the coast to engage any hostile forces in defense of Jewish settlements. They were strictly forbidden to launch any offensive measures. And any reprisals or countermeasures were to be aimed solely at combatants. These orders, Lieutenant Rosenheim thought, were so naïve they must have been issued by children. He had been placed in command of a unit of ten soldiers, all new Palmachniks like himself. They sang songs and ate halvah as they rode along. He shook his head. He had seen such esprit de corps before. He sat there, trying to memorize their names, knowing that by the time he did, most of them would already be dead.

They didn't get terribly far before trouble started. The

forward truck hit a land mine, throwing the men into the air. It was just a flatbed truck commandeered from a kibbutz, but the army had hastily armored it with steel plates sandwiched together with wood and concrete. Amazingly no one was hurt. Then the Arabs attacked. They were mostly villagers and not well trained, but there were a lot of them, and they were fierce. The radio girl, Malka, was hit immediately and fell into the mud. Heshel pulled her under his truck and began firing back. The men tried to use the trucks as shields, but the firing was intense, and several more people were hit. In the meantime, the soldiers of the lead truck were busy changing the tires, for in spite of the explosion, the only serious damage were blowouts on the front end. Against all odds, the "sandwiches" worked. When they were done with the tires, the men waved madly up the line. The drivers jumped in, and the trucks took off as fast as they could, the Jews clinging to the rails and firing the whole time.

They knew they could not make it to Revivim, so they turned back to Kibbutz Hatzerim. They camped there, awaiting news, or orders, whichever came first.

It was news, and it was bad. Thirty-five men trying to reach the Etzion Block with supplies were massacred. Their bodies, cut up and mutilated, were delivered to Kfar Etzion by the British in two truckloads.

The standing orders were changed. The Jewish forces would now go on the attack.

Lying in his bedroll that evening, allowing the rain slapping on the tent roof to calm his nerves, Heshel Rosenheim conjured up the lovely Fradl Moskovitz—strolling with her under a warm, dry summer sky, their arms locked together, her head resting on his shoulder. He watched the scene unfold, and plotted to himself how he might, in real life, win her back. Why not? Why not? He worked out scenarios. He imagined outcomes.

And then suddenly he realized that he was thinking in Hebrew. His inner voice was no longer speaking German.

In Hebrew he thought, My God, what is happening to me?

=========

By morning the rain had stopped, and he went out to shave. In his mirror he noticed someone staring at him, a new recruit, one of those fellows trained by the Palmach in the D.P. camps and shipped here in secret, by night, through the English blockade. Heshel lowered his mirror.

"Yes?" he said.

"Don't I know you?" the other said in Yiddish. "Were we together somewhere? I'm Levin."

"I am Rosenheim," he replied.

"Rosenheim," the man repeated, pondering. He had a thin, angry look. Heshel had seen it before. The haunted eyes. The nervous gestures. Soon to be replaced by the cool comfort of revenge. The kind that becomes a terrorist. "I knew a Rosenheim," Levin continued, "but that one wasn't you. You're not a sabra, though. You've been in the camps, yes?"

Rosenheim nodded.

"Maybe in the camps, then?"

"Anything is possible."

"Were you in Auschwitz?"

He had to say that he was. His sleeves were rolled up.

"Which camp? Which block?"

"Why ask me these things?" he said in Hebrew. "It's the past. It's over."

The man did not understand him. Instead he continued in Yiddish. "I was one of the lucky ones. Camp Three."

But Rosenheim said nothing.

"Well," continued the recruit, "I was in many camps. Perhaps

our paths crossed. Who knows?" He smiled in a friendly way. "I'm sure I know you." Then he walked off toward his platoon.

The company camped at Hatzerim all that day, but Rosenheim didn't see Levin again until they were at dinner, when he noticed him sitting with his crew at the far end of the dining hall. Levin looked up once and waved, but Rosenheim pretended he hadn't noticed. That was unwise! he thought, so he looked up again, and waved back.

But later that night he woke up from a dream: It was 9 November. All around him, flames. He was surrounded by dark figures. Above him floated the red banners, like sails carrying him to the Land of Perfect and Absolute Truth. Drifting down from the torch-lit sky, like angels, were a thousand black-sheathed knives. He heard a voice, far away, as if through a megaphone, but he could not make out what it was saying. It echoed off the corridors of men standing like pillars, holding up their salute to the Messiah of Pure Reason. The crowd screamed its obeisance. Then his own voice.

> Ich schwoere Dir Adolf Hitler! . . .
> *I swear to you, Adolf Hitler, Fuehrer and Chancellor of the German Reich, loyalty and bravery. I vow to you, and the superiors whom you will appoint, obedience unto death, so help me God. . . .*

SS-Mann! *he cried.*

He jumped up, awake—wondering—did I speak aloud? In which language was I dreaming?

He looked to see that his tent-mate was still asleep. But he thought he heard someone walking just outside. He stuck his head out. There was a group of four or five gathered around a little fire, smoking cigarettes and talking. They did not seem to notice him at all. But he thought he made out the figure of the little man with the angry eyes.

Alarmed, he slipped back into his tent.

This time Moshe was awake.

"Everything okay?"

"Just needed to piss," he said.

Moshe turned over and pulled his blanket over his head.

But it didn't really matter if Moshe had heard him or not. Or if the little Auschwitz man was listening at the tent door. The dream was a message. Even if no one was after him, their God would trick him into giving himself away.

=========

By now it was three or four in the morning. I couldn't sleep. I reached for the letter from the Holocaust people. I studied the letterhead and noted the phone number: Kaufman. Holocaust Archives. Never heard of them. And what's a memorial book? And who asked him to send this material anyway? Again it had to be that secret person—the key, the witness, the one who could unlock the truth. If I wanted the truth.

And that town, whatever it was—I'd never heard of it. Durnik. What kind of place is that?

I thought maybe a drink would help me sleep. I opened my father's liquor cabinet. No surprises there. It was empty, except for an ancient bottle of Dry Sack. It tasted like stewed prunes.

But someone did know the truth. Someone was feeding this to me, like spooning poison in my coffee, little by little. Why? And why now? What possible good could it do, even if it were true? He was a dying man. How could justice come at this late hour?

And what exactly did this "memorial" list mean? What did it prove? I knew what it proved. But couldn't there have been hundreds or even thousands of Heshel Rosenheims in Europe before and during the war. How many of them perished? Most of them. But some may have survived. One may have survived.

I had to call him, Kaufman. I took a bitter, dark swig of the sherry and dialed his number. I knew it was one in the morning there, I knew no one would answer, but I called anyway.

A thickly accented and ancient voice had recorded an awkward message asking me to leave my name and phone number, which I did. Immediately I wished I hadn't.

I was feeling a little sick to my stomach by now. What I really wanted to do was call Ella. Not possible. So I looked at the letter again.

Dear Mr. Rosenheim:
I hope this letter finds you well. I have enclosed the following photocopied document at the request of your agents in this matter, which I hope you find in good order. I shall have it delivered by messenger to your father's current place of residence, as instructed.

I shall have it delivered to your father. My God, I cried aloud. Did I have a sibling somewhere I didn't know about?

Right then I decided I had to stop. I could read no more. I could delve no farther. Enough! Enough! Enough!

CHAPTER 12

Just as I thrust the letter from my hand, the phone rang. I looked at it with terror. Could Kaufman have been in?

"Who is this?" I demanded.

"I can't sleep." It was Josh.

"Jesus, Josh, it's three in the morning."

"I know," he said sheepishly.

I was getting sick as a dog. The sherry was churning my stomach like a washing machine.

"What's going on?" I asked him.

"I can't sleep," he repeated.

I sighed. "Why can't you sleep?"

"I don't know," he said.

"Well, close your eyes and try."

"I did. It didn't work."

"Are all the lights out?"

"Yes."

"Then turn one on," I said.

"I already did that."

"Well, then, I don't know."

"Are you okay, Dad? You sound funny."

"You just woke me up out of a deep sleep, Josh."

"I'm sorry."

"Did you go have some cereal? That always works for me."

"I had a bowl of Cheerios. It didn't work."

"Well, no wonder! You have to use Trix!"

Hah! I thought. It wasn't my best, but at least I could still get a laugh. And this despite the fact it was four in the morning on the day I discovered Josh's grandfather was a Nazi war criminal.

And indeed, I could hear him trying to laugh. Though it may have sounded more like choked-off tears.

"It's all right," I said. "I'm not mad."

"I just couldn't sleep," he said.

"What's the matter?"

I could hear him thinking.

"School?" I asked hopefully.

"You keep on asking about school, Dad," he said. "It's summer, remember?"

"Right, right," I said. "Friends?"

"No. They're fine."

"Did you have a fight with Mom?"

"No, Dad. Why does it have to be something? I just can't sleep."

By which, of course, he meant he just wanted to talk to me because I hadn't been calling, and because when I did call I barely spoke, and because I wasn't home, and because I wouldn't let him come and live with me, and because I was a half-wit father who let them both leave. I guess he meant, instead of throwing that TV set at us, why didn't you follow us and make us come home? Why didn't you compromise and get a better house for Mom and why didn't you get a job that let you stay in San Francisco and make a decent living and have real furniture? But how was I supposed to answer these accusations? Could a father tell a son that he just didn't know how to do any better?

"Sleep is way overrated," I said. "Really. I get my best laughs at four in the morning. By watching reruns of *I Love Lucy*."

"*Dad . . .*"

"No, really."

He made a funny little sound, the kind of squeak boys make when their voices are changing, and when they can't quite get the words out. "Can I come out and help you?" he said.

"Help me?" I replied. "What makes you think I need help?"

"I don't know," he said. "Just."

"I'm fine," I told him. "You have to stay there and take care of Mom."

"She doesn't need me to take care of her."

"And I do?"

He fell silent then. I could hear my own breathing. It was raspy, overburdened. And my heart, it seemed to be flipping strangely in my chest, tingling in a weird way. It scared me a little, actually. And I was feeling more and more nauseous from the sherry.

"I just want to see you," he blurted.

"Me too, me too." When I touched my hand to my chest to stop the fibrillation, I felt something cruddy and dry on my shirt. I tried to scrape it off, whatever it was. Then I remembered I'd thrown up earlier. "I was thinking," I said, "when I get home we'll go to a ball game or something. What do you say?"

"Which one?" he said.

"Which one what?"

"Which game?"

"I don't know which game, Josh. Just a game, for chrissakes."

"I just wondered which game." He sounded beaten down again.

I started thinking about how something as ephemeral as a tone of voice, as nonlethal as a thing could ever be, had such destructive force—but only, of course, on the ones who loved you. Why would God make us this way, I wanted to know. When he was creating his world full of Nazis and Stalins and Genghis Khans—couldn't he have just left the tone of voice you use on your kid out of it? And I thought of my own father and the unconscious put-downs and snide remarks, the wry humor that deflected my advances, the furious anger that erupted without warning, the strong, fragrant hugs for no reason at all—and I felt myself retreat further and further from Josh. Of course my father had his excuse, didn't he? My father had his terrible secret to hide. To let me in might have exposed me to that frightful darkness, that twisted jungle of ugliness and crime. And so I held the phone receiver to my ear, and instead of Josh, I heard my father's voice, and I shuddered—and I wondered—what secret was I hiding from Josh? What secret chained the door between me and this sweet, blond-headed boy with the curly hair and the slight, lilting gait that sometimes made him seem, to me at least, as if he were skating on air across the playground, where others tumbled and fell?

"Dad? Are you still there?"

"Huh?"

"Dad—you're so quiet."

"Whatever game I can get tickets for," I said. "That's the game we'll go to."

"Sounds good," he said. "But I'm tired now. I think I'll go to bed."

A little later, I stuffed all the journals back in the Cheez Whiz box. I crammed the box in a corner between the TV and the sofa bed, and then I went into the guest room and fell into a deep, uneasy sleep.

CHAPTER 13

I've heard it said that in families there is no such thing as a secret. Which meant I must have known all along. Did I?

Was that why I used to lie in bed at night and wonder if my father was a secret agent for the CIA? It was a logical deduction. He was the only father out there protesting the Vietnam War. All the other fathers were *for* the war. The other fathers voted for Nixon. Mine voted for McGovern. Yet he was always going on about the plight of the Soviet Jews, so he couldn't have been a real leftist. Thus he had to be a CIA agent. QED. I found it kind of thrilling, in a twisted way. Plus it solved my problem: it was unseemly to hate him for being antiwar, even though really I did. I was only twelve when he started protesting—it was 1970 or so—

and I remember thinking, *Shave your beard! Cut your hair!* But if he was actually a CIA provocateur (though I could hardly have known that word at the time)—then, no problemo—I could hate him guilt-free.

But you always know, don't you? The secret in my house was the entire life of the house. Everything tiptoed around it, every evening of TV, every family supper, every bedtime. It didn't just come up once in a while, on the birthdays that were somehow sad, on the New Year's Eves, the Hanukkahs, the Rosh Hashanahs that left you feeling empty. It was every time you opened your mouth to say something and wondered if you should say it. It was every time they said something, and you wondered what else they weren't saying.

That's the Holocaust for you! At the time, I thought it was his suffering in the camps. I thought it was all the people he'd lost. I thought it was the horror of what was done to him that left him as a kind of sole survivor—for that's what they all were, each in his or her own way—sole survivors. Each one the only witness.

But the question was, did I know that the secret I thought was the secret wasn't the secret at all?

I had awoken sometime in the late morning with the sound of Josh still in my ears, and the fresh scent of soap whirling through my brain. I must have been dreaming about him. Perhaps it was the vision of him as a baby or a toddler, because he always smelled of soap then—or whatever that baby smell is, I don't know—but it made me want to take a bath instead of a shower, something I never do, or at least not alone. I sank into the warm water and rested my head against a rolled-up washcloth, as I'd seen Ella do so many times. I tried to allow myself to relax. Maybe I touched myself a tiny bit, but not really. It was just a passing thought. Instead I sat there and waited for the bath to happen, for the toxins to leach from my body, for the feeling of cleanliness to come over me, for the bubbles to caress me. I remembered bathing Josh when he was a little boy. I realized I missed him more than I suspected.

I tried to think back, to catch a glimpse of how I must have felt as a child of his age. I must have known. Karen must have known. And now, Josh must know. People think children are chatterboxes. But actually children never tell.

I slipped under the water, as if to wash away these thoughts. But secrets never, ever disappear, even after they are revealed. And that's the real secret right there. The empty space that never gets filled. The entropy of falsehood. The real secret is the secret itself.

I realized I never actually thought my father was in the CIA. That was really more my sister. She was younger; she had a bigger imagination. She also frequently suggested that my mother was once on stage, and that my father met her in a vaudeville theater. Mother was the most beautiful girl in the chorus line. She could have been a star, only she married and had kids.

"I don't think they still had vaudeville when they got together," I explained to her. "And Mom's a nurse. They met when he went in for a checkup."

"Then a nightclub," she said. She had recently seen the show *Cabaret*. She knew all the songs. Mommy was just like Sally Bowles. "She wore green nail polish and sang in her underwear." Then Karen giggled and sang "Money, Money" in a thick German accent. We were good at German accents.

As for me, I had also gone to *Cabaret* and was deeply impressed. I'd never seen Nazi uniforms in color before. There was something terribly attractive about those sharp brown shirts and colorful armbands, and the spectacular red banners that hung everywhere—with the white circles and jet-black swastikas. It was unsettling, confusing. Those boys singing "Tomorrow Belongs to Me." It sounded okay to me. There was such a disconnect between what they appeared to be and what I knew was coming. I wanted to talk to my father about it, but didn't dare. And anyway, he hadn't seen *Cabaret*. "Too trivial," he said.

But Karen had other fantasies as well. Aside from the run-of-the-mill lost-princess-adopted-by-caretakers scenario (brought on by the film *Anastasia*), she once decided that my parents were actually aliens from another planet. This was not a joke with her. She went on about it for months, maybe years. She was always looking for evidence, and often found it. If I was recalling this correctly, it all began with a dream she had, in which she went to lie down between Mom and Dad, and Mom's fingernails began to grow into talons and her skin turned green and pimply and her face looked more like a bird than a person. When she looked over at Dad for protection, the same thing had happened to him. He was a creature from outer space. She woke up screaming. We were still sharing a room then, that's why I knew about it, and when she told me the dream, it was so vivid it even scared me. Only she couldn't let it go. For her it wasn't a dream, it was a sign. That's when the evidence started turning up. An odd-looking glass bead she found in an ashtray became a device for interplanetary communications. Notes scribbled on bits of paper became cryptic messages about imminent invasion. Perhaps they weren't really speaking Yiddish to each other. Maybe it was Martian.

Eventually, of course, it was just a game. But underneath it, did she know that my father wasn't who he said he was? And my mother—what about her? Was she in on the secret, too? Is that why I played along? Is that why the two of us, one summer evening, plotted star maps to their home planet?

I made little eddies in the water with my washcloth, little vortexes twisting down into the murky bath. And then—oh my God!—it came back to me. She once said to me: "What if Daddy wasn't in the concentration camps at all? What if he was a Nazi instead? What if he was Dr. Mengele?"

Why was I thinking so much about Karen? I never thought about Karen. But there was something in her method that was a message to me. The collection of evidence. Clues. They were everywhere, I knew. In the drawers, under the beds, in the photo albums, stuck in hat boxes. I only had to have the courage to look for them.

I once went mushrooming with a friend of Ella's. He was French. "You can walk along for miles and see nothing, but once you see one, all of the sudden, there they are!" he told me. And it was true. I was standing beneath a live oak out at Lake Lagunitas and he said, "Look at your foot." And there it was: a chanterelle, as big as my fist. I had almost stepped on it. I stood frozen and silent, barely breathing, as if it were a forest creature that might startle and bolt, and then, slowly turning my head, looking right and then left and then round behind me, I saw them: little dots—or smiles, really—of gold and bronze, peeping from beneath the dark, sticky loam and shiny wet leaves, like newly formed stars, winking at me—for they'd been playing hide-and-seek, surrounding me as if I were *it* in a game of blindman's bluff. I laughed out loud, I was so dazzled and amazed.

Karen was telling me I needed to go mushrooming now. I needed to look at the ground in front of my feet, and I needed to be quiet and still, and search behind and to the right and to the left of where I was. Open your eyes! she seemed to be commanding me. Look!

The thought so nonplussed me I jumped from the tub. The

water cascaded onto the floor in a wild torrent and left a mess I'd have to mop up.

The phone must have rung while the water was running in the bathtub, because when I got out, there was a message from Kaufman, the Holocaust man. Forget him! I said. And anyway, I was suddenly incredibly hungry.

So I went out to The Charm and had pastrami and corned beef on rye, Russian dressing, slaw, no mustard. Then I took myself over to Starbucks for coffee, but she wasn't there.

CHAPTER 14

When I got home the phone was ringing. I knew it was Kaufman, and I didn't want to pick up. But when the voice came over the message machine, it was the nursing home. They told me to come quickly. My father was having a stroke. He was already on his way to the hospital.

About twenty minutes later I arrived at John F. Kennedy and was directed to the ICU. In a little while a young doctor came out to tell me Dad was stabilized. He'd only suffered a minor stroke. For a while he probably wouldn't be able to talk, but it seems he wasn't paralyzed. There could, however, be more dementia. He suggested his heart was weak, too. He asked me if my father had signed a living will. I thanked the doctor and went into my father's room. He looked shrunken, and with all the tubes and pipes attached to him, he might have been the space alien my sister dreamt about. There was a terrible smell, and the sound of the heart monitor beeping, which every so often spit out a ticker tape of vital statistics. His breathing was labored; his eyes were shut.

"Can he hear me?" I asked the nurse.

She said yes. Unless he was sleeping. But he is aware, she told me.

I sat there with him for a while. I spoke gently to him, nothing of any importance, just repeating my name, telling him I was there. But it was hard for me. And I found that I could not touch him. I should have been holding his hand, I supposed, but I couldn't. I made believe that I was there to comfort him—but really I was just observing him like you would some strange new species of insect—something large and repulsive, but impossible to turn away from—at least until you've had your fill.

At some point the young doctor came back in.

"He's such a good man," he said to me.

"You know him?"

"Not personally. But of course I've heard about him." He nodded as if I should understand this. Consolingly, he patted me on the back and proffered a supportive, courageous smile. Then he left.

I sat there watching the liquids go in and out of my father's body in tubes. The tubes were attached to needles stuck in his arms, and other wires were connected to electrodes on his chest and head, and there was some gadget on his finger with a wire protruding from it, and machines on the other side of these lines were plugged into the wall, and these signals were then sent to other machines, which, as far as I knew, were connected in turn to some central brain that monitored and maintained all the comings and goings into and out of his body, sustained the rhythm of his heart and the air in his lungs and the blood in his brain.

Dark thoughts passed through me, like bolts of lightning, sudden, and then gone.

"Who are you?" I said to him. "Who are you?"

I could see with my own eyes that all the universe was focused on keeping him alive, and always had been. It was as if he were one of those thirty-six "Just Men" legend tells us keep the world intact, without whom so much evil would arise that mankind would destroy itself in the blink of an eye. The righteous *Lamed-Vov,* they call them, the *Thirty-six.* Unknown even to themselves, their task is to reveal the hidden and redeem the world. It is said one of them might even be the Messiah. My father himself told me these stories. I had always thought they were stupid.

When I went home that evening I dragged the Cheez Whiz box back out into the middle of the Florida room, and opened the next of his journals.

=========

The weeks passed. The undeclared war continued. People were dying in large numbers. The Arabs attacked Jewish neighborhoods in Jerusalem but were driven away. A huge bomb exploded on Ben-Yehuda Street, killing fifty Jews. A car bomb blew up in the Jewish Agency building. The worst thing, though, was that the Haganah had to abandon the coastal road south of Tel Aviv. The Negev was now isolated completely, and along with it, Naor. Then even worse news followed. The road to Jerusalem was cut off. The city was under siege and constant bombardment.

And then came the month of April.

Heshel Rosenheim was attached to the Southern Command,

but had removed to Tel Aviv. Then one day most of his unit—and he with it—was merged into the force being assembled to open the Jerusalem road, and was thrown into the fighting immediately. After two or three days of it, Heshel found himself oddly elated and exhausted, and settled down to sleep with a bunch of other tired, bloodied men. At about six in the morning, after having had only a few hours' rest, he was awakened by an officer and told he was needed to reinforce a critical hill above the Jerusalem road. It was called Kastel. The Jews had finally captured it, but were now under attack by thousands of Arabs. They were almost out of ammunition and food. The site had to be held at all costs. Wearily, he picked up his gear and joined his unit.

One thing went wrong, and then another and another. These Jews were unused to large-scale warfare. They were disorganized, badly equipped. The armored car kept breaking down, and they could not progress without it. They did not arrive at the base of the hill till almost two o'clock in the afternoon, and by then the shooting was so severe it was almost impossible to reach the village. Some of the men made it up the hill. Heshel was not among them. He was pinned down in a little escarpment. Next to him were three dead soldiers. As soon as he lifted his head, he was shot at, so he lay there waiting, listening to the strange symphony of explosions, gunfire, screams of agony, and cheers of victory.

As he crouched there next to the bodies, he was struck by how different they appeared than the bodies of Jews he had seen in such abundance in his former life. These beside him were beautiful even in death—their muscular arms flexed, their still faces yet aglow with passion, their features not even particularly Semitic, with their tanned skin and their eyes, though frozen, blue as the sea. Already he could smell the urine on one of them who had failed to empty his bladder before the attack, but it was not unpleasant. He looked around for a way down the hill and to safety.

It did not take long before he heard the trampling of many feet coming over the hillside, and he braced for death. No, not yet, not like this, he cried to himself, cowering.

But they were calling in Hebrew—Let's go, let's go! Move! Move!

Some fell, but others were making it. It was enough of a chance. He took off, rolling more than running, down the rocky face.

When he was at the bottom and safe, he surveyed the men. There were no officers among them. Of the officers that had gone up, only he returned.

It was because of Shimon Alfasi, they told him. And they repeated his orders. All privates will retreat. All commanders will cover their withdrawal.

They looked at Heshel Rosenheim. At that moment he was their commander.

"Let's get the hell out of here," he told them.

But the words of Alfasi electrified the country. It became the new battle cry. Officers would always be first under fire, and last to retreat. And that, Heshel knew, included him.

=========

It was the next day that he ran into Levin.

"Rosenheim, right?" he called out in Yiddish.

Levin was not in uniform. Heshel's prediction had come true. Levin had found his way to the Irgun, or perhaps worse.

"Yes, I'm Rosenheim."

"Have you thought perhaps where we've met?"

"I'm sorry, but I don't remember you. I don't think we ever met."

"But we did, we did. Not at Auschwitz. Were you elsewhere? I myself was at three camps. I was also at Majdanek. Were you at Majdanek, Rosenheim?"

Rosenheim looked at him.

"You're one of those who don't talk about it," Levin said. "I'm one of those who can't stop talking about it."

"I see you are not in uniform."

"No," said Levin.

"But you are with a unit."

"Yes," said Levin.

"Good luck to you, then." Rosenheim moved away.

"We are all after the same thing," Levin called after him. "Wait!" He ran up to Rosenheim and grasped him by the arms. "It was Majdanek, wasn't it? Yes, I'm sure. What block were you in? What work did you do?"

Rosenheim wrestled free. "Leave me alone!" he cried.

He moved off quickly, trying to appear annoyed rather than afraid, but burned in his mind was the suspicion shooting from Levin's eyes like twin swords. He tried to calm himself, but all he could do was wonder how long it would take Levin to put two and two together.

If I see him again, he thought, I'll kill him.

=========

And he did see him again, a few days later.

He was once more separated from his unit, and attached to a platoon commanded by Yeshurun Schiff. They drove into the village of Deir Yassin on the morning of the eleventh, but the village had disappeared. What was left was smoldering under dark, billowing smoke. Bodies were piled up in a nearby quarry, many of them burned and charred. There were Jewish fighters among them, but far more Arabs, including women and children. There were more than a hundred dead, he reckoned, and they were beginning to stink.

Schiff screamed at the Irgunist commander. He called him a murderer. They went on this way for a while, arguing back and forth.

In the meantime, he spotted Levin. He was sitting alone, smoking a cigarette. He wore a bloodied head band, where obviously he had sustained some sort of wound. This time it was Heshel Rosenheim who walked up to him.

"I have seen this before," he said to Levin.

"Not the same," Levin replied. "We lost almost half our men."

Rosenheim stared at the man. "I do know you," he said. "I know exactly who you are."

"See, see?" Levin said triumphantly.

"You are the Kapo *in the* Sondercommando, *the one they all feared, the one as cruel to his own as if he were himself SS, the one who traded in flesh. You never withheld the lash. You withheld the rations. You betrayed the women who bore children. You threw your brothers into the fire. I do know you. I do remember you. Never, ever," he said, "seek me out again, or I shall expose you to your patriotic Stern Gang brothers, and see what they do to you."*

"What?" Levin said.

He had been speaking in Hebrew, and the man could not understand him—though of course he understood Kapo, *and* Sondercommando—*and Rosenheim knew that that was enough.*

But he repeated in Yiddish, "Never speak to me again, or I will tell your story and that will be the end of that."

And then he turned and walked back to his platoon. The men wanted to get out of that place as fast as they could.

==========

But even before Deir Yassin, Kastel had been abandoned by the Arabs, and the Jews took it back without firing a shot. None of it made any sense.

Thus, too, with the road to Jerusalem. It was open for a week or so, and then it was cut off again. The Arabs revenged Deir Yassin by massacring seventy-seven doctors and nurses on their way to the Hadassah Hospital. Battles flared up, died down. Towns were taken, lost.

The important centers of Haifa, Safed, Tiberias, and Jaffa were also either abandoned by the Arabs or overrun by the Jews, and they became Jewish cities.

Many people on both sides were killed. But Heshel Rosenheim survived.

CHAPTER 15

He knew it really wasn't over with Levin. He knew Levin was one of those people who never let anything go. He was the kind of person who mulled things around endlessly, thought everything through and through, examined the issues from every possible angle, and always came out with the same answer: he was right in the first place. That way he might never feel one iota of guilt.

But had not Rosenheim so often done the same thing himself? Had he forgotten so completely that he was born not Heshel Rosenheim but Heinrich Mueller? Had the statistics he kept so assiduously not, in fact, pertained to people? People scurrying about in rags, covered in filth, clinging to their dinner bowls, limping through their miserable existences in ill-fitting shoes that turned their feet into pulp? Had not other numbers simply disappeared into the ovens by stepping to the right instead of the left, or the left instead of the right—and had he not recorded them as well? Had he not pawned a gold fountain pen, a diamond ring, a leather jacket, purloined, he thought, from the Reich, but in fact stolen from some fellow whose name had once been painted on a shop window, some woman who once drank tea from china cups, some young man who once thought he would become a chemist or a music teacher or even a doctor of philosophy? Had he not allowed the whole of that well of despair to grow invisible, numerical, abstractive, mathematical? Where in that sum was his guilt?

Yes, Levin would be back. And Rosenheim would have to deal with him. But in the meantime he was caught up in the war.

On May 14, at nine-thirty in the morning, the last of the Etzion Block of kibbutzim fell to the Arabs. The Jews who surrendered were massacred on the spot. On the same day, May 14, the British ended their mandate of Palestine, and all but a few of their troops were evacuated. In the U.N., three resolutions to make Jerusalem, with its Jewish majority, an international city were rejected by the Arab nations, who demanded all of Palestine be Arab.

At five o'clock that evening, in the main hall of the Tel Aviv Museum, David Ben-Gurion declared the birth of the state.

No one in Heshel Rosenheim's platoon who had gathered round the radio had any idea what the state would be named. Zion? Judaea? Herzliya? But when Ben-Gurion uttered the words State of Israel, *it was as if he had given a name to each man and woman's own secret yearning, and a kind of electrical charge ran through them. They held hands. Breathlessly, they listened to the Declaration of Independence.*

They listened as Ben-Gurion recalled the ancient ties to the land where their spiritual and political identity was forged, giving birth to all their cultural and religious values, to the Bible itself, and how though exiled, in each generation for two thousand years, the people kept faith with the land, striving to return, and how they did return, reviving the Hebrew language, building their towns and villages, making, in his words, the desert bloom. They listened as he recounted the promises of the nations to help them establish a homeland, and the catastrophe of the Holocaust which only proved how desperately such a homeland was needed, a land open to every Jew, allowing each to live in dignity and freedom, finally becoming masters of their own fate. They listened, and their hearts filled with hope as he declared a nation grounded upon justice and equality for all, regardless of race, religion, gender, safeguarding all the holy places, Muslim, Christian and Jewish alike, living as brothers with their Arab neighbors, and when he pleaded with these neighbors to live with them in peace, to join with them in building a new way of life, the Jewish soldiers shook their heads. They knew it was not to be.

Then, as they heard the crowd in the Museum Hall go wild, the platoon cheered too. They hugged one another and tears streamed from their faces.

Heshel Rosenheim sat in the corner watching them. In some strange way, he realized, he was responsible for all of this—for the darkness and now for the light—that he, and all the Germans, were tied so closely to this people and its fate, that they had always somehow been kin. He did not feel good about this. He felt deeply ashamed.

"Rosenheim!" someone called out. "Come over!"

He smiled wanly and stayed put.

"I was just thinking," he said, stroking the barrel of his Sten gun, "tomorrow the Arabs will attack."

"True, Hesheleh," another replied, "but now at least they know we are real men."

=========

I had come back to the hospital in the morning, and was sitting in the lounge waiting for them to finish sponging him off. He was already out of the ICU and very quickly recovering, almost, the nurse said, as if he hadn't had a stroke at all. I found my way to the little glassed-in waiting room at the end of the hall. They had comfortable chairs there, a table with some magazines on it, a television set tuned to the Cartoon Network. Across from me a small family sat quietly with blank faces. They had cried themselves out, and talked themselves out too, I guessed, because they looked like the kind of family that never shuts up. There was a youngish woman among them, slender, long fingernails, probably the daughter. Her hair was disheveled, and she had no makeup on, but her jeans were skin tight and her midriff was exposed. I wanted to be aroused. I should have been aroused. But I wasn't. In a minute I'd have to go back in and see my father, and I wasn't looking forward to it. I knew now he was going to die, *Lamed-Vovnik* or not—perhaps not today, not right now—but soon. I was running out of time.

The young woman suddenly lay her head in her mother's lap, just like a child would, even though she must have been around twenty. Her mother was not someone I'd like to lay my head upon—she was wearing a Disney World T-shirt and pink pants. She was grossly overweight. She wore running shoes. But there it was—all in that simple gesture: the mother stroked her daughter's ratty hair, and they both closed their eyes as if communing with some deep, spiritual source. They were a family.

I opened a magazine and tried to read about how to manage your portfolio, which was something else I did not have.

=

"Mikey."

He was sitting up in bed, smiling.

"How you feeling, Dad?" I asked.

"Funny," he said, "I thought I saw Israel here. Crazy. Like a ton of bricks—that's how. It's all these goddamned tubes. I've even got a goddamned tube up my whatsacallit. Can't wait for them to take that one out. That's going to be fun."

His words were slurred, but I could understand him well enough to squirm at the thought of having a catheter removed. My squirming seemed to make him feel better.

"I'm fine," he said, but softly.

"You had a stroke."

"So they tell me."

"They don't think it's too severe. With a little rehabilitation you'll be good as new."

For the moment we had run out of things to say, so I sat down on the little plastic chair and looked around. It was a double room, but the curtain was drawn between him and whoever was next to him. From the other side I could hear someone moaning softly but continuously, the volume rising and falling on the tide of each failing breath. I also noticed there were flowers in my father's room. I, of course, hadn't sent any flowers.

I drew my chair closer to his bed.

"I was thinking about things last night," I said rather casually, "about you and Mom and us kids and being Jewish and everything."

"We tried," he said.

"I know. But it's weird, isn't it, how you and Mom were so involved with Israel, but I just didn't know anything about it?"

"Of course you do."

"Like how it became a state. I don't know that."

"What are you talking about? We always go to Israel Independence Day, don't we? You have all those little flags, remember?"

"Not really," I said.

"You don't remember singing *Hatikva*?"

"I think I knew two things. I knew 'they made the desert bloom' and if you swim in the Dead Sea you float like a cork."

"We should have made you go with us. You didn't want to. Next time."

"No, I did want to go. You never took me."

"We never took you?"

"It was like you didn't want me to see something."

"What wouldn't I want you to see?"

I didn't answer him. Instead I said, "Frankly I think the Palestinians should have a state. I think what Israel is doing is awful."

"History is not so simple," he said.

I looked at him.

"But what do I know? I never studied it. I run a business. I make a living."

I report this conversation as if we were strolling in the park, but actually it came out in driblets and sudden spurts as he struggled to make himself understood, rested frequently, took little sips of Gatorade through a plastic straw, and drifted away and then back to me on the shifting sands of his dementia.

After one of these breaks, when I saw he was ready again, I scooted my chair even closer. "How come you never told me much about Grandpa and Grandma?" I asked.

"What are you talking about? We go there all the time."

"No, no. Grandpa and Grandma Rosenheim. Your parents."

"We can't go to them, Mikey. They're dead. So we go to Bubbie and Zayde." He was referring, of course, to my maternal grandparents, who had lived in Newark and had been dead for many, many years now.

"Did they die in the Holocaust?" I asked.

"What are you talking about? We just had Pesach there!"

"Your parents, the Rosenheims."

"Why are you suddenly asking me this? Who remembers?"

"You don't forget if your parents died in the Holocaust."

"I don't talk about it."

"But I need to talk about it."

"Why all the sudden? You never wanted to talk about it before."

"No, *you* never wanted to talk about it."

"I don't know how they died," he said finally.

"Then how do you know they died?"

"They're not here, are they? They died. Why go into it?"

"In the concentration camp?"

He nodded, but without conviction, I thought.

"Which one?"

He looked at me impatiently. "Auschwitz, I think."

"Not Majdanek?"

"Where did you even hear of Majdanek? No one ever remembers Majdanek. They say Treblinka. They say Auschwitz. Buchanwald. Who ever brings up Majdanek? Only you."

"It existed, didn't it?"

"Yes, of course it exists. They all exist. I can give you a list of every one of them if you want. You want? Chelmno, Sobibor, Treblinka, Belzec, Dachau, Sachsenhausen, Ravensbrück, Flossenbürg, Neuengamme, Gross-Rosen, Mauthausen, Stutthof, Nordhausen, Natzweiler—did I forget something? Birkenau, that is part of Auschwitz. And your Majdanek. And you think that's all? Did I say Bergen-Belsen? Did I mention Theresienstadt? Do you think that's all? That's all they know about. But there are more. They come and they go in a night. On the banks of some river, in some ravine, in the woods behind the town. They come with their trucks and their guns, and with buckets of lye. And of course," he added with, I thought, special bitterness, "their account books, their ledgers. No deed goes unrecorded. But then they erase it. They burn it down. Bury it. Everywhere you look—yesterday, they were there. Believe me, there is not an inch of ground not stained with Jewish blood."

He was shaking with rage. Outside, a small cloud passed over the sun, darkening the room. I felt my throat tighten like a clamp.

"You were in Auschwitz, right?"

"I am not in Auschwitz!" he cried.

"Not now, Dad. I mean before." I grabbed his emaciated arm and held it up. "You have the tattoo. They only did that at Auschwitz, isn't that right? So you must have been in Auschwitz. Or did you get it somewhere else? Tell me, did you get it somewhere else?"

"I don't know, I don't know. I might have."

"Dad!" Now I pushed his arm right in front of his face. The faded blue-black numbers seemed to loom ever larger on his sad, shriveled flesh. "Where did you get it?"

He eyes widened as if he had never seen it before, and he started weeping.

"For God's sake, Dad, tell me who you are!"

A nurse suddenly rushed past me toward the patient behind the curtain. He must have been pressing the buzzer. I could hear him cry, "They're yelling so loud! They won't stop yelling!"

And then she came round and looked at me.

"Is everything all right?" she asked.

"Yes," I said.

"You realize that your father just had a stroke, don't you?"

"Of course I do."

"You need to keep it calm in here."

"But it has been calm in here," I said. "I think he was imagining things."

"Mr. Antonelli?"

"Yes. Maybe he's oversensitive to sound or something. Or

maybe he was dreaming. He's been moaning the whole time. We were just talking."

"Oh," she said, "sorry."

"No problem," I said.

"But your father does need quiet. And so does Mr. Antonelli."

"Of course," I said.

I smiled sheepishly at her, hoping she'd feel I was full of remorse even though I just told her I hadn't done anything wrong. I didn't know what the logic of that was exactly, but it seemed to work. It was as if she and I had a little conspiracy going. Crazy Mr. Antonelli. Silly old people with tubes stuck up their dicks.

"We'll be really quiet," I whispered.

She nodded at me, and assured Mr. Antonelli that everything would be fine now.

After she left, I settled back into the green plastic chair.

"You won't get away with this," I whispered to Heshel Rosenheim, but I don't think he understood me. On the contrary, he seemed to relax. He asked me for the cup of Gatorade, and I gave it to him.

"That's a good boy," he said.

Maybe he'd forgotten the whole conversation. I watched him drink, then took his cup. I smiled at him.

"Tell me about your parents. They were born in Durnik, right? In Lithuania."

"Lithuania? No. We're from Berlin."

"What did he do for a living?"

Dad seemed to like this question. He snuggled himself in his pillows and smiled.

"Papa was a professor of languages, oh yes. He was a genius, your grandfather. He was a great expert in Finno-Ugric languages, but of course he spoke everything. All the Romance and Germanic languages. He taught at *gymnasia*. But a very good one. The best one. And he wrote for many leading journals, and he even lectured at the university as a matter of fact, and at other places, too. Oh yes, I was jealous of Papa being away all the time, and all the professors and students coming over and me not being allowed to stay and have tea, because with tea came the special cookies my mother made." He looked so happy, recalling the taste of his mother's cookies.

"You inherited your ability with languages from him, I guess."

"I'm not so good with languages," my father insisted.

"What about your mother?" I continued.

"Mama?" he smiled. "Never was there one like her!"

"What did she do?"

"Do? She was a mother!"

"But I thought Grandpa taught at the university. Now you say it was *gymnasia*. Why?"

"I don't know why. I was only a boy. It seems to me he also knew Sanskrit. Indo-European languages. It seems to me he was working on something with that."

"Where did you live?"

"A beautiful place!"

"A house?"

"No, of course not. An apartment. We had—oh, it was big—with a whole room for the nanny. I once sneaked in there," he laughed. "My bottom paid the price for that!"

"How many rooms did you have?"

"On the ground floor there was the pastry shop. At night, you could smell the baking, and in the morning we could run down and get strudel or little cakes, marzipan, Sachertorte, Linzertorte. Everything you could dream of, they had. For a penny you could get little cookies filled with jam. We would take them to class with us and eat them for lunch. In the parlor, there was a big clock, and I loved that clock, and every evening before dinner Papa would wind the clock with this big key, and only Papa could wind it, that was the rule!"

"You said you had a nanny?"

"Of course."

"So you had money."

"I don't know. We never went hungry, we had beautiful clothes, every year a new pair of shoes. White cloth on the table, the curtains of lace . . ."

"How many were you?"

"Hmm?"

"How many brothers and sisters?"

"I told you, I told you. Your auntie Mootie, she was the youngest. Your auntie Reggie, she was the older. And then, you know, the baby died, he was just a few months old. And there were cousins and uncles and aunts."

"You had a cousin Hans, right?"

"Did I?"

"Yes, didn't you? You had a cousin named Hans, and he suggested you join something—do you remember?"

"I don't remember."

"What did 'Mootie' stand for?" I asked, when he failed to recall cousin Hans, the one who suggested he join the SS.

"Mootie is Monika," he replied. "And Reggie is for Regina."

I knew these names, of course. I knew these stories, too. But sometimes they changed. That was the thing. Sometimes Mootie stood for Mona. Reggie sometimes was Rachl. Sometimes there was Linzertorte, and sometimes there was kugel. When I was little these things didn't seem to matter. Now they were the details on which everything hung.

"What was the street you lived on?" I tried again to connect him to some real place, some real existence. Maybe I could look it up. Maybe I would go there and ask all the old people if they remembered this Jewish family that once . . .

"Who remembers?" he answered.

"You don't forget a thing like that. Come on, what street?"

He sighed.

"Mikey," he said, "I'm tired."

"Just one more question. What street did you live on?"

"Oy, Mikey, ask your mother."

"I can't ask her, Dad. Tell me the street you lived on."

He rubbed his eyes and when he looked up, they were clouded over and red, like bisque.

"Alexanderplatz," he muttered. "Number Twenty-five."

"Do you remember the name Mueller, Dad?"

"Mueller?" he said.

"Yes, Mueller," I repeated.

"Sure," he said sleepily, "I remember that name. But it's like Smith," he went on, "everybody had that name."

His strength had been amazing, but finally he fell asleep. He seemed so small and unprotected in that huge bed, unshaven and dressed in that paper-thin hospital gown with the little blue flowers on it, and snoring so unnaturally, as if the molecules of air had grown too large for him to swallow. Without meaning to, I had begun to look for clues. My heart ached in my chest to such a degree I had to sit down again and catch my own breath.

My cell phone rang. I thought it would be Josh, but it was Kaufman, from Los Angeles.

I couldn't place him.

"From the Holocaust Library," he explained in his thick accent. "I tried first the one number and then this one you left on my machine." His voice was as frail as butterfly wings. He was concerned that I hadn't gotten the materials.

No, no, I told him, I had gotten them. He wanted to know, then, how he could help me.

I had to think about that. I looked over at my father, sleeping.

"I have some questions," I said at last.

Actually, I asked him many questions. He told me, first of all, what a memorial book is—a list of the dead and sometimes also the survivors from a town or a shtetl. Each has its own memorial book, he explained. Compiled from oral accounts, from Red Cross lists, from German documents. They are not always one hundred percent accurate, but are fairly reliable. Rosenheim? Well, it is a German Jewish name, not terribly common, but not unique either. One would expect most Rosenheims to live in Germany or Austria, but there is no reason not to find them in Galicia, or in Russia or Poland either, in fact anywhere. Durnik? It was in Lithuania, in fact, not far from Amdur. It no longer exists, he said, a shtetl of perhaps eight hundred or a thousand souls, of which about fifteen are known to have survived the war. It was liquidated on March 17, 1942, its inhabitants transported to the Vilna ghetto, and later sent to various concentration camps. Several escaped and went to live with the partisans, of which only one survived. The only Heshel Rosenheim? In all of Europe? No, no, there were probably many, though Hershel (with an *r*) would have been a more common name than Heshel. Majdanek? It was the worst of the worst. It still stands, by the way, he said. One of the few that remain. You should go see it. Mueller? A very common name. Heinrich Mueller? Don't you mean Heinrich Müller, head of the Gestapo? No? He was at Majdanek? We can see if we have any mention of him, it should be on the computer, but again these lists are incomplete. But in answer to your question about Heshel Rosenheim, yes there were others, I can see them on the screen right now, but that was the one you requested. The one from Durnik. Otherwise I would have given you—oh, let me see—well, we have seventy-three listings just right here, not to mention the Hershels, and then if you want variations on the spelling of the last name.

"I asked you for Durnik?"

"Did I make an error? I'm terribly sorry."

"No, no. But it wasn't me."

"It was not you? You are not Mr. Rosenheim?"

"Yes, I am. But I think someone was using my name."

"*Gott in himmel,*" he said. "Should I call the police?"

I told him not to do that. It was probably a cousin or something. Is it possible, I then asked him, if Heshel Rosenheim actually survived? That the list was wrong?

"Of course," he said. "Anything is possible."

He called me about fifteen minutes later. I'd been sitting there looking at my father the whole time, frozen to the chair. The minutes could have been counted in the heartbeats in my neck—like a time bomb. Hello again, he said. Yes, there was indeed a Lieutenant H. Mueller mentioned in at least one document as having been at Majdanek sometime between 1943 and 1944, but it was unclear what his duties were.

"What happened to him?"

"I'm sorry, I don't know. There is no record."

"How can we find out?"

"We'll never know what happened to him, Mr. Rosenheim. That's the way it is with most of them. They rose out of the masses to do their dirty work, and faded back into the masses when it was over. He has probably lived a normal life. He was a plumber or a baker or a car salesman, he had a family, and as far as anyone knew he had spent the whole of the war at the Russian front as a truck mechanic. Walking down the street, one of his victims may run into him and not even recognize him—in fact, he'll buy his new car from him and give him his money and shake his hand and go home and tell his wife about the nice fellow who sold him his car. I'm sorry to tell you this, Mr. Rosenheim. It seems so unfair. Perhaps there is a story in your family, about some guard named Mueller who harmed your relative, your

Heshel Rosenheim, who beat him or tortured or murdered him, and that is why you want to find him and punish him. Well, I tell you: you will not find him, and if you find him he will not go to trial, and if he does go to trial he will not go to jail, and if he does go to jail they will release him in a year because of his old age, if he is even alive anymore. I am not telling you to forget it. God forbid you should forget it. Not one of us should forget a single sentence of it. We should remember it always, and teach it to our children and our children's children. But I do advise you not to hold on to it. I do advise you to let it go, to, yes, remember that it happened, but not to live with it as if it were happening to you, in your own life, in this very day. I hope I've been some help to you, Mr. Rosenheim," he said.

Silently, slowly, I folded the cell phone and put it in my pocket. My father, like a beached whale, was gasping for air and spewing back foul vapor from his mouth hole. Suddenly, I could not stand the sight of him. I lurched at him, fists clenched. The heart monitor clicked happily its message of life. In the hall, nurses and orderlies scurried by on missions of mercy. But something rose up in *me*—something familiar and dark, like an oft-repeated dream which comes to you in different guise, only, at last, to reveal itself as the obsession of your every night—and I felt my jaw grow rigid and steel-like—and I raised my fist above my father, brushing against the lifelines of fluid that led to his arm, his heart, his brain, his soul, and I held it there, my fist, shaking, threatening, ready.

"Hey you!" I heard a voice from behind the curtain. It was Mr. Antonelli.

I jumped. Startled, I fell back against the curtain and found myself in Mr. Antonelli's side of the room.

"What is the matter with you?" he cried.

"What do you mean?" I said.

"All this noise! All this noise! Can't you be quiet for a minute?" He shook his finger at me. "There's something the matter with you! You need to have your brain examined."

Then he turned over, and presented me with his back.

I fled from the room.

Then a very strange thing happened. I went out into the vestibule and ran right into that woman, the poet from Starbucks.

CHAPTER 16

"What are you doing here?" I said to her. I must have been terribly agitated, because she put her hand on my shoulder and attempted to comfort me.

"I just thought I'd stop in and see your father," she said gently.

"What?" I said.

I suddenly couldn't remember why I was in the hall, why I had run out of the room. The *ping! ping!* of the hospital intercom—*Blood gas unit to 349!*—made me think I had momentarily and impossibly materialized on a submarine. How on earth did this woman know about my dad? She knew me only as Mickey Rose, not Michael Rosenheim, I was sure of that. And even if she did know my real name, what was she doing here anyway? I had one lousy conversation with her in a coffee shop. Was she following me? Stalking me?

Suddenly she embraced me and told me how sorry she was. She knew what it was like to lose a father.

She was rather tall, and when she grabbed me, my head was tilted downward and my nose got pressed into something incredibly soft. Her blouse was remarkably silky, considering it looked like it had just come off a camel, but, more important, I hadn't been this close to a breast in two or three years, and in spite of my confusion and panic I didn't pull away. Her smell, utterly foreign, was also painfully familiar, and it entered me like an oar through water, propelling me forward into her bosom almost against my will. In a warm, consoling voice she explained that her mother (as it turned out!) lived in the same condominium complex as my father. Wasn't that amazing? Not the same building, but down the road, in the town houses. The town houses were newer and more expensive, and they were two stories high—so anyone who lived there had to have a good retirement plan and two working legs. She had told her mother about meeting this comic, Mickey Rose, and her mother had said something like "Oh, *him*" (but in a nice way, she assured me, a very nice way) and explained to her who I really was, and who my father was, and that my father had had a stroke and was at JFK.

"A bunch of us got together and sent flowers," she said.

"A bunch of who?" I muttered into her collar, my cheek glancing upon her neck.

"His admirers, I guess," she said.

More admirers. How on earth had a war criminal managed to get so many admirers? And Jewish ones at that! And how any of them knew he was in the hospital was beyond me. Was there some sort of Heshel Rosenheim Emergency Broadcast System? The poet lady made a move toward his hospital room.

"He's asleep now," I said.

"Oh," she replied. "Well, I don't want to bother him. But you look like a wreck, poor thing. Maybe we should get you something to eat."

She took my hand and led me down the corridor to the elevator, and then put me in her car. We drove around awhile, looking for someplace that wasn't a chain. We never found one.

Finally I suggested we head back to The Ponds at Lakeshore.

Why I brought her home I will never know. Was it the tenderness of her gesture, the way she hugged me, almost like a child? Or the (I had to admit it) thrilling sensation of those thick, yielding breasts and the heady scent of slight nervousness mixed with Chanel that had risen through the fabric of her blouse like ether? I was a fool. I barely knew her. She wore Birkenstocks. I was in love with my ex-wife.

When I opened the door and let her in, I glanced through to the Florida room and my heart sank. The journals were there for anyone to see. I pointed her to the kitchen and closed the door.

There was, of course, next to nothing in the refrigerator, nevertheless she managed to put something together and set it before me at the little breakfast table. I hadn't sat at this table once the whole time I had been at my father's, but she set a place for me there, so I sat down. She seated herself across from me and watched me eat. I imagined my mother and father must have played out this scene countless times. She was a stranger to me, but I liked the easy, familiar way she had about her. She had not asked me where things were in the kitchen. She just found what she needed and went about her work. She didn't chatter or make small talk, which I also appreciated. And I didn't feel like she expected me to talk either. She wasn't waiting for me to say anything. She just sat there with a contented look, and sipped some tea.

"Do you want to see something?" I said.

"Sure," she replied.

I got up, took her hand, and led her through the dining room and the living room and out into the Florida room. The Cheez Whiz box was still in the center of the floor. It was egregiously watermarked and moldy, the way old boxes get after they've been left out in the rain, and I noticed an almost animal-like smell emanating from it. It was like a dead body, exhumed and still rotting, wanting nothing more than to be put back in the ground.

She stood there quietly, looking.

Some of the journals were stuffed in the Cheez Whiz box, but others were scattered about the floor. They, too, gave off an unpleasant smell.

"I'd open a window," I said, "but it's always so fucking hot."

She nodded. "Perhaps it will rain soon."

"But then you can't open the windows anyway."

"It's a problem," she said.

I waited for her to ask me what all this mess was, but she didn't.

"Do you want me to tell you what these are?" I said.

"If you want to," she responded.

I looked at her. She looked back at me kindly, her hands folded near her waist. The smell in the room was suffocating. I wanted to smell her again. Not this.

"What kind of poetry do you write?" I asked.

She raised her eyebrows—she must have been surprised by my question.

"Would you like to read some?"

Why would I want to? What if it was awful? But of course I said yes.

She walked over to my father's bookcase, the one we had passed in the living room, the one filled with books entitled *The Jewish Book of Questions, Love Your Yiddish!, Chaim Weitzman*

—*Man of Honor,* translations of *The Mishna, The Zohar, The Book of Job*—and from among these, strangely, miraculously, jammed in with a few other slender volumes I had never noticed, she pulled out a slim paperback and handed it to me.

"My mother probably gave it to him," she said. "I noticed it on the way in. My mother gives a copy to everyone she meets."

I now had to look at her book. I opened it to the title page and noticed her list of prior publications on the flyleaf. There were many. Very many. And I suddenly felt that I had even vaguely heard of her.

"Read it later," she said, "if you feel like it."

I put the book down on the table. I was confused about books at that time anyway. I didn't know what to think about them. For instance, just then I recalled those kisses among the orange groves.

Impetuously, I again took April's hands in mine.

"Can I ask you a straightforward question?"

"Sure," she said.

"What do you look like without all those clothes on?"

"I thought you wanted to tell me what all that stuff on your floor is," she said.

But she let me draw her closer to me, so close I could taste the loose strands of her long, silvery hair and feel the moisture on her back through the fabric of her skirt.

"Oh that," I said. "My father is a writer, too."

It wasn't my greatest performance. I came in about thirty seconds. But I couldn't stop touching her, I just couldn't stop touching her, and that seemed to make her happy, because at some point she smiled at me, stroked my face, looked me deeply in the eyes in an open and fresh way, and I knew that right then I could have said whatever it was I wanted to say to her—no questions asked, no judgments even. I took a deep breath.

"What?" she urged.

She was so close I could see little specks of gold—maybe like mushrooms—dotting the circles of her sea blue eyes.

"Nothing," I said. "I just think I better get back to the hospital."

She drove me back, then took off, as I asked her to.

I went upstairs. More flowers had arrived. Dad was asleep.

I sat next to him for a long time, thinking.

The nurse stopped by at some point and informed me that he was completely stabilized, and though there was no telling what might happen next—how fast, how slow, as she put it—they would be releasing him back to the nursing home sometime the next day.

"He looks so thin," I said.

"Really, he's fine," she said.

The tubes had been removed and the monitors unplugged. They had given him something to eat, too, because the tray was still on the table, and I could see he had eaten well and heartily, his plate wiped clean. He looked so serene, almost angelic, except for the dark rings under his eyes which reminded me of all those pictures of Eichmann.

Then the social worker came in to describe his physical therapy and how Medicare wouldn't really pay for any of it.

CHAPTER 17

As they sped southward, he sucked on an unlit cigarette and considered his options. He had been pulled back into the Negev Brigade a few hours earlier, thrown into an advance unit, and given command of a small squad—five men whom he had never seen before. They were now riding in a lorry crowded with twenty or thirty Palmachniks, but silence reigned. The weather had again changed, and now the Negev was hot and dry. A khamsin was blowing up from the south, smacking against the open truck bed and pelting the soldiers' cheeks with sand, filling their mouths and forcing them to keep their eyes squeezed shut. Those who had them tied kaffiyehs *over their noses and mouths, and the others turned their faces away, but the dust found them anyway. It was impossible to smoke, which made the gloom even more complete.*

Heshel Rosenheim dug some sand out of his ears. Most of the men, he had noticed, were wearing their khaki shorts because of the heat, and now their legs were covered with red welts. He still preferred trousers as being somehow more military, though he did recall that Rommel's Afrika Corps wore shorts. But that was different. They also had tanks. The Jews didn't. No tanks, no artillery, no combat aircraft—virtually no heavy weapons at all. They were running down to face ten thousand Egyptians armed with several tank battalions, regiments of artillery, armored cars, many hundreds of Bren guns, innumerable mortars and rockets and fighter planes. It was ludicrous. He was just happy that some of his men had managed to get new boots. Heshel still wore his old ones, but by now they felt like he was born in them.

Someone tried to start a song, but it was quickly choked off by the wind and sand. They continued along in silence, their eyes shut tight. Even if they could have opened them and looked up, they would not have been able to see anything, not even the sun. It was utterly obliterated. But they were not without gratitude. The clouds of dust protected them from snipers.

It was May 15, 1948, one day after Independence. The Arab armies had already begun their invasions. From the north, the Lebanese and the Syrians. From the east, the Iraqis and the Arab Legion of Transjordan. And from the south—after first bombarding Tel Aviv the night before—the Egyptians. The situation had been made clear to Lieutenant Rosenheim when the junior officers were briefed by their commanders earlier that day. The objectives of the Egyptian army were two: to capture the Negev by driving through Bersheva to Hebron, where they would meet up with the Arab Legion, and simultaneously to advance straight up the coastal highway and take Tel Aviv in a matter of days. And what, Heshel wondered, was there to stop them? There was nothing between Gaza and Tel Aviv but a few small kibbutzim. Most of the Haganah and Palmach were defending Jerusalem. The rest would have to be diverted to fortify Tel Aviv, which was completely unprotected. If the Egyptians made a successful dash up the coast, all would be lost. It was up to the kibbutzim to hold off the Egyptians until Tel Aviv could be defended, and up to a few small units of the Negev Brigade to help them.

It was, Heshel knew, an impossible task. And yet he found himself volunteering. He was not exactly sure why, but it did occur to him how easy it would be to surrender his squad to an overwhelming Egyptian force, after which, having been taken a prisoner of war, he could reveal his true identity and offer his not inconsiderable talents to the Arab cause. It seemed a logical course of action.

Someone in the lorry again tried to rouse the men with song—this time it was a little fellow up forward, more protected by the cab. He managed a few lines from a tune they all knew about a young man coming upon a beautiful girl at a desert well—offering to draw water for her flock—one of those silly love songs that Heshel found so saccharine and somehow hopeless. A few of the boys tried to join in, but again the vortex of sand filled their mouths, and instead of singing, they were spitting and gagging. The wind was so loud anyway, they could barely hear the engine, and if anyone had to bark an order, it would have been too bad, because no one would hear. They probably wouldn't even know if someone was shooting at them.

Heshel opened his eyes for a few seconds. Utter nothingness. Behind them were clouds of dust, in front of them clouds of dust, and they were driving along as if in a dream, when you suddenly realize you are nowhere, and there is nothing, and you are alone, and around you is only the dim suggestion of some former reality, some place to land. That's usually when you wake up and see you are in bed, and everything is really as it should be, and you are really all right.

He snorted, blowing the sand out of his nose, and closed his eyes again.

All the days of his life he would remember this moment, when he had stepped out of the world, and out of time, and was reborn when the wind cleared.

But at that moment he did not know that, and all he thought to himself was: My one responsibility is to stay alive.

Which, had he thought about it, was exactly what the inmates at Majdanek said to themselves, lying in their own excrement, dreaming of their next scrap of bread.

=========

At some point the truck could go no farther. The drivers had lost the road and the wheels had gotten stuck in deep sand. They pulled tarpaulins over the truck bed to make a tent, and camped within it as best they could, waiting for the wind to stop.

=========

They crawled out like prairie dogs, sniffing the air.

The sky was still muddy, but the air was calm. Looking about, they could not see the road at all. They must have strayed by miles. The best they could do was head in a westerly direction until they ran into the highway. The commander cursed that they had lost a whole day. He ordered the men to push the truck out of the sand. The heat was ungodly, but it was much better to be doing something than hiding like rats under that miserable tarp. They gathered round the lorry, pushing and tugging, while others placed scraps of wood beneath the rear wheels. It was a desperate task. The lorry just sank deeper. They decided to rest the engine.

"What's that?" someone said.

In the sudden silence they heard the distant grinding of another engine, and what seemed like shouting. They looked up. Those with binoculars searched the horizon.

"Look!" one of the commanders said. "They're stuck worse than we are!"

It was a group of Egyptians. They had three Jeeps and a personnel carrier buried up to their headlamps, and they were running around just like the Jews had done.

"Hey!" one of the men called out in Arabic, waving his shirt. "Need help?"

"They can't hear you," someone said.

But apparently they could see them, because just then three Bren carriers appeared on the horizon. These had no trouble negotiating the sand dunes.

"Shit!" cried the commander. "You—set up a perimeter. The rest of you—get this fucking vehicle moving!"

But the Bren carriers didn't advance. They just sat there, pointing their guns at the Jews.

"They're afraid of us," someone said.

"I doubt that," Heshel replied. "They're just waiting for something."

Through his binoculars, Heshel could see the Arabs rushing about hysterically, trying to get their Jeeps moving. As he panned across to the Bren carriers, he could see an officer seated beside the gunner. He was drinking tea.

"On the contrary. I think they are very confident, indeed," said Lieutenant Rosenheim.

=========

It took a good half hour to extricate the lorry from the sand and get out of there. The poor Egyptians were still struggling, but they waved good-naturedly when the Israelis (as they now called themselves) drove off. One of Heshel's men answered their wave with a salute of gunfire that rose harmlessly into the brown desert sky.

They arrived at Nir Am late in the afternoon, having missed two days of the war.

=========

The Palmach had set up makeshift headquarters in the underground bunkers at Nir Am. Most of the men had never been in a bunker before, but Heshel had, and he knew the smell, the odd feeling of affinity one acquires with creatures like termites and moles, and the fear, almost worse than being out in the bombardment, of not knowing when the end might come, or who of your friends or loved ones were already without arms and legs. He knew, as well, that it would get much worse down there, that soon the stench would be unbearable and the emotions would boil over like scalded milk.

They gathered round a table that had maps laid out upon it, and the commander explained the situation. Two kibbutzim had already been assaulted by the Egyptians—Nirim, the one closest to the Egyptian border, and a religious settlement named Kfar Darom. Both miraculously repulsed the invasion. In the case of Nirim, which faced tank assaults and heavy artillery, they triumphed with two pistols, two mortars, seven Italian rifles, two Stens and one Bren gun. Half their eighty-odd people were killed or wounded, but not as many as the Egyptians suffered. The situation was similar at Kfar Darom.

The men cheered, but the commander remained ashen-faced. The Egyptians, he told them, were simply bypassing Nirim and Kfar Darom—wasting their time there had been sheer foolishness, he said, but good for us, since it gives us more time to prepare. The real battle would take place at Yad Mordechai, only a few miles from where they now sat cramped together in the dark of the bunker. Yad Mordechai was the key, he said, and it must be held at all costs. It sat directly in the path of the Egyptian advance. After that was only Naor and Ashdod, which was largely Arab anyway. Once taken, the road to Tel Aviv would be wide open, and then the war, and the dream of two thousand years, would most likely be over. But if Yad Mordechai could hold out, even a few days, defenses could be prepared for Tel Aviv. It would be no picnic, he told them. Not like Nirim. No, he said, the Egyptians won't give up so easily this time.

He asked for volunteers. Each knew what was at stake, and they all raised their hands. He made assignments, but to Heshel Rosenheim he said, "No. You're from Naor, are you not? I'm going to send you there, you and a few men."

"But they may never attack Naor," he replied.

"So what are you worried about?" the commander said.

=========

Naor had changed greatly, and yet the air was the same, the dry, sweet smell coming off the desert and the vague saltiness of the not-so-distant sea. As he jumped from the car, Heshel Rosenheim saw immediately the watchtower, his watchtower, which dominated the farm, was now fortified with sandbags. Squinting, he saw the figure of a man in the tower, but it was a stranger, someone from the Haganah. He now surveyed the compound with the eyes of a soldier. Defensive posts had been established around the perimeter, basically foxholes hardened with cement and sandbags. They were not connected with trenches, as they should have been, though a few trenches had been dug closer to the center of the kibbutz. Several rows of barbed wire had been laid around the circumference of the village, reminding him more of a concentration camp than a communal farm. He was interrupted by a hand on his shoulder.

"Yekkeh!"

It was Avigdor, the sabra who used to mock him, calling him by his pet name. "It's our little German!"

They all came out to greet him.

"My! How he's changed!" they joked, tugging at his uniform.

"What's the Palmach coming to?" someone laughed.

"Thank God you're back," added another. "The books are a mess!"

He felt a strange happiness at seeing them. Each face held a story for him, a memory of peeling potatoes in the kitchen, or raking the barn in the early afternoon, or settling a dispute over how many times a pair of shoes can be repaired before new ones are authorized—faces he had seen through the canopy of orange branches, or across the table at dinner. And for all that, he did not really like them.

He looked around for Moskovitz, and finally saw her, standing off, in a pair of army trousers and an incongruous pink blouse. He thought vainly, she put on the blouse for me. She was smoking a cigarette, brushing back the ringlets of her dark hair that kept escaping from a hastily tied bun. She looked heavier, ruddier than he remembered, stronger. He wanted to make his way over to her, but they were all hugging him, each one in turn, and when it seemed none was left but Moskovitz, she merely smiled, crushed her smoke, and went back inside.

CHAPTER 18

Even though he was not actually under Haganah authority, he accepted his assignment as commander of Post 4, a dugout on the northeast corner of the settlement in view of the experimental banana groves and the fields of alfalfa that bordered them. Above him loomed the watchtower with the kibbutz's single Bren gun. It would be the first objective of any Egyptian advance, which meant he would be in the main line of fire—not exactly what he had hoped for. Of course, if he were the Egyptian general he wouldn't bother with Naor. It was far off the main road, even farther than Nirim or Kfar Darom had been. Much more strategic was the hill just to the west which in fact overlooked the coastal road and was not even occupied. It was known only by number. He might have suggested this to the Haganah commander—why tempt them with Naor? Put a garrison on the hill and let them fight it out there. But he kept silent.

His squad had brought some weapons with them. Several Sten guns, a mortar, a bag full of antitank mines. One of his men, Dovid, was a sapper, and the two of them walked together, smoking cigarettes and laying the mines. They had gotten to know each other a little, and Heshel liked him. He was from Provence, but had been secreted over the Pyrenees during the war and raised quietly by Spanish nuns. Even though he was now only seventeen, Heshel felt they might be able to talk to each other, if for no other reason than they had both eaten pork.

"They'll come from there," Heshel said to him in French, pointing to the line between the banana trees and the alfalfa, which was still low to the ground.

Dovid indicated a pattern with his hand, and Heshel nodded, and they began to stroll along, stopping now and then to bury a mine and carefully mark its location on a map. It was a useless occupation—if the Egyptians did bother to attack, these few mines could never stop them from breaking through.

"Save some for the flanks," he said anyway.

"You seem melancholy," said the sapper.

"Don't I always?"

"Yes, you do."

Heshel laughed at this.

"But why?" asked the boy. "Here we are in our own land, doing the most important thing. Not sitting in some apartment somewhere drinking tea and complaining about the weather. What could be a better life than this?"

"I don't know, Dovid," he said. "Perhaps being home with a cup of tea would not be such a bad thing."

"For someone your age, I guess."

"I'm only twenty-seven," said Heshel.

"A Jew can't sit at home anymore!" exclaimed the boy. "That would be the worst thing I can imagine—to have all this happening and not be a part of it. You would miss everything! And think of the millions who died so that this day might be possible. And think of how they died, Lieutenant. Walking like sheep right into the ovens. Digging their own graves and waiting for someone to shoot them in the back of their heads."

"Yes, yes," Heshel said. "I remember."

"I guess the world just can't forgive us for introducing them to God!"

"That's nonsense."

"It's true. No matter what we do or what we say, they find a reason to hate us. We bring them the word of God, so they conclude that we're the devil. Can you explain that?"

An ancient voice rose up in Heshel Rosenheim. It's the way you separate yourselves from everyone! it said. The way you think you're better! The way you cheat the Gentiles! And how you lust after money! It's your greed and lust! It's your need to control!

Angrily, he looked into Dovid's eyes. They were gentle even for all the fire of his young words. Heshel turned away. He saw his men feverishly digging trenches in the pitch of night, and spotted in the distance the lanterns of a small group of women braving the banana fields to thin the new sprouts so at least some might grow and prosper in spite of the tanks and firebombs; and he turned at the sound of two boys laughing as they lugged huge milk cans filled with water into the dining hall, as if that flimsy structure might withstand even one round of artillery.

"No," said Heshel, "I cannot explain it."

"That's why, for me, this is the happiest time of my life."

Heshel handed the boy another mine.

"I'm glad," he said. "Put this one over there."

With all his heart he still wanted to get away. Yet he remained steadfast and precise with his work. He laid the mines as carefully as he could—to protect as best he might these foolish creatures whom God had abandoned to the likes of him.

=========

Moskovitz was obviously trying to avoid him. She did not venture out to Post 4, nor sit near Heshel Rosenheim at dinner, nor join any group of soldiers where she might find him. She was working in the children's house, and she slept with them in the shelter. In those days, they still came out to play for a while in the daylight. They played rounds of football or volleyball, and the little ones had the sandbox and swings. Heshel somehow found himself wandering over to the playground. But he stood back, looking on as she watched over them. There were two or three infants there as well, in strollers or bassinets. Sometimes he saw her holding one or another of them. She seemed so natural with them. He desperately wanted to speak with her, but did not dare. He waited, and hoped, but for what he did not actually know.

He said to the commander, "Why are they here? Shouldn't the women and children be evacuated?"

"Bad for morale," was the reply.

"Ridiculous."

"Yes, but those are the orders. Anyway," he added, "it's what the women want."

=========

He decided he would not speak to her unless she spoke to him.

In the meantime word arrived that, to the south, Yad Mordechai was under attack. Those on Naor redoubled their efforts, building more shelters, digging more trenches. During the night they somehow erected a pillbox at Post 2. There was a Haganah radio on the kibbutz, but it did not always work, and news from headquarters or Yad Mordechai came intermittently, broken by hours of silence. In bits and pieces they learned that Yad Mordechai had sustained some four thousand bombs from Egyptian planes and heavy artillery in the first three hours of battle alone. There was not a building left standing. Then leaflets were dropped calling upon the kibbutzniks to surrender. But of course they didn't, so the shelling began again, even more intensely, and then suddenly there was silence—for the infantry had finally advanced.

Through the static, Heshel could hear the constant explosions broken by bursts of automatic weapons. The Israeli doctor had gotten on the radio, begging for help. He wondered if the Red Cross might come. Someone else called for reinforcements. It was clear none was on the way.

On Naor, no one said a word. Most went back to their desperate work. As for Heshel, he wished he were at Yad Mordechai. That way he could give himself up and be done with it.

Yet by nightfall, they learned, the Egyptians had somehow been driven off. They gathered again by the radio and listened in silence to the casualty list. It seemed endless.

Then someone remarked, "They can never surrender."

Everyone knew he was referring to the massacre of the Jews who had surrendered in the Etzion Block.

"That was not the Egyptian army," Heshel heard himself say.

"In any case," the man said, "surrender is not an option."

And with that he loaded several boxes of shells into his arms and walked out to his post.

In a while, only the radio operators were in the shelter. Everyone else had gone back to work, taking their suppers with them. Finally, Heshel turned to go. Moskovitz was standing in the doorway, studying him.

"Why so ready to surrender?" she said. Even in the gloomy closeness of the shelter, the whiteness of her skin seduced him.

"I didn't say anything about surrender," he said.

"I must have heard wrong," she replied.

"I merely said that the Egyptians are not the same as the Arab Brotherhood. They are a disciplined army. They respect the rules of war."

"You hope so."

"I do hope so. For all our sakes!"

"Heshel," she said, with a sad little smile, "let's not fight."

They walked out into the trench and climbed up onto the lawn near the children's house. Even with the heavy scent of spring in the air, he could pick out the natural perfume of her skin, like some sort of wild desert honey. They felt their way along the slender pathway.

"I hate these blackouts," she said.

What exactly did she want? he wondered. What exactly did he want? They had but one moment together, that was all, one night, one embrace. Other than that, they were strangers, weren't they?

"Do you think we will all die?" she asked.

"Of course not," he said, caught off guard.

"I don't mean the whole nation. I mean the kibbutz."

"I don't even think they'll attack here. It would be a waste of their time."

"Then we will have to attack them, won't we?" she said.

She sighed and lowered her head. Her hands were now tucked in her pockets. She looked different, somehow, her cheeks thicker, rosier, her hips wider, more feminine. He had to resist reaching for her.

"Don't worry so much," he said. He smiled at her, trying to be encouraging, but he doubted she noticed.

They had arrived at the shelter near the children's house. It was underground, so the metal door lay flat upon the earth. With two hands she yanked it up, revealing a set of stairs leading below. He could see a light, and hear the clamor of children and the voices of women speaking in consoling tones. The smell of dinner drifted up—tinned beef and sausages, he thought—and the aroma of burning kerosene. The children sounded unafraid—giggling, arguing, as if nothing were out of the ordinary. He wondered briefly if he would ever have children. The thought had never occurred to him before. He looked at Moskovitz.

"My post," she said. "At least for tonight."

He held the door for her.

"You look good in a uniform," she remarked. And then she slid down the stairs and out of view.

=========

Hunkered down in his foxhole, he tried to stretch his legs. He wanted more than anything to take off his shoes and go to sleep. But it was impossible with Dovid and Ari chattering on. In time of battle, this hole would be manned by four men plus himself. Tonight, the others were hurriedly enlarging the trench so that Post 4 would not be so isolated. Dovid opened his shirt and pulled out a bottle of red wine.

"Mukhuzani!" he declared. "I got it from some Czechoslovakians. Where they got it, I don't know, but I traded it for a block of halvah. Idiots."

He drank some, passed it around.

Heshel held the bottle to his lips. It was coarse and bitter, but he swallowed it anyway.

=========

They heard on the radio that Yad Mordechai was in a panic. It became clear that the presence of women and children was a mistake. Fear of rape and atrocity at the hands of the Egyptians made some go mad. One distraught man ran around the kibbutz shooting all the farm animals, the cows, the mules, the white horse named Atziel that everyone loved. Some of the young girls refused to stay inside the shelter anymore. Others cowered under the beds. But by then it was too late to evacuate.

On Naor, they called a meeting. Heshel listened with relief as the commander ordered the women and children removed that very night.

Lorries began arriving around midnight. The mothers took their children first, kissing their husbands good-bye. Most people tried not to cry. Then the wives without children got on. But some of the single women decided to stay. There was the radio operator. The nurse. Two women who suddenly formed themselves into the kitchen brigade.

Heshel saw that Moskovitz was not getting on the lorry.

"Get on!" he commanded.

She laughed at him. "Why should I get on? I'm a single woman. I have the right to stay if I have an essential job."

"What job is that?"

"I'm the assistant PIAT operator."

"We don't even have a PIAT."

"One is coming in tonight," she said. "I have to be here if something happens to the operator. What good is an antitank weapon if you don't have someone who knows how to fire it?"

"Fool!" he cried.

"Don't worry," she said, walking off, "I'll stay out of your way."

CHAPTER 19

I was exhausted from everything. From reading. From visiting a father who told me nothing. From feeling I had to call April, and yet not doing it. The doctor had said something about a living will. I had no idea if he had one. I'd have to search his files. And while I'm at it, I thought, I might as well get the rest of his things in order. Box up the books. Call the used-furniture man. I wanted to get rid of everything. I began the arduous task of going through the house, room by room, drawer by drawer. I started in the dining room, by packing the china into boxes. I picked up a dinner plate—the good china, my mother used to call it, so ornate it could have made Catherine the Great blush—and I remembered clearly how Ella reacted the first time she had seen it. *Jesus,* she whispered, *I hope we're not inheriting these!* and then how she said to my mother, *Oh! What a beautiful table!* It was the first of a long run of inconsistencies in our marriage. My eyes then fell upon the rose-colored candy dish that had graced our dining table for as long as I could remember, its edges scalloped with real gold, now chipped and worn—and suddenly I tasted the Bartons chocolates they used to keep there when we were kids. Did they even make Bartons anymore?

The chafing dish told me of the parties my parents used to give—usually to raise money for my father's latest cause, Israel Bonds or saving the last Jews of India, but it also came out on New Year's Eve when they sometimes had people over—and I remembered one year sitting on the landing, poking my head through the banister, trying to stay awake, watching them, me in my cowboy pajamas, listening to the din of adult conversation—so loud and incomprehensible, like waves crashing onto the shore—when suddenly my father rushed up, grabbed me in his arms and carried me downstairs, presenting me to the crowd like the crown prince; and even now, recalling the smell of scotch on his breath and the warmth of his hands through my pajamas made me weak in the knees.

I found Karen's old violin, which my parents kept as a kind of memorial, leaning artistically against the buffet. When I opened the case, it gave off a damp, musty smell—like the Cheez Whiz box. Since the violin was always there, I'd never noticed it, and actually had forgotten she had played it. I'd forgotten she was musical as well as comical, as well as literary and delightful and perfect. I tried like hell to remember one tune she had played. I couldn't. But, really, did it matter what tunes Karen played, if she played at all? Perhaps I was misremembering even now. Perhaps it wasn't Karen's violin. Perhaps it was my father's. Perhaps he wasn't a Nazi, or an Israeli, or a wallpaper salesman, but was actually a concert violinist. Or had wanted to become one. Or had forgotten that he was one. I looked at the violin. My God, I thought. It's not hers. It's mine.

It was true. For several gruesome months my mother insisted I learn an instrument. The torture ended when I told her that Mr. Jarâs—he was French, and thus suspect to begin with—liked to touch my bottom. But I was lying. Even now when I thought about it, I convulsed with shame. How could I have lied to my mother? And such a terrible, inhuman lie. No wonder I had blotted it out so entirely.

Very soon the apartment was cluttered with candlesticks and dessert trays, water pitchers and embroidered napkins, school photographs and kitchen utensils all waiting to be put in boxes. And then it struck me. These were not the innocent accumulation of a typical family life. These were the very clues I had been looking for! I stood there sunk up to my neck in stuff, and felt intoxicated.

I had to triage the evidence. For instance, a death's-head insignia would have more title to my attention than, say, my mother's Hummel figurines (girl at well, boy with sheep) or her Revere Ware frying pan with the handle you always had to screw back on. Where to start?

Over the past weeks, the intensity of my feelings about my sister, Karen, had grown from a benchmark of almost zero to something close to boiling. It was disconcerting and unexpected. It led me to believe she was hiding something from me. That's why the first thing I did was move the candy dish and lay out her things on the dining table: her scrapbook, her junior yearbook (she never made it to senior year), a pile of drawings my parents had saved going all the way back to when she was two or three, a little jewelry box that held an assortment of cheap necklaces, earrings,

rings, and pins. Among them was the high school ring she had never worn because it didn't arrive until after she was dead. Next to the jewelry box were her toe shoes, worn and yellowed, the points darkened with rosin now turned black, a shoe box full of photos of her friends, almost none of whom I recognized, and then her diary. Her diary from the year of her cancer. It used to sit next to her bed, a simple black sketchbook with a thick cardboard cover sealed only with ribbon, once pink, now brown. I remembered looking upon it with dread. Even now I dared not open it. Nevertheless I put it aside; it was a clue.

Along with this I found something else. Her hospital wristband, with her name, blood type, and case number typed on it. This also I set aside.

I chose not to analyze or interpret or even feel anything at this stage—in fact, that was the most important thing of all, not to feel anything. I was collecting data, that's all. I had to keep a clear head.

Thus I ferreted out my father's little collection of Ella-nalia. There was of course the wedding book with its myriad of unidentifiable relatives and former friends. A manila envelope filled with birthday, anniversary, New Year's, and Hanukkah cards she had sent to my parents over the years, signing both our names. I was surprised to find quite a few items of clothing she'd left in the guest room. When I first came upon them, I had the sense that I was looking at a ghost—that the empty dress on the hanger could hop down and saunter away. I gathered her dress in my hands and felt tears rise in my throat. I also found several pairs of shorts, a sarong, two bathing suits, mismatched socks, wooden sandals, and a straw hat. I laid them out on the couch. From the kitchen I took the Wüsthof chef's knife that she had bought so there would be at least one sharp knife in my father's house. It was, of course, dull. From the bookshelves I gathered a handful of murder mysteries and best sellers which I remembered her reading out by the pool or beside me in bed. Each of these items was like a talisman to me, a sacred object. I tried to find her scent on the clothes, but instead I got a nose full of mildew. I had the sense that there was no meaning in any of these items, and I did not mark them as evidence. However, I did find myself putting her sundress aside so it might breathe some fresh air.

I thought of my mother.

Somehow she had played no role in this. How was that possible? Everything around me, the sofa, the dining table, all the silverware, the china, the choice (oddly, none too good) of wallpaper, the chandelier, the illuminated wall unit, the buffet, the very sheets on the bed, the bedspreads, the carpets, the incongruous Louis Quatorze chests of drawers—everywhere I looked, there she was, but where was she? Why was she silent all that time? Would she remain silent now?

I had a picture of her in my mind, a small woman, dwarfed by my father, her long red hair done up in a bun, her house dress tied with a bow, her slender figure bent over my crying baby sister, or striking a casual pose while stirring the pot with her long wooden spoon. I could also see her later in life, when she went back to nursing in her creamy white shoes and white stockings, her figure fuller now, and her hair tinted, but still reddish, cropped much shorter and plastered with hair spray. In those days I suppose I held her in a kind of contempt, as teenage boys often do, and yet could not quite get around how much I needed her. I craved her comforting embrace, and no doubt still wanted to fold myself into her bountiful maternal flesh, but every word out of her mouth seemed idiotic to me, and when she hugged me, I cringed.

I found her hat. The one that floated across the pool. I picked it up with careful fingers, barely able to touch it, not wanting to disturb it. I placed it aside, for it was the only clue of her I had.

Of Josh there were many, many reminders in this little house, but I left them where they were, except for a copy of his last report card which I had taken with me from San Francisco for no particular reason at all. I found it crumpled in the pocket of my linen sports coat.

I now turned to what I thought of as the main course—my father. I took down his plaques from the walls, and pulled out several more boxes of them from the closets. Commendations. Meritorious Service. With Thanks from a Grateful Nation. Man of the Year. Letters from Presidents of the United States.

He was a one-man Jewish National Fund. He saved Ethiopian Jews, Yemenite Jews, Indian Jews, Iraqi Jews, Soviet Jews. He raised money, organized, fixed, schmoozed. One commendation proved he really did work on the Nuclear Freeze, even though I know he was secretly proud that Israel had The Bomb. There was a newspaper photo showing him protesting the Vietnam War, and yet I found he also donated to the creation of the Vietnam War Memorial in Washington. He even had, in his most recent commendation, a letter from ACT UP, for his "tireless efforts in support of equal rights for Gays and Lesbians and for combating complacency in the battle against AIDS."

He was faultless. None of these were clues.

I had run out of room on the tables, the couches, the chairs, so I set out his other various treasures on the floor. His two rams' horns, which he had learned to play and did so, much to my consternation, on the High Holidays, his five menorahs, his ritual spice box and candleholder, his collection of commemorative Israeli coins, his Israeli stamp books, his three-dimensional historical map of the Holy Land, his special prayer book which was small enough to keep in his shirt pocket, yet contained every prayer for every possible occasion, including, for instance, the prayer for seeing a great work of art for the first time, the prayer for washing your hands when you get up in the morning, the prayer for if you happen to walk past the kitchen and smell a fragrant spice, and about which he always said, "This book is yours,

Mikey, when I'm gone," as if I might want it. But there it was, on the carpet, right next to his miniature Torah (which of course was never supposed to touch the floor, but that was not my worry just then) and his books on Zohar, his seven-volume set of the Talmud which had stretched across an entire shelf, his miniature reproduction of the Chagall Windows which had stood on a little stand next to the telephone, and, most hated of all, the music box in the shape of the Ten Commandments that played *Hatikvah,* the Jewish National Anthem. I found, as well, a pile of browned and fragile advertisements for his wallpaper store in Hillside, New Jersey, announcing Father's Day Sale, Back-to-School Sale, Mother's Day Sale, After Christmas Sale, Veterans Day Sale, and, finally, Going-Out-of-Business Sale.

None of this was useful to me.

But I did find his driver's licenses going back to 1953, several U.S. passports, his Social Security card, various bank statements and passbooks from financial institutions that no longer existed, expired insurance policies, and, buried in a shoe box with old photos of my mother on the beach—probably at Coney Island, her legs stretched out, her back arched, pin-up style—his citizenship papers. 1954. Newark, New Jersey. By order of . . . And beneath them their marriage certificate. 1949. Newark, New Jersey. An embossed invitation. The Avon Manor. Four P.M. Pressed within it, a boutonniere. And beneath that, a little envelope stuffed with items not in English, a train ticket, a note, a torn photo, a list of names.

These things I did put aside. These were clues.

I rifled through every drawer, every carton, every shelf, under every bed, above the refrigerator, behind the dressers, in the backs of closets, atop the highest shelves to find anything, anything, anything. Whatever seemed important or mysterious I placed in my corner of clues. And when I had done all that, and sifted through the wreckage of our family's hopes, separating the useful from the un-useful (based almost exclusively on how it felt to hold the object in my hand—if it gave me a sharp, unpleasant sensation just above the groin, or if I saw my hand shaking but didn't know why, or if it seemed to want me to put it down before I had a good chance to look at it—I knew it was a clue)—and, as I said, when I was done with all that, I went into the guest room to rest. I had to make a pathway to the bed and clear off a lot of junk from the covers—books, papers, drawings—but I believed, as I lay between a stack of *Commentary* magazines and an old adding machine, that I was on my way to finding the truth. Turning my head, I could see into the living room. Everywhere were piles I had organized by category. Items pertaining to Judaism, items pertaining to school, items pertaining to sickness and death, items pertaining to expressions of love. It was like looking at my own, personal, primordial soup. I had this feeling that all I had to do was reach out and give it a little stir, and life would miraculously appear in the form of a one-cell me. And if I was patient, that cell would grow and divide and multiply and evolve, and sooner or later would slog its way out of that mess and into the light of understanding.

I let out a deep breath and relaxed upon the pillow. I fell asleep, but I had terrible dreams.

CHAPTER 20

The next day I decided to drive down to Miami. I threw on my favorite Hawaiian shirt and pair of beachcomber shorts, filled up the tank with Super, and jumped on the highway. I still had much to do in the apartment, but I had a friend there I'd been meaning to see anyway and I was swept along on impulse. We'd met in Vegas when he was opening for a fifties comeback band and I was doing the lounge at the Hilton. Our relationship was simple and clean. I gave him funny jokes when he was dry, which was almost all the time, and in return, he could score just about anything I needed to keep me being funny. I never really went on stoned, but afterwards, it helped me relax. It's hard to sleep on the road. But we liked each other, and I needed a change of pace, a friendly face, and a little help.

I met him in a Cuban bar called Julio's. He himself wasn't Cuban, he was Puerto Rican, but he liked calling Julio's "his office." He laughed at this every time he said it. I thought it was a good thing he had gotten out of comedy.

We sat at "his table."

"You're not going to carry that out to the car like that, are you, man?" He had not the slightest Latin accent in real life, though on stage he put it on so thick, even Latinos couldn't understand him.

I unfolded a little green gym bag. Its fiber sparkled under the spotlights that illuminated the table. "I thought this."

"That's good," he said.

"You think it's too obvious?"

"Don't worry about it. Have some sangria."

He poured himself a glass.

"You seem different," he said. "Normally you're a nervous wreck."

"I am?"

"Well, yeah. Only now you're even worse. It's like freezing in here with the air on, and you're sweating like a pig."

"I am?" I touched my forehead. "It's just this fucking Florida."

"Yeah," he said rather philosophically, "you either love it or it hates you." He laughed at his own joke. "So, what's this thing about clues? Is it a bit or something you're working on?"

"I told you about the clues?"

"What's the matter with you? Just about two seconds ago. So is it a new bit?"

"Yeah. I think so."

"Yeah," he nodded, mulling it over, "I like that. Clues. Like before I broke up with Sylvia, there were clues everywhere, man. I was just a blind motherfucker. But you could make a great bit about that. Like when you notice she is always falling asleep just at the moment you go down on her. That's a clue." He thought that was funny, and he smacked the table. "Or when you come home and she's wearing these huge, like, diamond and ruby earrings, and you say, where did you get those? and she says *Sears*—that's a clue. Actually," he added, "any time they say Sears it's a clue." He looked up at me. "Feel free to use any of my material."

"I will," I said.

In a little while we made our good-byes and I zipped up the gym bag. He walked me to the door, his arm around my shoulder, the stale smell of last night's beer corrosive in the damp, semidark air of Julio's Hi Hat. When he pushed open the door, it was like a hydrogen bomb had just gone off on Collins Avenue, it was so bright. I could no longer make out his features, but just his presence comforted me. For one thing, he reminded me that, at least by comparison, I was actually a pretty funny comedian. For another he was maybe the only person in the world right now who would actually come through for me.

"Clues!" he said in parting. "It's a great idea."

"It's not just clues," I told him, "it's proof. I want proof."

"Proof of what?"

I thought about it. "Proof of everything."

"Funny!" he bellowed. "You are *funny,* man! See you on *Letterman*!"

The drive up from Miami was uneventful. I drove just over the limit. The bag was in the trunk, under the beach chairs that hadn't been used in ten years. By the time I pulled into the lot of my father's building, evening was settling in and the sun was casting long, lethargic shadows along the asphalt. As I reached the end of the front walk, the elevator, screaming and complaining the whole time, reached the ground floor and painfully slid open its door. Two old couples emerged, the ladies first, the gentlemen after. They were nicely dressed. The men wore suits—dark ones, not pastel for a change—and the women wore pretty dresses.

"*Gut Yontif,*" one of the men said to me.

"What?" I said.

"Happy New Year," interpreted his wife.

"It's *Erev Rosh Hashanah,*" the second woman explained. They all smiled at me.

"Oh my gosh," I said. "I didn't realize. Already?"

"It's early this year," she said. "Perhaps you'd like to come to shul with us? There's always room for another!"

The first woman took me by the arm. I inhaled her sweet, expensive perfume mixed with the scent of discount hairspray. For some reason, I liked how she smelled. Perhaps it reminded me of my mother. "It must be hard for you," she said, "to be away from your family this time of year. Look, we could wait. You could change."

"I'm not religious," I said. "But thank you."

I put out my hand to stop the elevator door from closing.

"Have a good holiday," I said.

"There are services tomorrow, too, you know," one of the women replied. "Come if you like. We're Gitlin, 316 . . ." and the door closed, locking me in.

The elevator creaked upward, lurching and bouncing, finally delivering me on the third floor. Down below, they were still making their way through the parking lot. "His name is David," I heard one of them say. "No, no, I think it's Joel or Jake . . . something with a J."

Then they got in their cars and drove away.

=

Standing there, leaning over the railing, I watched the cars disappear down the long, palm-lined drive. At this very moment, and three thousand miles sunward, I knew Ella had already begun the arduous task of getting Josh ready for services. She had to do it in stages, giving him plenty of time to refuse to go, argue about what to wear, allow him to walk around in one sock and one shoe, grow panicky because he couldn't find his favorite tie (he only had one), stop everything to e-mail several friends on important matters, and call his friend Sam to arrange where to meet and how best to sneak out and be back in time for the blast of the shofar. All this would slide off Ella's back as if it were actually some sort of fragrant oil. She would be amused by him, and he would be edified by her, and in the end Ella would glow with hope for the new year. "Isn't it nice to have a fresh start?" she would be saying, placing a jar of honey on the table, and an apple, so that when they got home it would be ready for them. For the sweetness of a new year, she'd tell him, the same words every year.

I looked down at my shorts and sneakers. How was it this new year came without me?

I closed my eyes and tried to wish them a sweet, good year, but what was a good year? The year I lost Karen, which also meant losing my father as I knew him and watching my mother turn into an old woman before my eyes? The year Ella walked out of my life and took Josh with her, and I didn't do anything about it, anything that made any difference? The year my mother died, and I got a phone call just before I was supposed to do a matinee in Cleveland, and had to go on anyway, and had one of my best shows ever? The year the doctor said the word *Alzheimer's*? "Al's what?" I asked.

And now *this*?

Exactly which year was it that was a good year?

I set my gym bag inside the door and went back outside. I didn't want to be in the apartment. Everywhere I looked in that apartment screamed *Jewish*. I strolled around to the town houses, which were on the other side of the golf course. The parking lots were virtually empty. I wondered which of these units was April's mother's. The two of them would already be at temple. They would have driven over together, made their way down the aisle, her mother introducing April to all her friends—Yes! The Poet!—How wonderful she could be here! they'd say, Happy New Year! they'd say, feeling perhaps a twinge of remorse that they had once again failed to read her books. Then the chanting would begin, the rabbi would step forward, the prayer books would fall open, and the sound of Hebrew would fill the room with its strange, unsettling powers.

I continued down a little flower-lined path. The town houses were nice, but they were all the same. And except for the few Gentiles who lived there, all were dark. Even the nonpracticing Jews seemed to be hiding. I alone walked down the garden lanes.

Everything was so good before! With Ella. With Josh.

I tried to recall how Ella and I sat beside each other in synagogue, I dozing off, she fervently singing, but in the end turning to each other and offering that blissful New Year's kiss—*L'shana Tova!—For a good year!* But it was hazy, hazy. Then suddenly I remembered something else—as if it were yesterday!—playing with Josh in the living room when he was, what? no more than two—no he wasn't even speaking yet—I couldn't be sure. Funny to remember that, I thought. It wasn't even that it was so much fun to pile up blocks and knock them down, and pile them up again and knock them down again, or watch Josh tear out pages of magazines and crumple them in his little fists, or read to him the same six pages of that alphabet book over and over and over again, but I felt good when I thought about it, so good.

I laughed. Why did I suddenly remember that? Why that? And like a sword thrust, the rest of it came to me.

I had come home and found Ella lying on the kitchen floor—frozen except for the thrashing of her arms and the rapid blinking of her eyes—and the baby, Josh, screaming his head off, his bowl of mashed carrots spread out beside him like splattered orange paint.

She came out of it as soon as I took her in my arms.

"Oh my God!" she cried. "Where's the baby?"

I was terrified. I ran to dial the ambulance.

"I don't need an ambulance," she said. "I just need my pills."

"Pills?"

She told me where they were. Sobbing, she explained. She had "a mild case" of epilepsy. I was flabbergasted.

"Epilepsy?"

"I'm a horrible mother!" she sobbed.

What was it that made her hide it from me? I now wondered. At the time I thought she must have been ashamed, like a person with a venereal disease. I didn't want to embarrass her about it. So I just said to her, "But don't the pills keep you from having seizures?"

She said they made her feel depressed. She had been feeling strangely disconnected. She thought she might feel better if she stopped taking them.

The town houses disappeared behind me as I rounded the swimming pool.

I had remembered it as a moment of supreme happiness, one of those rare and special interludes with Josh. But actually I had just led Ella, weeping and inconsolable, back to the bedroom, laid her down and watched as she turned her back to me, much as Mr. Antonelli had done. Then I ran back to calm Josh, who was still howling in terror.

Karen was right. There were clues everywhere I looked.

=

For the first time the heat broke, if only just a little. There was the hint of a breeze coming in from the east, and I accepted it with gratitude. Darkness also began to cover the sky, and I was grateful, too, for the balm of invisibility it gave me.

The prayer book says that on Rosh Hashanah the Book of Life and Death is opened. On Yom Kippur it is closed, and our fates are sealed. Between the one and the other we have ten days to repent, change our ways, make restitution. Then they blow the shofar—and, well—either you made it or you didn't.

So today my father's book was opened, and my book was opened, and so was Josh's and Ella's and April's. I did wonder about those few Italians I noticed down on the eighth tee getting in one last round before the sun dropped its ball into the Gulf. Maybe they were in a different book.

When I got home, I dialed Ella to wish her and Josh a Happy New Year. I knew they wouldn't be in. They'd already be over at her mom and dad's. They'd all be going to temple together. I left a message. I told them I loved them. For Josh's sake I lied and said I had to run off to services. I'm going with the neighbors, I said, the Gitlins in 316.

I hung up and closed my eyes. I don't think I said a prayer, but I did wish to God this would all soon be over. The apartment was an incredible mess, but I found a way to slide the gym bag under the guest bed. Then I reached for another one of my father's journals.

That would have to be penance enough.

CHAPTER 21

The last survivors of Yad Mordechai could hold out no longer. That night, a small detachment of armored cars went down to wait for anyone who could escape through the Arab lines. Heshel Rosenheim had called on the radio to volunteer to go along, but they told him to stay put. He was no longer clear why he did anything. He only could not resist the impulse to volunteer. Yad Mordechai had held out four days. Tomorrow the Egyptians would march into the settlement, guns blazing, and find it abandoned. They would be flush with victory. They might take an hour to celebrate. Then they would rush on and take Ashdod. After that, they would find their way to Naor, or they might bypass it. But he knew they could not bypass it. It was not in their nature. They needed to destroy it. He understood why.

The Nazis had often done the same thing where the Jews were concerned. No town was too small. No rag of a Jew unworthy of their undivided attention.

Around four in the morning, the report came in from the front. About a hundred survivors. Many wounded. Many of them women and small boys. The sky behind them lit their way, bright with the fires of what once had been their homes. Some came carrying stretchers. Some carted the wounded on their backs. Some did not make it the last kilometer. There were three stragglers, two women carrying a man on a stretcher. The waiting soldiers could make them out as dark figures moving erratically down the path. But then they heard a sentry call out in Arabic, and the footsteps stopped. Up on the hill, silhouetted against the fires of Yad Mordechai, they saw the three being led off under guard, and then they heard shots.

Heshel did not know why this news stabbed so painfully into his own heart, but Dovid, standing nearby, put his young hand on Heshel's shoulder.

"It's all right," he said to Heshel. "At least they didn't go like sheep."

He nodded to Dovid, but what was he really thinking?

Later, he found himself alone, seated on a stool in the milking shed. He never did know much about livestock, but he liked the smell of the barn, the dark aroma of manure mixed with the bright grassy heather of hay and alfalfa, and he was somehow comforted by the snorting and mooing of the cows as they went about their business, doing nothing, thinking nothing, merely enduring, or perhaps even enjoying, their simple existence.

"They will never be seen again." That is what the voice on the Haganah radio had said. In some ways these words were more terrible than the news of the fire bombings, the tank attacks, the victims blown up or shot down, the panic in the doctor's pleas for help. Why was that? Why was it worse to be

led a few feet to the side of the road and dispatched with a pistol against your forehead, than be torn to bits by shrapnel or ripped apart by Bren fire? Death is death. And yet not. Because they were not afraid of dying. Anyone could see that. But when they heard of these three, the two women carrying the wounded man, and how they were stopped, and how they were led aside, and how they were executed in a burst of gunfire (all three at once? the man in the stretcher first? or last? stoically? with tears? with cries for mercy?), there was such a silence in the room, such gasping, and off to the side, behind quivering hands, such tears flowing—and not just from the women's eyes—that it stunned them all, including Heshel Rosenheim, as if their own loved ones had been murdered before their very eyes.

He sat there listening to the cows swat their tails and lick their noses. In a minute or two the milking would have to begin. He knew the schedule of the kibbutz better than anyone. He realized, of course, that it was a mistake not to evacuate the cows with the women and children. They would die here. During battle, no one would milk them, no one would feed them. And then they would get blown up or burnt to death. It's just that no one had thought of it. When they come in this morning, they will all realize their mistake. They will wake up with a start at five in the morning and say, Oh my God! The cows!

He closed his eyes, the better to feel their living presence. And that is when he remembered.

=========

Heinrich Mueller arrived by train to Lublin on November 2, 1943. He had been on leave for two weeks after vacating his post in Bergen-Belsen, and had traveled first to Berlin to visit his family, and then to Vienna, which he had never seen. He spent four days there, during which he ate great quantities of pastries, and had numerous sexual intercourses with prostitutes. He visited the Hofburg, the Kunsthistorisches Museum, and Schloss Schoenbrunn, but mostly spent his time in the cafés and night clubs. He was not deprived of company, as there were always groups of cavorting SS men who invited him to join in. He even went dancing with a group of town girls who attached themselves to some young officers like himself, but out of a sense of honor he had not had sex with any of them, though without a doubt, he told himself later, he could have. There was one in particular who seemed to like him, and he thought about her all throughout the train ride to Lublin. He had gotten himself a first-class berth, but he could not sleep. He had written her name on his ticket, but he hadn't had the courage to ask her address. He reproached himself all night long. Upon disembarking the train, he flagged down a car, threw his duffel in the back, and arrived at his post by midday. It was depressing, after the gaiety of Vienna and the beauty of the girls, the excellent food, the fine Austrian wine, the endless rounds of beer, to be shuffled into the commandant's office by a dour-faced adjutant, to be shuffled out again after a quick salute and a few meaningless inquiries, and to be shown a desk with no window and a bunk in the officers' quarters that was but a straw mattress on a steel frame, a few inches of private space that contained a miniature writing table, and, off to one side, a minuscule closet. It was a terrible, foul-smelling place; the air was dark even now at midday, whereas the sun had been shining only a moment ago in town. On top of that, his heart sank when he met his immediate superior, Wippern—a man with no imagination and plenty of ambition. One could never advance under such a person.

The very next day, Mueller was taken across the highway, to be shown the lay of the land, as Wippern put it.

"You're in luck!" Wippern said. "Today is a big day! Big action today. Lots to see!"

As soon as he crossed the road, he could hear the loudspeakers blaring music, but beneath that, something else.

"What's that?"

"That's what I'm saying!" snapped Wippern impatiently. "Big action today! Harvest Festival! That's what we call it."

As they walked toward the main field, the field that joined the two camps, he saw hordes of men and women stripped naked, their clothes thrown into piles, which others loaded onto carts. It was a pleasant day, not too cold at all, and the sun was shining brightly in spite of the gray cloud that hung over the camp. The music was incredibly loud, but as they walked farther, the mask of music grew thin, and he began to hear bursts of shooting and screaming. It was coming from an area behind several large buildings, one of which was clearly the ovens.

"I thought I heard convoys coming in last night," Mueller remarked.

"Yes, some crackerjack units. Special orders from Berlin," replied Wippern, rubbing his hands together against the damp morning air.

Mueller watched as groups of a hundred or so of these naked people were herded like cattle through a narrow causeway of barbed wire. They ran along, trying to cover themselves. The women put one arm in front of their breasts, the other between their legs. Why bother? thought Mueller.

"Rosamunda!" the loudspeaker sang. "Give me a kiss!"

"It's a good thing you're here," said Wippern. "There will be a lot of paperwork tonight. A lot of head counting, a lot of shoes to deal with."

He winked.

He pointed out the various fields and blocks, told him where the Soviets were held, where the Poles, where the Jews, where the women.

"We just got in a huge crop from the ghetto in Warsaw," he said as a way of explaining what was going on. "Leftover from the riots, you know. Can't have that type around, can we? Next thing you know there'll be trouble here too!"

"How many?" asked Mueller, thinking ahead to how much work he had to do on his very first day.

"I don't know. Ten thousand, maybe, from Warsaw. Plus all our useless Jews in Camp A."

"It will be a long day," Mueller sighed.

"Attitude is everything!" advised Wippern.

"I only meant—"

"Never mind," Wippern said kindly. "I know what it's like to come back from holiday."

They walked until they reached the gas chambers and crematorium. The music had gone dimmer here, for which Mueller was grateful, but now the sound of automatic weapons, barked commands, and human screams filled the air.

"Let's take a peek," suggested Wippern.

Mueller went along beside him. Not far beyond the crematorium they had dug several huge trenches, four, perhaps five, meters deep. They lined up the naked Jews and commanded them to climb down into the trench. There they were ordered to lie down atop a row of dead bodies—those who had come only moments before. They did what they were told. Amazing, he thought to himself. They did not seem to him at that moment the arch villains who had almost destroyed Germany in their plots to rule the world—the puppet masters of Roosevelt and Churchill, who had started this war. Only we could have broken them! he thought. The operation was wonderfully orderly, yet their nakedness disturbed him, he did not know why. It was particularly hard to watch the women lie down on the row of corpses. It offended, somehow, his German sense of chivalry, to see their asses lined up that way, and, after the Sturmbannführer nodded and the guns went off, to witness their defecation, or worse, the way their bodies writhed under the pressure of the bullets in a mockery of coitus. He knew he must not close his eyes, but he felt himself grow faint, so he pulled out his handkerchief and made a show of blowing his nose. When he uncovered his face again, he saw a lieutenant briskly walking the perimeter of the trench, finishing off any left alive with a deft pistol shot to the head, although with some he did not seem to bother, since, Mueller assumed, the half-dead criminals would be buried or crushed in a matter of minutes anyway. Indeed, a second later another group of naked Jews was led to the trench, and they too lay down upon the row of bodies, and they too were put away in a red flood of gunfire.

Mueller looked around and noticed Weiss, the commandant, on a little rise a few meters away, seated in his camp chair next to which was set up a table upon which breakfast was being served. The table was covered with linen, and the attendant poured coffee from a silver urn. When they saw him, Wippern and Mueller rose to attention and saluted, but Weiss did not notice them, and after a while Wippern suggested they stop fooling around and get back to work.

And they did have a lot a of work, too! The special units left Lublin that evening, and Wippern and Mueller had to do the accounting. It was a tedious and laborious task, but when it was finally done, they could report to Berlin that the population of Majdanek had been reduced by 18,400 Jews. They had decided to round off for convenience.

That night, the Poles in Block 3 were heard celebrating. But Mueller was exhausted and oddly aroused. He knew it was the moral thing, the right thing, the necessary thing for the Reich, for all of mankind. But he could not stop the queasiness rising up in his throat. It cannot be right, he thought, to dispose of so many potential workers while they still might be useful to the state.

Thus, he was much relieved when Wippern assigned him to Camp B, the work camp. It was actually the harder job, which is no doubt why Wippern gave it to him, but now, at least, he might be spared the sight of so much waste.

=========

The cows were becoming restless, full of milk. Heshel Rosenheim got up from his stool and walked over to the stalls. There were no milking machines on Naor, they milked by hand, and he thought he could do it as well as anyone. He grabbed a bucket and slid it under Rifka. There were only five cows, and their milk was mostly used by the kibbutz. They made kefir, curds, simple cheeses, butter. He grabbed a teat and started to squeeze. She jumped a little, but he got it under control, and soon was milking smoothly. He felt calm again, peaceful.

It is not that he had forgotten. One cannot forget such a thing. It is that he had never associated it in any way with himself. He had been an observer, that's all. He had done the numbers. And, in fact, until tonight he had mostly remembered about the hours and hours of paperwork, if he thought about it at all. It was just one day in the life of those days. People were killed in the camps every single hour. The gallows were never empty. Every night the gas chambers were filled to overflowing. And there was never a single second that the crematoria ceased belching out their fetid plumes of human smoke. It was normal. It was nothing to worry your head about. Yet the three people shot by the side of the road at Yad Mordechai had made him see it differently. Terribly differently.

He recalled now a little detail. Those trenches had to be dug up a few days later. It was the stench. And for health reasons, of course. So they ordered the few Jews left to dig it all up and set fire to the bodies right there in the trenches, and when that was done (he knew this because he logged it in his books) the bones were crushed to powder, and the ash and the bones together were loaded into burlap sacks, and the sacks were put in the warehouses, and in the warehouses the sacks were stamped with the word FERTILIZER, *and the fertilizer was put on trains, and the trains took it to farms in Germany and Poland, in France and Belgium, in Italy and Greece.*

He remembered Moskovitz, back in the D.P. camp, picking up some dirt in her fingers and saying how the very earth was sullied—what did she say? contaminated? cursed?—he could not recall. But he thought, yes, it is true, there is not an inch of soil in all of Europe unsanctified by Jewish blood.

Rifka kicked a little. He had been squeezing too hard.

"Easy, girl," he said.

Tears began to roll down his cheeks—at the thought of hurting her.

"I'm sorry," he said to the cow, rubbing her haunches and making little cooing sounds in her ear. "Sorry girl, I'm sorry."

CHAPTER 22

I put down the journal and walked out onto the catwalk. The cars with their American flags and Mogen David bumper stickers were back in their assigned spaces. The first evening of Rosh Hashanah had come and gone. I wondered if it meant anything. I wondered if God's book was really open, and if He was thinking about all these people who owned these cars, and if it really mattered to Him what they did or thought or said. I doubted it highly. The time of judgment was supposed to be upon us. I found myself laughing at this.

I would have liked to call the Simon Wiesenthal Center. Or Mr. Kaufman at the Holocaust Archives. I would have liked to set the wheels of supposed justice in motion. But what justice? God loved him.

They had slept through the crime of the century—both of them, God and my father. They had felt no pain. Why should either of them wake up now?

And, of course, in the world of Nazi criminals Heinrich Mueller was as insignificant as one of his beloved *Sachertorten*. Even if the Allies had captured him back in 1945, he probably wouldn't have done any time. He was just a bookkeeper, they would have said. He was as nobody as anyone could ever be. A nothing. A zero. Not worth the time. And if, today, in some incomprehensible act of revenge, they did deport him, so what? He wouldn't even know he'd left the country. He lived in the world of *Leberknoedel* and jam-filled cookies now, as if none of it had ever happened. It was too late for justice. Too late for anything.

I saw it all so clearly. He was a coward, that's all. And stupid. If he'd just let himself get caught in the first place, he'd have had a normal life. If he had just been a little less clever, I might have been born in Hamburg or Bremen and not been raised on his manna of bitterness and guilt.

I wanted God to come down as a pillar of fire, reach out with His awesome hand in fury and vengeance and erase my father's name from the annals of man. Like Amelek. Like Pharaoh. Like Haman.

It was a hot, sticky night. The breeze that tried to cool our little stretch of Florida had given up. Even the breeze knew it was hopeless. I could hear the alligators crying in the canals. Frogs were clinging to the walls of the building, and two palmetto bugs were casually making their way along the edge of the walkway like an elderly couple at the mall. They seemed to like each other. They made me think of my mother and father. My father. God had chosen him, that's all there was to it—if there was a God, that is—chosen him to bear the guilt for all of them. For all of us. Perhaps he *was* the reason the world had been able to move on, to free itself from an endless cycle of retribution and bloodshed. Perhaps he was a Just Man.

I must be going nuts, I thought.

I looked at my watch. It was two in the morning. I was drunk with sleeplessness, that's all.

But I was too restless. I got into the car again, and this time I drove to Lake Worth, crossed the causeway to the ocean, and parked near the beach. I climbed down onto the sand and took off my sneakers and socks, and, holding my shoes in my hand, I made my way out to the surf. The moon was full, the stars were out in full regalia, and I could see far along the beach a world of shadow and foam. The lights from the boardwalk spilled onto the sand here and there in garish swaths of sickish yellow and sallow green. The water splashed on my feet and tugged at my toes as it sucked its way back into the sea. As the surf retreated, it left behind rows of shells and bits of stone, which in daylight would be brightly colored and shiny. I had forgotten seashells. We didn't have much of that back in San Francisco, where the ocean guarded its treasures more closely. I picked up a few, then threw them back, wondering about the creatures that once lived in them. Where did they go, once they gave up their little happy homes?

The ocean seemed to have no end, but I knew that somewhere out there was Cuba, I mean, if I turned my head to the right—but I was looking straight out into the darkness, and straight ahead, if I remembered my geography, was . . . was . . . I wanted to say Spain, but that wasn't correct. It was Africa. Liberia. Senegal. The Ivory Coast. A place as distant and foreign as any place could be, and it was right in front of me, invisible only because my eyes couldn't see that far, at least not in the dark.

All I could think of was sailing away toward that nightmare of foreignness, to a land where no one would know who I really was.

I turned to go back to the car. Walking along, I noticed a conch shell half buried in the sand. It was mostly broken, but I picked it up anyway. I didn't know why. Probably because the exposed, pink insides reminded me of something. I sat for a few minutes in the car with the motor off, trying to repress the anxiety that was rising in me. Without thinking, I lifted the conch to my ear, and was surprised that, broken and partial as it was, I could still hear the echo of the ocean in which it had once lived. To me, that was beautiful. I sat there with the windows rolled up, listening to this little version of the ocean for a long time, while outside, the sea itself pounded against the shore in absolute silence.

CHAPTER 23

I had already taken all the pictures down from the walls—the Chagall print of the old Jew wrapped in his black-striped tallis, the tapestry of Jerusalem as it might have appeared in the days of Solomon's Temple, the little watercolors of Arab shepherds resting their flocks among the cedar trees. Now I moved the couch away, revealing the rest of the wall, which, hidden from the sun, was two shades darker than above. I stood back and admired the smooth, vaguely salmon-colored space ("White Rose," Mother had called it), and thought of one of those war rooms in cop movies, where they tack the clues up on the wall. That was exactly what I had in mind. I opened a fresh roll of masking tape—the man at the store promised me it wouldn't pull off the paint—and reached for my first piece of evidence.

It was a family photo, but whose family was not entirely clear. I believed it to be a photo of my grandparents. I had found it in a box of dozens of antique photographs of people in European dress, almost entirely from the turn of the century. In this particular photo, the resemblance of the sitters to my father—the sharp nose and long earlobes of the man in the picture, the soft, sleepy eyes of the woman—was uncanny. They might as well have jumped out of the picture and pinched me on the cheek, crying, *Bubele!—my dear little grandson!* Although they might also have said *"Liebchen!"* instead of *"Bubele!"* for the couple was rigorously nonsectarian. The woman sat rigidly on a divan, and the man stood beside her, one hand rakishly poised on his hip, the other protectively, or perhaps possessively, guarding the back of the sofa. The difference in their postures was remarkable. She was stiffly upright, head reared back like a horse on a short rein, shoulders erect, and though her legs were hidden under a long, flowing hem, her bosom was prominent enough to strain the lace of her bodice. Her hair, too, was perfected in a tight bun with but a single strand escaping round her left ear. She might have been the picture of nobility, had she not been so relentlessly bourgeois. He, on the other hand, slouched in a cocky, relaxed posture, bright-eyed and radiating energy. Frozen though he was in time, you could feel him fidget, anxious to get going. I could practically hear him cracking jokes between his teeth, ready to fly once the powder flashed. Perhaps I took after him. Behind these two disparate figures was a painted backdrop of trees and parkland. What an odd aesthetic, I thought, to put a divan in a park. I wondered what they were trying to convey—and did in fact convey to each other—that had become lost in the ruin of generations? I stared in wonder at the photograph, looking for its clue.

I found it in the beautifully and rather self-possessed imprint embossed in the lower-right-hand corner of the dark gray cardboard frame into which the photo had been set: *Adolf Zucker, Photograph, Hundestrasse 15, Berlin.*

Very well then, my grandparents—for who else could they be?—had lived in Berlin. I taped the photo to the wall, in the very center of the wall, in fact. Beneath it, I pressed a sticky Post-it on which I had written: *Grandparents. Berlin. Year? Greta. Wilhelm.* Then under that, in parentheses, I added: (*Golda? Velvel?*). My father had at different times called them by different names.

Next to this I taped the letter from Mr. Kaufman of the Holocaust Archives. I circled the word *Durnik,* the town in which the Rosenheims once lived. Under this I wrote the word *Victim.*

It was completely possible that all of them were victims. It was completely possible that all of them had perished in the same way, that they were even cousins, or brothers. Only one thing was certain. They were not from the same place. But for the moment I left unresolved the fate of the two people in the photograph.

My father had variously told me that my grandfather was a philologist, a high school language teacher, a professor of Romance literature, an expert in Finno-Ugric. This now did not sit so well with me. If he was a philologist, he was so just at the time they had gone crazy sorting out the Indo-European roots of Western language. Not coincidentally they called this root language "Aryan." Their imagined etymologies enabled them to glibly reify for themselves remote, mythological times, conferring nobility on their own sad, dull, modern words, and, by extension, on their lives as well. They created this world of Aryan purity in the comfort of their studies, warmed by their Persian rugs and cosseted by their thick velvet curtains, not willing to see how their trains of thought might one day turn into cattle cars filled with real people.

I stuck another Post-it below the photograph. *Mad Scientist.*

I would just like to add that I was once thumbing through my father's OED and found that the Indo-European word for *salmon* was *lox*. If I could see the idiocy of that, surely they could, too. Maybe that's why the man in the photo seemed so jittery.

I reached for my next piece of evidence. It was a train ticket I had found in that envelope filled with foreign objects. It was a ticket to Vienna. Or perhaps from Vienna. It was only the barest stub, so very little could be gleaned from it. Torn away were the basics: the date, the station. I looked for a clue.

I found it near the top edge. *Wagon-Lit* 2-4-4. I taped it to the wall about two feet above and to the right of the photograph of my grandparents. It needed to be nearer the outer circle of this story. Under it, I attached the note: *Car 2, Compartment 4, Seat 4*. My father had written that he had been on vacation in Vienna. Perhaps this was his ticket. I added the words: *To Majdanek? From Belsen? Childhood vacation before the war? Trip with Mom after the war?*

It was such a small shard of a ticket that no markings such as the German Eagle or any National Socialist symbols remained, and it had been crumpled and it sustained water damage, too, but it chilled me to look at it. Trains of any sort in this context were too brutal to contemplate. Perhaps I should have studied it more closely, but I taped it to the wall and reached for the next piece of evidence.

This was Josh's last report card. In my day, report cards were actually cards, with little boxes printed on them, and each teacher wrote down a grade in one of the boxes, and only occasionally a comment in the single line provided. But Josh's report card was four pages long. Each teacher felt obliged to write a short essay on his "positives" and "negatives." Josh of late was pretty much in the negative column. "Not working up to ability." "Shows little enthusiasm for his work." "Sloppy." "Late with homework." "Seems preoccupied."

I taped it up in the far right corner, as far away from the train ticket as I could find. I put a Post-it beside it and wrote the words *Possible trouble at home.*

Next to his report card I attached, with a great deal of effort, Ella's sundress—the one I had found hanging in the closet and that mysteriously had no body in it. I tried to remember when she had worn it, and I had no idea whether this really happened or not, but I saw her come up to me at the swimming pool, and I seemed to remember she was carrying a large rattan purse with ivory-colored handles, and I also remembered sandals because her toes were bright red, and she said something to me, something like we're all going now, are you sure you don't want to come with us? I probably just made that up. But I scribbled on the yellow Post-it: *Where it all went wrong.*

Then I turned around looking for another clue. My eye was caught by something I had not put in the clue corner, actually. It was April's book of poetry. It was poised on the edge of the couch, sending out waves of grievance because I hadn't even opened it, let alone read it. Why I reached for it at that moment I don't know, but I did. I studied her name on the cover. April Love. That was more ridiculous than my stage name—and of course there was no one named Love in the condo directory. (I checked.) She must have come up with it in the sixties. I imagined her at Woodstock, forcefully shoving flowers in everyone's hair. (I, by the way, was still in grammar school during Woodstock.) And by the time the eighties came around she must have published so many things under that name it was too late to change it. Her real name was probably Lubovnik.

The book was called *Indefinable Ecstasies*. I paged through it. It was kind of Ginsberg-y, Whitman-esque, filled with emotional excess.

But I was struck by a line of a poem she called "Questions Number 4." It was:

If I am blind, what is that light?

It was one of those poems filled with questions like *Can I cry if I have no eyes?* and *Who said my first word?* It seemed to me I had seen poetry like this before. Or maybe I'd read her stuff sometime and just didn't remember. In any case, it got under my skin, that line, and I didn't really know why except that's how I felt. *If I am blind, what is that light?* It was like that scene in my father's book—the one when he is sitting in the back of that army truck with the sand storm raging about him, and the whole world blotted out, yet there he was, racing on . . . to where? He wasn't even driving. He couldn't see, couldn't hear, couldn't even feel. And yet he knew that he had experienced something beyond his four senses, and beyond his intelligence, too. That was the time in the story when I felt I knew him, if only just a little.

But I did not think this was a clue, and I was about to put the book down when I noticed the inscription on the flyleaf. It was addressed to my father, but it wasn't signed by her mother as she had claimed. It was from her. *My dearest Heshel,* it read. *For everything past and everything future. With deepest and enduring affection, April.*

It was dated two years ago.

I tore out the flyleaf and taped it to the wall.

She was the one.

I ran out of the apartment, along the gangway, waited impatiently as the elevator snailed up from the ground floor, hopped down the stairs instead, and jogged over to the town houses. It did not take long to find the house of the woman with the famous poet daughter. The name was Bloomfeld, as it turned out. April herself answered the door. She seemed surprised and happy to see me.

"You found me!"

"Can we talk?"

"You look upset. Is your father all right?"

"He's fine, he's fine."

"You want to come in?"

I could see her mother on the easy chair straining to see who was at the door.

"No. Let's go out."

I couldn't think of anywhere, so I suggested Starbucks. It was ludicrous, of course, but I had to think fast. We took her mother's Continental. Traffic was thin because it was the second day of Rosh Hashanah and the conservative and orthodox Jews were still at services. Starbucks was mostly empty, too. Automatically we went to our table—I thought of it as our table even though we had sat at it exactly one time before. I watched her pry the lid from her tea and blow on it. I had to admit I had grown to like how she looked, and even now in the flush of my anger and anticipation, I noticed how her hair glistened in the sunlight, silver with age as it was, and how her long, fine neck emerged like a bouquet from the cup of her silken collar. There were indeed wrinkles on her skin, particularly when she bunched up her forehead in thought, but they no longer obscured the lovely structure of her face.

"What is it with you and my father?" I finally asked

It was weird, she told me, how things happen in life. Being a writer, she had an obsessive need to create meaning where none actually existed. But sometimes, she said, stories really happen, sometimes the circle actually closes. Fortinbras enters stage right and carts the bodies away. April spoke like that.

Thus, it turned out that it was not entirely accidental that her mother had moved to The Ponds at Lakeshore some years after April's father had died. In fact, it turned out that April's mother had known my father for many years, and that she felt she owed him a debt of gratitude. Learning that he was widowed and alone, she felt impelled to be near him, to try to repay this debt, to help him if she could. That's why she bought one of the town houses.

"Debt?" I said.

"Your father walks with angels," April replied. She took a sip of her tea. I myself held on to my coffee cup as if for support, like it was bolted to the table. I watched her closely. The tea had moistened her lips.

Many years ago, she went on, my father had helped them. Her own father had been a physician, but he had gotten into some sort of trouble and had lost his practice. There was some misdeed. Maybe abortions. Maybe embezzlement. Maybe alcohol or drugs. She was unclear. Maybe they needed something to glue them back together. Maybe he'd already gotten back on his feet, and they wanted to move on. Anyway, they were desperate for a child. They knew there were war orphans in need of homes from all over Europe, but, with his background, they had been turned down by all the agencies, including the Jewish ones, or whoever it was who arranged these things. But somehow or another, by talking to someone who knew someone who said something to someone, they found their way to the one man who could get them a child.

"My father?"

"Your father. He found me. I think he actually went over and got me himself."

"You're a concentration camp victim?" I blurted stupidly.

"Actually, I don't know," she said.

She was found in a convent orphanage, but if her parents died in the camps, or in some ghetto, or as partisans, or in a bombing, or of starvation, or simply abandoned her—she had no clue. She had always felt that my father knew, even though he always claimed he didn't. But he had treated her so kindly for as long as she could remember, lavished her with such tenderness and generosity, that she dared not press him. In time, she forgave him. And truthfully, sometimes she was grateful for his silence. What possible good would it do? she often thought. He had saved her. Given her a new life with good parents. Why dig up the past?

She smiled up at me, her face alight, I supposed, with the memories of that happy childhood.

"So Mother wanted to help him in his later years," she said.

But a strange thing happened. It was actually April who spent time with him. And each time she came to visit her mother, she found herself spending more and more time with him.

"At first I would bring your father something for dinner. But it seemed like every woman in Florida beat me to it. His freezer was always stuffed with roast chicken, flanken, brisket, you name it. I would come in, and there'd be deli trays, nova, layer cake. Apparently he was popular with the ladies," she shrugged.

"Why didn't you tell me you knew him?"

"To my parents he was a god," she said, as if she hadn't heard me. "When they told me my story, he was always the leading man. How I arrived, speaking no English, holding his hand. How my hair was in braids, and how I used to hide from everyone, except him. How I wouldn't eat anything except noodles, until he taught me to eat plums. And always how the good Mr. Rosenheim had gone himself to find me, how he had brought me here, how he had arranged for my papers—not that I knew what that meant—how he had come to visit every time there was trouble with me, speaking to me in my language, just a little, to calm me down. I don't remember any of it, really. I was five. I mean, I do have some memories, but they are so vague. Virtually all of my memories begin here in America, as if nothing happened to me before that. It's remarkable really. I can't remember speaking any other language. I don't even know what language I spoke. It's all gone. I asked your father. Where did I come from? What language did I speak? He would answer, 'Who remembers?' "

"Well, you must have been speaking German, or Yiddish," I said.

"Or Polish, or Hungarian, or French, or Greek, or Italian," she said.

And it was true. My father knew many languages, at least a little. And the children came from everywhere. I remembered now that there were others among my parents' friends—a girl from France, Michelle; a little boy from Poland, I couldn't remember his name; another girl from somewhere. . . . Had he brought them all over? Had he begun his long, pathetic attempt at absolution by saving the Jewish children of Europe?

I was lost in these thoughts when she said, rather desperately, "Perhaps he did actually do some research on me. Or maybe he already knew who I was. After all, he was the one who dug me up."

She looked at me with bright, anxious eyes.

"I was thinking," she said, "maybe he mentioned something about me in those journals you were looking at."

"You haven't read them?"

"Me? No," she said.

"But you were the one who brought them to my father's room at Lake Gardens. You're the one who called Kaufman."

She looked confused.

"You were the one who brought the box to my dad's room, right?"

"No," she said. "I'm not sure I know what you're talking about."

I slumped down in my chair. I had been thinking, assuming—and I was more and more sure of it with every word she spoke—that I had finally solved the riddle. That my answer was right in front of me—the box delivery, the inquiries to Kaufman, the invisible friends coming at odd hours. It was all April. But now I realized that all I actually had in front of me was another question.

And she was still waiting for her answer. She was hoping with all her heart that I had unlocked the key to her identity. That it was all there in those books I had been reading. That I was the one to answer *her* question.

I took her hand.

"No," I said. "Nothing. He hasn't mentioned you at all."

She looked down at the table, then bravely up at me. The moisture from her lips seemed to have journeyed up to her eyes.

"Oh well," she said.

When I got home I decided to take a rest. I made some space on my father's La-Z-Boy and reclined it. From where I sat, I could see the clues on the dining room wall. My eyes found the flyleaf from April's book. It had been a good clue, but not the right clue. I yawned and turned onto my side, cuddling into the chair. I opened my eyes a slit, just to situate myself, and there, on the table, where I had left it the day before, was one of my father's journals lying two inches from my nose.

CHAPTER 24

A few days after the fall of Yad Mordechai, the city of Ashdod was taken. The same day, the bombardment of Naor began.

The man who called himself Heshel Rosenheim sat in his foxhole behind the little concrete bunker that had been built a few days before and marveled at the weather. It was lovely. The skies were clear, the days a pristine, translucent blue, the nights starry and moonlit. The bombs came in waves, an hour of intense fire, an hour of silence. Then the bombing would recommence. Each wave was more violent than the one before, and soon most of the kibbutz was reduced to rubble. The watchtower was cut in half, and though the Bren gun had been saved, the operator was killed. He was the first to die. His body, without its legs, fell from the tower and landed near Post 4. In the hour of quiet they hastily buried him together with his legs, in the sand on the edge of the perimeter. Others tried to repair the damaged bunkers and reinforce what was left of the Bet Am in the center of the kibbutz—once it had been the dining hall, the meeting place, the school house, the movie theater—but now it was mostly a shell, though the blue-and-white flag still flew above it, tied to an exposed steel beam. Most people hid in the shelters during the bombings that followed, and casualties were fewer. Heshel Rosenheim remained in his foxhole, though, and it was assumed it was because his was the first line of defense. But the truth was, he was happiest there. It was not that he wanted to die—he still intended, in fact, to surrender to the Egyptians at the first opportunity. It was simply that he could no longer face being in such close quarters with all those Jews. He could no longer look them in the eye.

He rested his Sten gun across his knees and glanced over at Dovid, who would not leave his side, even when ordered. When the bombing stopped, Heshel would stand up and stretch, then commence to reinforce the bunker that protected his little round of turf. In the foxhole with him were some boxes of ammunition and a small supply of Molotov cocktails, and on his belt two real grenades—familiar ones, German M24s. From time to time he would send young Dovid through the trenches to bring back a little food and something to drink from the makeshift kitchen that had sprung up in the shelter. Once he even brought cold chicken. Another time some pita and a nice tomato and cucumber, which they ate in slices. The water tower had been pummeled into debris, so water was carefully rationed. Dovid sometimes brought juice or soda pop instead, which was fine with Rosenheim. He watched the boy march across the lawn which was now cratered like the moon, his arms full of booty.

"Are you still happy to be here, Dovid?" he asked.

"I am the happiest man on earth," he replied. "Or the moon!"

When the bombs started falling again, they ducked down. Heshel ordered the boy back to the shelter, but he wouldn't go. Or maybe he didn't hear. It was so loud they both went deaf for minutes at a time. They played cards, cursing each other wordlessly when one or the other lost a hand.

In the evening, the bombing let up for quite a while. The Egyptians were having dinner, they supposed. An older fellow, Yitzhak, ran around trying to fix the electrical system so they could light the encampment, which, except for the shelters, had been thrown into darkness. Several Haganah teams built makeshift bunkers in the burned-out Bet Am, while others roamed the perimeter to repair the barbed wire. In the lull, a small group of reinforcements arrived, bringing with them the PIAT. Heshel watched as they leapt from the Jeep, one of them carrying the small rocket launcher on his shoulder. Moskovitz came up to him and shook his hand. It was obvious she was explaining that she was to be his assistant. The PIAT operator looked familiar.

Christ! he thought. Levin.

=========

They brought the PIAT down to Post 5, which was about twenty yards from Heshel's Post 4. Moskovitz, walking with Levin, listened carefully to his instructions. He looked up at her as he spoke, leaning into her. Watching their silhouettes move through the moonlight, Rosenheim bristled, but he did not stir. They disappeared into the trench, and he went back to contemplating the stars.

After a while there was a halfhearted barrage of mortar and small cannon fire, but then the night grew calm again. Ari and

Pinchas came to relieve him, and he made his way along the trench line toward the Bet Am, smoking. He could hear voices coming from the shelter nearby; he could hear the plaintive cry of a cow in need of milking—they had set them free, but most had wandered back, and they waited among the ruins, mooing in distress.

He walked past the little detachment of reinforcements seated together round a small kerosene burner, drinking tea and eating black bread spread with jam. There were three of them, Irgunists. Probably no one else left to send, he thought. It was a matter of where to find a PIAT. It could be an effective antitank weapon from close range, but they were tricky to use, spring loaded, difficult to aim. You needed an experienced operator. He thought he felt Levin looking up at him, but he couldn't be sure. He continued along in his leisurely way.

"Rosenheim!"

The voice was unmistakable. He turned.

"Who would have thought I'd find you here?"

"I live here," Heshel replied.

"A kibbutznik!"

Heshel tried to look through him, but could not get past the jumpy, hungry eyes.

"To think we'd be fighting together!" said Levin in Yiddish.

"What do you want from me?"

Levin just smiled. "Since our last . . . conversation," he replied, "I've been thinking."

"Have you?"

"Yes, I have. I have. Racking my brains actually. Trying to place you. You may recall you made up a story about me. Do you remember? You made accusations, unfounded accusations. As if it were a crime to survive. Perhaps I did steal someone's bowl, or someone's shirt, so what? We all did. How many shirts did you steal, Rosenheim?"

"What do you want of me?"

"No one survived without stealing, without having friends in the kitchen, without smuggling contraband, without having patrons, without skills. So how did you survive? I wondered. I asked myself that, I thought about that." He tapped his forehead with his finger to let Heshel know exactly where all this thinking had taken place. *"You see what I'm getting at, Rosenheim? You said I was some sort of criminal, but really, I'm a hero, aren't I? I survived. They couldn't kill me! Of course, luck is part of it, certainly. Luck is always very important. But no, you needed more than luck, didn't you? To survive more than a day, a month, more than three months, a miracle. Who survived more than three months, even in the work camps? One or two—the chosen ones. They did what they had to do. They were forced to do what they had to do. Who, after all, could remain human there? We were all reduced to some criminal state, some sub-human state. So I thought to myself—why this outburst from Lieutenant Rosenheim of the Palmach? I tested and retested my memory, I went down every little alley, looked both ways at every little crossing—Rosenheim, Rosenheim. Ah! I did know a Rosenheim! Yes, I told you that once. He was a shoemaker, so he was saved for a while by fixing the shoes that were sent to all those poor, needy Germans. But you know shoes—they just pile up! They filled the warehouses from top to bottom. So enough with fixing shoes! The shoe fixing was over! This Rosenheim, he knew what that meant. He knew it was shoes or gas. But he was smart, too, this Rosenheim, and he found another job. I couldn't remember. I knew him only briefly, of course. What job did he get? I racked my brains! I remembered! They sent him across the highway. Outside the barbed wire. To work in an office. Every day he marched off with his little commando—two or three of them, I think—he even got a clean uniform, and shoes with leather soles, and a shave, once a week!—so he shouldn't stink*

up the place, right? I remember watching him—it came back to me—watching him march off holding his bowl and his spoon—out in the morning, back in the evening—sitting all day in the warmth of the office, having his extra ration of bread and his soup from the bottom of the pot where all the cabbage was—and you know what? I hated that Rosenheim. I did. I hated him with every shred of my being. I regret that, but I did." He shook his head sadly to indicate regret.

"Why are you telling me all this?"

Levin sneered, "Do you remember when you threatened me at Deir Yassin?"

"I remember."

"I could not understand all your words, but I understood all that anger. You were at Majdanek, all right. But you were not that Rosenheim. So who were you?"

Heshel was acutely aware that he should not have stood there so long listening to this—it was an admission of something—but he found he could not pull himself away. Levin himself did not interest him. And his story was also nothing—he knew it all too well himself. He was not even afraid of jail or execution anymore. Something else terrified him. If he were exposed now, what would it mean? That's what he asked himself. When he listened to Levin he barely remembered who that SS-Mann was in the office across the highway—he could not recall his voice, or his thoughts, or his desires any more than he had been able to recall even the slightest detail of the real Rosenheim's face.

"So who am I?" he insisted.

"I'm still working on it," replied Levin, with a sly wink.

"Perhaps I'm just who I say I am."

"No. No, I don't think so. You stole his name. I'm just not sure why. Were you in his commando? Were you a spy? A murderer? I can't recall. But it will come to me. Because you see,

I know your face. I just haven't sent my brain down the right street yet." He smiled again, his little threatening smile.

Heshel crushed out his smoke and walked away at last. His hands were shaking and his heart was pounding, but he felt compelled to turn around and face Levin once again.

"What happened to him?"

"Who?"

"Rosenheim. The Rosenheim you say you remember."

"Who knows? I'm sure he's dead."

"Why?"

"He was soft."

"Soft?"

"I saw him share his rations more than once."

"Why would he do that?"

"Maybe some part of him had remained alive. Maybe he still had a soul."

"Then he was better off dead."

"Exactly," said Levin, who went back to his comrades and poured himself some more tea.

=========

He tried with all his might to recall one thing about the prisoner, Heshel Rosenheim, but he could not.

Perhaps a vague, dim face did appear before his eyes. The sunken cheeks, the dark, overgrown brows, shaven head, neck like twisted hemp, gaunt fingers with long, shit-colored nails—nothing special at all, nothing to particularize him, nothing.

But then creeping up from some dark hole in his fevered heart, a voice.

"But what should I say?" it seemed to cry. "About what in particular?"

It washed over him, thrilling and horrifying at the same time—this voice—for that was the one thing they could not burn out of them. Their voices—implacable, immutable, like fingerprints of their souls, holy in their absolute and irreducible separateness.

But it was less than air, less than a dream, and he could no more hear it than he could see the face, or the man behind the face. The voice simply melted into the lowing of the cows, the chatter from the bunkers, the flapping of the bats that sometimes swept like storm clouds across the fields.

CHAPTER 25

I didn't know how many days passed, but I kept building up my wall, one little clue at a time. He'd been calling me "Israel" a lot lately, so I wrote the name down. *Israel!* he'd say. *It's good to see you! Israel, can you turn on that lamp! Israel, have a cookie!* It occurred to me that he was seeing some sort of angel or something. Maybe Israel just stood for the whole Jewish People. Maybe in his crazy mind he believed he was finally a full-fledged member of the tribe. Anyway, I taped the name *Israel* to the wall about midway between the train ticket and Josh's report card, near the ceiling. I attached a Post-it, but I left it blank. I knew it was a clue, but I didn't know what it might mean, not in the slightest.

For instance, a day or two before, I had gone to see him.

I had asked Lamar, the orderly, to bring in some soup, and now I held the plastic spoon up to his lips.

"Papa," I said, *"iss ein bisschen suppe."*

He opened his mouth. He had heard me.

A little bit of broth found its way in. He opened his eyes. Wide and sightless like gardenias floating in bowls of gray water.

"Israel!" He smiled.

"Hey, Dad," I smiled back tightly. "It's Michael." I wondered if I'd ever hear him say my real name again.

"More," he said in German. *"Kann ich bitte . . ."*

His voice was reedy, insubstantial, but for all that, present. As usual, he should have been worse, but he was better.

I fed him another spoonful. And then another.

"You're hungry," I said. "That's good."

"I feel good now you're here," he said with a voice thin as wafer.

"You've been speaking in German."

"I am?" He shrugged. "Who can tell anymore?" He studied me with those foggy eyes, thick-lensed, creamy. "You don't look so good, my Mikey."

"*I* don't look so good?"

"Well," he said, "I'm no beauty queen, either." What he actually said was I'm no *Schönheitskönigin*. He was somehow lost between then and now, like a ghost trapped in a mirror.

"We have so much to talk about," I said to him.

"Yes, we do," he said.

"Do you think you are up for it?"

"I can try," he said.

"Then let's try," I said.

"Okay," he said, "let's try."

His face tilted benignly toward me, and he suddenly remarked, "Did you know that the word *holocaust* is Greek? It means a *burnt offering*—when the oracle would place the sacrificial bull on the altar and burn it in its entirety, until nothing was left but ash. Not a bite left to eat. Not a shred of skin or hide to make a scrap of clothing. Not an ounce of anything left for any useful purpose whatsoever. Burnt to nothing. That is what *holocaust* means."

I must have known that, since I had briefly studied Greek in undergraduate school when my ambition was to be a philosopher, and yet it did come as a surprise to me.

"Tell me more," I said.

"You know everything there is to know."

"Then tell me about you," I said.

"Memories come and go. Sometimes I think I'm still there. Sometimes when a bell goes off I think it's the siren in the camp. You know what *selektion* is?"

I did. It was when they divided them into those who would stay and work, and those who would go directly to the gas.

"Sometimes when they announce bingo I think it's *selektion*. I can smell the ovens, hear the footsteps of the prisoners—God in heaven! you cannot imagine what is that sound. A thousand feet all at once—quick step! quick step!—sloshing through the mud . . ."

"How do you feel then?" I said.

"How can one feel? A nightmare from which one cannot wake."

"Why is it, do you think, you were never selected?"

"That's the great mystery, isn't it, my love?" he said, trying to fill his wooden lungs with air. "That's what I live with. Why not me? There's no answer, Mikey. Death itself is not fearsome, my darling boy. Only hatred and cruelty. Only the human mind, that engineers such wholesale destruction. They say to destroy one life is to destroy an entire universe, yes? What is it then to destroy a universe? Death is nothing—but what is fearsome is to look into the eyes of a man who has no human feeling, and see yourself reflected there. He is nothing, you are nothing. God has flown the chicken coop. That is what is meant by terror."

"I feel that way," I said.

"What way?"

"That God has flown the coop."

"No! No!" he cried with great agitation. "That's the thing. That's the thing to actually understand."

"What is?"

"We run from Him, not the other way around." Then he wagged one finger at me. "Plus, He always catches up, my little one. That's His game. You run. He catches." He pointed to his oxygen tank. "As you can see."

He made an attempt to wink at me, but it was more like he closed both eyes and then had a very tough time opening them again.

I could see how tired he was. More than tired, the kind of tired that only happens once in a person's life. I wanted him to rest, but I was too afraid to let him go. Not until we spoke of it.

But before I could say anything, he suddenly reverted to English and announced, "It's really about you, I want to talk."

"Me? What's to talk about me?"

"Well, for one thing, are you happy?"

"Happy?" I said.

"Ya. Happy."

"How could I be happy?"

I looked at the floor. "I've lost Ella. I can't seem to connect with Josh. And then you."

He shook his head. "Don't worry about me," he said.

"No!" I said. "Those journals you wrote. I need to know, Dad. I need the truth. Can't you see that? Can't you see how desperate I am for the truth?"

"Yes, desperate. That describes you." Somehow, he reached out with his hand, the translucent skin bereft of all fat, his fingers corroded with arthritis, and laid it upon mine. "Don't be so desperate, Michael. Everything is all right. That's what I'm trying to tell you. Everything you need, you have. Or you can get just by snapping your fingers. You know how to snap your fingers, don't you? You don't need to go, go, go. Always go, go, going. That was you, even as a little boy. Looking everywhere. Never finding." He wheezed out a little laugh. "It's all in that crazy *keppela* of yours," he said, trying to jab his finger at my temple, but his touch was as light as snowfall.

"I don't know how to be anymore," I cried. "I'm totally confused."

"Not the end of the world," he replied, sinking back into the crumpled bedsheets.

"They think you should go to hospice," I said. "Are you ready for that?"

"I'm happy here," he said. "I won't take long."

"Oh, stop!" I said.

Again he laughed. "I'm telling you, death is nothing, Mikey. Nothing. After what I've seen."

Finally! I thought.

"Then tell me what you've seen."

"Everything a man could see. Everything you should never see."

"The camps."

"The camps."

I held my breath and forced myself to take his hand, this hand that pulled me back to safety when I leaned out too far that time on the Staten Island Ferry; the same that caught me as I careened out of control down those rapids on the Russian River, snatching me out like a ripe plum just before I hit the rocks; and the same that often was raised in anger but never, ever came down, and yet was strong enough to crush walnuts in its bare palm when, after the dishes were cleared, the grown-ups sat around the table talking politics. It was the same hand that today was like flatbread, dry, brittle, lifeless—I could have cracked it in half with a flick of my wrist, and now I held it and waited. A minute ago I might have been repulsed by this shadow of a hand, and by this rancid smell that seemed to float around him, by the sunken, bony eyes—but now I wasn't. I wasn't at all. I felt something else. I couldn't exactly say. But I sensed I was closer to him in this depressingly stupid, two-bit nursing home than maybe I'd been in my whole adult life.

"Tell me," I said as gently as I could, "in the camps. Which side were you on?"

He looked at me for a long time, and nodded as if he had told me the answer, but his lips had never moved.

"Why won't you tell me?" I whispered.

"Like everybody else," he barely said, "I was on my own side."

Almost immediately he fell asleep, as if he could no longer carry the burden of speech. I let go of his hand and set it carefully at his side, stood up, arranged his blanket and tucked it in, brushed his hair back with my hand the way he liked it, straight back, the long white tendrils pressed behind his ears, and gently I ran my hand along his forehead and down his cheek.

Back at home, at his apartment, rather, I could not see how anything on my wall made any sense. What else could I do? I picked up another volume of his writings, and ruefully began to read.

CHAPTER 26

They sat together speaking in Yiddish, Moskovitz smoking a cigarette and Levin absently wiping down his PIAT. Lieutenant Rosenheim watched them with growing annoyance. The moon had moved across the sky, and soon it would be dawn. With first light the attack most likely would begin, and before that he expected a heavy bombardment, the likes of which few of these people had ever seen or even imagined. Over the hours of this night he had thought about many things; he had planned with his cadre how best to meet the enemy advance; he had gone over in his mind variations and permutations of attack and defense; he had tried to bring to mind the many people who were counting on him, the people who had somehow become his friends; he thought long and hard about his own plans for surrender, and what ultimately he would have to do about Levin, but mostly he thought about Fradl—or Yael, as she was now called. Levin was flirting with her; it was obvious. He watched to see how she reacted, if she touched him, or leaned in toward him, how she laughed—politely or seductively. She mostly seemed to keep her distance, as if she sensed how dangerous he was—but then, all of a sudden, she would giggle like a little girl, or allow him to light her smoke.

But it would all be over soon, he told himself. The whole charade. In death or surrender, he would once again be Heinrich Mueller. The name sounded as foreign to him as Heshel Rosenheim once had.

Finally Levin got up and made his way into the darkness. Probably to relieve himself. Heshel grabbed his Sten and cantered over to Post 5. He slid down next to Moskovitz and asked for a light. She looked at him briefly and without feeling, and then gave him the hot end of her cigarette.

"Have you ever been in battle?" he asked.

"I'm not afraid," she said.

"I wish to God you had gone with the others."

"Why? Don't you think I can handle it?" Impatiently, she spit some tobacco onto her fingers. "I wonder where Levin is?"

"I don't like him," Heshel said. "He's a fanatic. The worst kind."

"You don't even know him."

"I know him well enough. He was at the massacre at Deir Yassin. A man with no regrets. What kind of man is that?"

"I would think you're jealous," she said, "if I thought you were capable of any feelings whatsoever."

She said this so matter-of-factly, so without a hint of cruelty, that it pierced his gut like the sharp end of a bayonet.

"He thinks we were in the lager *together," he picked up the thread as best he could. "He's wrong about that, by the way, we were never in the camps together. He has me mixed up with someone else. But he won't leave me alone. He keeps badgering me. If I were you, I'd be careful around him. He's not stable. In battle, you want to be with someone stable."*

"Why the sudden concern?" she asked.

"Fradl . . ."

"Don't call me that."

"I want to talk to you."

"Too late," she said. "Here he comes."

"Walk with me."

But Levin was upon them, and Heshel had to move aside to let him come down. Levin's lips convulsed into a small caustic smile. "Do you want a break, Yael?" he said. "Go ahead."

"I'm fine," she said.

Heshel wanted to take her by the arm, by the hair even, and drag her away, not even knowing what he would say to her, just to be near her, drink in her presence. It was suddenly clear to him. In the last vestiges of night, he saw what he was looking for.

"No, really," she said, "I'm fine here."

Briefly he closed his eyes and sighed. Then he jumped up and ran back to his post.

"Wait," she called after him in the half whisper of those under watch.

He heard her and turned around. She was splendid, standing up, the first rays of sun red-hued on her olive skin, bringing the gleam back into those dark eyes, and rimming her hair, wild and black, with fire.

"Put on your helmet!" he cried back at her. For he could suddenly hear the whistle of shells and the drone of aircraft coming in for the kill.

==========

It was an enormous bombardment, unlike anything they had experienced before. They all hid in the shelters and trenches or under their makeshift bunkers, shaking uncontrollably, their eyes shut tight, their fists clenched over their ears. Those who were caught in the Bet Am were killed within the first moments, hit with incendiaries and a massive barrage of artillery. The fields of alfalfa were ablaze, the bananas were leveled and burning, and the orange groves were hollowed out, the few standing trees leafless and broken. Heshel had seen Moskovitz dive into her foxhole, but after that he could not tell if she was alive or dead. They had no walkie-talkies, and few dared lift a head above the trench line. They stayed put and waited for the silence that would announce the Egyptian assault.

But Heshel couldn't wait any longer. Three of his men had made it to the post before the bombardment, and he signaled them that he was going out to check on Post 5. He dashed through the trench and then jumped up on solid ground a few yards from Fradl's post. Standing thus he could see what no one else could—the world on fire, the twisted earth studded with body parts like strange new vegetation, the banana trees like fountains of flame, the precious soil charred black with soot, the main house virtually gone from sight, and fire coming up beneath it as if from the ground itself, like demons rising from hell. He saw the plane coming, a German Stuka, and jumped into her foxhole just as it began to strafe.

"Where is she?" he said in horror.

"I don't know," Levin replied breathlessly. "There were wounded over by the Bet Am, so she ran to them."

"Wounded? There's nothing there. Why did you let her go?" He grabbed Levin by the collar and started shaking him.

"She's supposed to be with you! That's her job! She's the PIAT assistant! Why did you let her go? You're her commanding officer!"

Levin pushed off Rosenheim and collapsed onto the dirt floor. "She wouldn't listen," he moaned. Pathetically, he looked up at Rosenheim. "I'm sorry. I'm sorry. You think I want to be here all by myself?"

Rosenheim was panting, filled with rage, his face contorted and blazing.

"You fucker!" he cried. "I should kill you! You pig!"

He was looming over Levin. Levin was pulling himself back into a protective ball, like a dog . . . when suddenly he lifted his face and, with swiftly changing expression, eyed Rosenheim with a kind of detachment that turned suddenly into a look of triumph, as if he had just solved a difficult mathematical equation.

"You spoke to me in German," he said, rising. "And I cowered out of habit, didn't I? To my old master. Right? I cowered like a sheep, like a dog, to the sound of that German. A voice I have not heard in some time, except in my dreams, every night in fact, in my dreams. And I begged for mercy, didn't I? And you, with your German, with your very special German—my God! Now I do know you! I do know you!"

It was Levin who was now backing Rosenheim into the corner, pressing closer, jabbing at him with his finger, spit flying as his words cut across the burning air. His face was a lantern.

"I remember you! You were not with my friend Rosenheim, you were not in his commando. No. You were his SS keeper! You were der Buchhalter, *yes? The bookkeeper of Majdanek! I remember you! Counting shoes! Counting eyeglasses! Counting wedding rings! Counting gold fillings! Yes, I remember you! Marching out to greet the new shipments—of food for you and gas for us! Strolling up and down the boxcars you had us load*

with hair and trousers, shoes and silk underwear, making little checkmarks on your bill of lading, stopping only to kick some mud from your fine boots, all that loot on its way to Berlin and Leiden! What a hero you were! How could I ever *forget you? What? Nothing to say now, Mr. Palmach man? Skulking about the warehouses, watching us from afar, afraid almost to show your face—but I saw your face! We all saw your face. Oh . . . what's this? Are you going to kill one more Jew now? Haven't had enough?"*

For Rosenheim had pulled the cocking lever on his Sten, and was pointing the barrel directly at Levin's head. "You can't tell anyone," he said.

Levin laughed.

"Why, because you'll tell them I was a Kapo*? And a trustee at that. And a cruel one? All right, I was. So what? Who will believe you, and who will care? How do you think half these people survived? By being nice? Don't you recall anything of what you did to us? What you turned us into? Is it all to be forgotten with a change of name? Is it all to be washed away with a few good deeds? Unless of course you're a spy . . . Oh!" His eyes brightened even more. "What else could it be? How else do they know where to hit us so easily? Oh yes—and at the glorious battle of Deir Yassin—where* we *lost more than they did—attacked on every side!—gunmen hiding behind children, women firing from beneath their burkas. . . . But you—you could see only their suffering and not ours. A spy!"*

Around them the sky was on fire, the bombs falling, yet they were standing up in the foxhole, their heads and shoulders visible above the embankment, eye to eye, the Sten pointed at Levin's face, a bit of oil *dripping from the end of the barrel.*

He had to decide what to do.

Suddenly there was silence.

The bombardment had ceased.

Everyone would now be running to their posts—in one second the place would be a beehive, soldiers and kibbutzniks scurrying along the trench lines and across the fields.

"It's now or never," sneered Levin.

It would be now, he decided. His finger tightened.

But then Levin's head was gone. A fountain of red shot up from his shoulders, three feet into the air, raining down on Heshel and covering him in hot, sticky blood.

"Tanks!" someone cried.

Levin's headless body fell upon him, propelling him into the dirt and out of harm's way. But he was confused, disoriented. He hadn't fired. Hadn't shot him. He squirmed out from under Levin. There was no head to be seen anywhere.

"Oh dear God!" It was Moskovitz, jumping into the foxhole.

"It was the tank," Heshel muttered.

"Oh my God," she said again. Her hands were shaking, but she bent down and covered the body with a tarp. Then she caught her breath. "Where's the PIAT?"

"The PIAT? What PIAT?"

She tried to calm him. "We have to stop the tanks, Heshel! I need the PIAT."

He saw it sticking out from under Levin's feet.

"You've got to get back to your unit," she said to Heshel.

"I'll stay with you."

"No," she said firmly. "I don't need you here. They need you."

But she pulled him close until there was no space between them, not an inch, so close he could feel her breath enter his own open mouth, and she looked into his eyes, and then, with sudden, swift resolve, she kissed him, she kissed him now as she had once before under the fragrant, blossoming orange trees, holding his blood-soaked face in her hands, and fitting her lips over his to feed him the love of her mouth.

"It's all right," she said. "Now, go,"

He did as he was told. With soaring spirits, he ran back to his men, firing as he went in the direction of the advancing Egyptians.

CHAPTER 27

Suddenly the weather changed and the rains started falling—incessantly, it seemed—hot, tropical rains with high, violent winds that sent the palm fronds flying through the air like snapped-off propellers. They landed noisily upon the pavement and piled up upon the grass, turning quickly into rot. Deep puddles impeded the sidewalks and flooded the roadways. It was best to keep away from the canals. People often drowned in them, their cars slipping down the embankments and disappearing into the silent waters, their screams unheard behind sealed windows, their last words inhaled by the fish.

Then the rains would stop suddenly, the heat would return in a matter of seconds, and just as suddenly the skies would turn black again and down it came in torrents so heavy it hurt when it hit you. I found it more oppressive than when it was just plain hot, and I hated Florida more than ever. By now I saw no way to go home. I felt as if I might have to stay there forever.

Also my wall was filling up. After I had tacked the name *Israel* in the space between the train ticket and Josh's report card, I had gone on to find some old *Life* magazines with pictures from the war, from the liberation of the camps, and from the Nuremberg Trials. My parents had saved only these *Life* magazines. Why? I taped them in the inner circle, and wrote under them: *World History/Family History?* I searched the images for signs of my father. There were none. I went to the library and got a book about concentration camps and Xeroxed the pages on Majdanek. I taped these to the wall also. Among them was a photo of Colonel Weiss. It went on the wall with the words: *White Tablecloth, Silver Coffee Urn.* There was no mention of these details in the article, but the mass execution my father witnessed did indeed happen more or less as he described. I added *Eyewitness or Eye Research*? These were not really clues; nevertheless I needed to hang them on the wall. I taped the most recent phone bills from his room in the nursing home onto the wall. There were no calls to L.A. *He could not have called Kaufman,* I wrote. I stuck up a map of Berlin. I circled Alexanderplatz, where my father said he had lived as a boy. It was a main square. Under it the Post-it read: *Not likely.* I tried to find even one of my father's forty-two-volume set of the *International Military Tribunal at Nuremberg,* but they had disappeared. Instead, I attached my parents' wedding invitation, their framed wedding photograph, and a picture of my father on the beach in 1952. I wrote: *Shirt on at all times. Fair skin? Bullet holes?* I put up the picture of Karen I always loved. It was when she was about thirteen or fourteen, pubescent cheeks, goofy smile encased in braces, hair parted in the middle and hanging straight down like Cher's in the 1970s. I studied her face, trying to remember what Karen was really like at that age, tagging along, mouth still sticky with peanut butter and chocolate.

Two days before I was to leave for upstate New York my mother had called.

"Your sister is sick," she said.

Okay, she's sick, I thought. So? It did not really register with me. Even the word *cancer* had very little meaning for me. I wasn't even sure she used that word. Possibly she said she has a growth of some kind. Maybe she used the word *tumor*. In fact, my mother was quite cheerful. To my few questions she answered only in the positive. The doctor says Karen is young and strong. The doctor says he can probably get it all, and she'll be fine. They don't make any promises, of course, but he doesn't seem too concerned. She vaguely explained some of the procedures: they're going to try this, and then if that doesn't work, they'll try that. But I shouldn't worry. She said that quite a few times. I shouldn't worry. Finally I reluctantly asked if I should cancel my plans. It's just summer stock, I said. Comedy. Ridiculous! she said. No reason to come home. Everything's fine. Enjoy yourself. Then Karen got on the phone. She also insisted I go to the Catskills. She was going to come and see me! As soon as she got just a little bit better. We told jokes. Then she laughed and gave my father the phone. "Mikey," he sighed. I remembered that explicitly—*Mikey.* Even now, as I heard the faraway echo of that plaintive cry, my heart shriveled. What did he mean by that sigh? What was he trying to tell me? But then he said, Why come home? What can you do?

So off I went.

Karen was seventeen. I was only twenty. Still.

Even now, when I thought about my sister's illness, I had the distinct impression the diagnosis and outcome were virtually instantaneous, as if it all happened in a day. But of course it actually groaned on for a year. I tried to recall the months and months of torturous surgeries and treatments—the chemo, the radiation—but even now it all blurred into a vision of her sparkling eyes, her intrepid cheerfulness—how when she went bald, she insisted I draw a happy face on the top of her head. Why did I blot out the weeks of nausea and pain, the emaciation that seemed to come on in a single night, and her final bizarre madness when the cancer, which had begun so far down below—in her barely used ovaries—jumped ship and coursed through her brain, giving rise to the hallucinations that, in spite of everything, made us all laugh. Even now it came to me only in bits and pieces, flashes, vignettes, as if it were a secret I had been keeping from myself, revealed only in hints and innuendo. I had evaded her suffering by painting it over like artists sometimes do when they move a figure from one side of the canvas to the other, or change a frown to a smile. I now realized that I had seen her suffering no more than Heinrich Mueller had seen the suffering of Heshel Rosenheim. No, I said, no. Not the same thing at all.

In any case, I went back to the wall and taped Karen's hospital bracelet to a spot somewhere near the note I had written to Ella asking her to reconsider, but which was returned unopened. I always carried it around, just in case one day she might want to open it. I put the bracelet on the wall, but honestly I didn't know why. In fact, under it I wrote simply: *Why?*

The wall was now almost completely covered with evidence. I stood back and studied it, drawing invisible lines of connection between objects, erasing them, and then frantically sending out vectors to other points on the wall. It was here, it was all here. All I had to do was—

The doorbell rang.

It was Mrs. Gitlin, from 316.

She had a casserole cradled in one hand, an umbrella clutched in the other, and her feet encased in clear plastic galoshes. She smile beatifically, revealing bits of lipstick on her upper teeth.

"It's Jonathan, isn't it?"

I smiled down at her. I smelled brisket.

"I'd like to have a word with you," she said brightly.

She waited for me to let her in.

"The house is kind of a mess," I said.

She shrugged the shrug of a woman who's seen it all, and isn't about to be deterred in any case. "A man living by himself. What else is new?"

"It's just not a good time," I said.

There was a crack of thunder, and the wind whipped up, catching the underside of Mrs. Gitlin's umbrella. It tugged at her so violently it almost lifted her off the walkway. I found myself rescuing her and pulling her down. Rather taken with my gallantry, she handed me the casserole.

"Just a little something," she said.

It must have weighed eight pounds.

"Thank you," I said, "but I couldn't."

"Of course you could!" she replied, rising on her toes to look past me into the apartment, but I moved to block her. For once I was glad I played right guard in high school.

"Well, thank you!" I said, and waited for her to go.

"May I ask you something?" she said.

"I guess so."

"Well," she began, touching with her long arthritic finger the elegant Jewish star that hung on one of three golden chains around her neck—I noted a Tiffany bean on another, and a big, fat diamond on the third—"we were talking."

"We?"

"The girls. And also my husband and the other husbands, too.

Although to be honest, there aren't all that many husbands anymore. Well, we were thinking about you. We know you are going through a very hard time. What could be harder?" She looked at me consolingly, and I could tell she wanted to hug me but held herself in check. "We know you are all by yourself up here in this apartment and surrounded by all us old people. It must be so boring. Who wants to be with old people?"

"I'm fine," I said.

"We also know, to tell you the truth, that one day in the not so distant, if you know what I mean, our own kids will be doing what you're doing right now. . . ."

"I'm sure not for a long, long time," I assured her, and started to close the door.

"Be that as it may," she replied, putting herself between me and the door frame, "but all we have here is us—old people, that's all we have, and though I know it's boring for you, we thought, well, that Yom Kippur is coming up. And we don't want you to be alone. We talked it over. So here, we got you a ticket. It's free, you don't have to pay a thing. And you can sit with us. With the Mosemans and the Futernicks and Harry and me—we sit together. We have good seats, right up front. It's a lovely temple, you'll love the rabbi—it's a woman! It takes a minute getting used to, but even my husband likes her now. One could not say she's beautiful, but she's very, very smart, and such a good speaker! Now we don't have a big cantor or a choir, but it's a lovely service, and there are some younger people who come too, and I'm sure you can meet them if you want, and then afterwards, there's the *oneg,* and then we thought you can come with us to break the fast. We all go over to Charlie's Crab. You're not kosher are you?"

"No, I'm not kosher." It was obviously very important to her, otherwise they'd have to change reservations.

"And you don't have to worry about the cost of that either. It's on us."

"I couldn't possibly . . ." I stammered.

"Don't be ridiculous. It's Yom Kippur. You're doing us a favor. Maybe He'll give us another year or two for this!" This caused her to laugh with great delight. Then she looked me in the eye with a kind of tenderness I had not seen since my mother died, with eyes, though perhaps bordered with too much mascara and pearlescent eye shadow, still vibrant and blue and full of fire and hope. "It would be a *mechayeh*. You know what that is? A joy! You'll be doing a good deed." She placed the ticket in my hand. "We'll see you tomorrow, all right? We all meet downstairs. Kol Nidre starts at six. So we meet at five-thirty."

Tomorrow? I thought. Ten days have passed already?

She looked at me seriously now. "If you're not there, we'll understand, and we'll leave without you. But we want you to be with us. It would be our pleasure." Standing there in her raincoat and galoshes, her umbrella bouncing in the wind, she reached out and squeezed my hand. "Be strong," she said. "It's something we all go through, if we're lucky."

I knew what she meant by that. She meant if we live long enough to see our parents die, rather than the other way around, the world is as it should be.

Then, bunnylike, she scurried down the gangway towards number 316, her see-through plastic booties barely skimming the surface of the water under her feet. I thought of my mother then. She and Dad had it the other way around. And I thought of Josh, too. If I lost him, only then I would know pain.

I went inside and put the casserole down. I threw the ticket into the rose-colored candy dish, where it would stay long after tomorrow had come and gone. I already knew how it would go: the two Gitlins and the two Futernicks sitting in the car, waiting. Harry Gitlin, the husband, anxious to leave, growing more impatient by the millisecond. They would get into a spat because she'd be saying, just another minute or two, he'll be down—just one more minute! But sooner or later even dear old Mrs. Gitlin would have to give up on me. Oh well, she'd say to Harry, what can you do? We tried! Delirious to have been right for a change, he'd console her. You can't save everybody! he'd say, throwing it into Drive.

Later that night, I went back into the kitchen. The casserole seemed to look up at me with plaintive Jewish eyes. I was hungry, so I thought, why not? I'll give it a try. It turned out it wasn't brisket after all. It was something they liked to call Chicken Divine—chicken breasts baked with broccoli and a sauce of Campbell's Cream of Mushroom Soup. I looked at it suspiciously but popped some in the microwave. I brought it out and sat down at the dining room table and took a bite. It was actually delicious. As I sat there eating, I could study my wall of clues in the living room just beyond.

My eye found itself drawn to the little train ticket that I had put up a few days before. I set down my fork. Stepped closer to it. It was just above eye level, and I had to stand on tiptoe to view it. I must have been less than an inch from it. I was being silly, there was nothing. But then I thought I saw a blue color bleeding through from behind, as if someone had written something on it, which long ago faded away. I pulled it from the wall and turned it over. There was a trace of writing there! Very small, very fine, created with a remarkably precise hand, now blurred with years of erosion, moisture, traces of mold; and the tops of all the letters were cropped away—but there it was. GvH.

GvH. I wondered what that could mean.

I stared at it a long time. I tried to think back—what had he said? What had he written?

And then it hit me. G. von Hellman. The girl from Vienna.

CHAPTER 28

Not Frau Hellman. *Fräulein.*

I was suddenly overwhelmed by the need to take a shower. I threw my plate into the sink and ran into the bathroom. I scrubbed my body with Ivory Soap, shampooed my hair and shaved, all under the bracing needles of the Shower Massage. My father had loved his Shower Massage. *Ooooo,* he would croon when he mentioned it, *Ahhhh.*

I looked at the clock. It had somehow become night.

I thought about him lying there. Dying. It's time to go, I thought.

I put on a pair of khakis, a pale yellow golf shirt, and my linen sports coat. I wanted to look respectable. In fact, I looked pretty much like him.

I knew I needed the stuff in the gym bag, but I couldn't remember where I'd put it. I looked everywhere for it, frantically digging through the piles of discarded evidence, throwing photographs, notebooks, ashtrays, and shoehorns right and left, cursing, wailing, begging, and finally dissolving into tears. Then I saw its iridescent green strap peeking from under my bed. I pulled it out so carefully you might have thought I was rescuing a child trapped in a culvert. I unzipped it, felt around inside for what I wanted, put the stuff in my jacket pocket, zipped it back up. I stood up, looked around. The apartment seemed totally unfamiliar to me. Everything was a wreck. What had I been thinking? It was like waking from a dream. And yet it was all too familiar. I knew I had been here before. But when? As I rushed towards the door, for some reason I pulled Karen's hospital bracelet off the wall and shoved it in my pocket too.

The phone rang.

Oh God, I thought, he's dead! But it was April.

"I was worried about you," she said. "I haven't heard from you for days. Are you okay?"

"I have to go to the nursing home," I muttered. "I have to see my father."

There was a discernible catch in her throat. After a minute she asked, "Do you want me to come with you?"

"No," I said. "I'll call you."

She said she would be thinking of me, and we hung up. Vaguely I realized I did not have her phone number.

I moved toward the door, but the phone rang again. Jesus! What does she want? I thought.

But it was Josh. His sweet voice, like an angel whispering in my ear, like the heavenly stranger at the tent door. Something urged me to invite him in, to *beg* him to come in if I had to, to fete him with delicacies and fine drink.

"Josh! Kiddo!" I said instead.

"Hi, Dad."

He waited for me to say something.

"Sorry I didn't call today," I finally said, tossing off the first thing that came to my mind.

"Or yesterday," he said.

When I spoke to him, I felt like I was drowning, but not in water, in mud. No thrashing about, just stuck and sinking.

"How were services?" I went on stupidly.

"Boring," he said.

If I were my old self I would have said, "Yeah, I know. Who needs heaven?" I would have gone into my rap about how nice Sodom and Gomorrah really were and why having your wife turn into a pillar of salt was not necessarily a bad idea—I had a great bit about it that I used when I toured places like Arkansas and North Dakota, actually—but instead I just asked, "How was dinner with Grandpa and Grandma?"

"Boring," he repeated.

"Come on, Josh! It was fun, wasn't it?" I insisted desperately.

"Not really," he said. I could hear him waiting for me to tell him I'd come home and save him from having to go to temple on Yom Kippur.

"Listen, I have to go see Grandpa Rosenheim. He's not feeling well today," I added.

"Hey, I was thinking about Frau Hellman," Josh said cheerily.

"What?" I said.

"Frau Hellman. The mayonnaise lady."

"Yes, Josh, I know who she is."

"Maybe Grandpa's worried he's going to die. You know, *Hell*man. As in *hell*. It's psychological, Dad."

I shifted impatiently. "I guess that's a possibility."

"Or maybe it was his girlfriend. Before Grandma."

I heard myself cough. "Yes, that's also possible."

"But shouldn't he be thinking about *Grandma*?"

"I'm sure he is. Why are you obsessing over this?"

"I don't know, I was just thinking about it."

"Well, try thinking of something else, okay?"

"Like what?"

"I don't know, Josh. For heaven's sake—"

Instantly I regretted scolding him, but I had to leave. Time was running out.

"I have to go, Josh," I said. "I'm late for seeing Grandpa."

"It's okay, Dad," he said.

His little heart was trying so hard to be valiant. I loved him. I wanted to hug him. Protect him. Maybe in some strange way that's what I was doing, protecting him, but from me. When I look back on it, I'm absolutely sure I intended that Josh have a childhood of honesty, love, and security. But at that moment I concluded you simply can't give something you've never had yourself, even if you always thought you had.

I promised him that when I got home we'd spend so much time together he'd get so sick of me he'd send me on a one-way ship to Patagonia.

"Where's that?" he said.

I was honest with him for once. "I haven't the slightest idea," I said.

Then I asked him to put his mother on.

"She's probably busy, Dad."

"Put her on," I said.

I must have been breathless, because she sounded horrified. "It's your father!"

I said, "No. I want to talk to you about me. I need to tell you something about me. I need to tell you something very, very important. I want to come clean."

She didn't miss a beat.

"But I don't need to hear it anymore, Michael. I don't care."

Instead of coming in through the front, I found a side door, and before I knew it, I was standing in the dark, forgotten space at the far end of the hall near the stairway no one ever used. No one could see me there. The night crew moved like ghosts themselves, barely visible, like beams of light, their white shoes descending like snowflakes, their voices muffled under the hum of the water-coolers. I watched their comings and goings. In and out of the broom closet, the dispensary, the bathroom, the patients' rooms. I had the strange sense I had been here before, too, but all I wanted at the time was to stand there in secret and watch, secure in the shadow and quiet. Then I roused myself, went outside, and came back in through the front doors.

Nurse Clara was on night shift. She appeared to be waiting for me, even though she could not have possibly known I was coming. But for once she looked at me kindly, took me by the arm, and led me aside, her monster breast pressed against the sleeve of my jacket. In her other hand, she grasped her equally large, black wooden cross as if to ward off the evil demons that followed me into the nursing home. She held it in front of her as we walked, clearing us a safe path.

"I wanted to warn you," she said in her serpentine southern drawl. "Physically, you will have to be prepared." Her eyes were teary. "We were going to call."

"Physically."

"There's been a pretty big change."

"I see," I said.

Nurse Clara took my hand. "I'm sorry," she said. "We all love your daddy."

"Yes I know," I said.

She was right.

The fat under his skin seemed to have melted away. The arms sticking out of his short-sleeved gown were like branches of willow, the skin weeping down in long flat sheets, the bone eerily visible. His face had become birdlike, with sallow cheeks and pointed beak, and a strong, sour smell rose from his corrupting flesh, like rotting fruit. He no longer resembled my father at all.

I did not want him to die that way.

I closed the door, lowered the light until it was no more than a glimmer. I slowly walked over to the window and lowered the blinds. Then I quietly pulled the curtain around the bed. The hooks made a swishing noise against the runners. I stood there over him. It was our private world, the most alone with him I had ever been, cut off from everyone and everything. All we'd ever said to each other, done to each other, hoped for each other, seemed very far away. The only noise was the echo of his oxygen mask and my own hushed breath. I came closer. I stood as still as a statue, watching him. I studied the dark scrolls running down his face, crisscrossing his skin, each wrinkle set there for a purpose—to teach us the folly of hope, I supposed. I looked at his mouth, drooped open and toothless, the same mouth once so full of wisecracks and patriarchal wisdom and an endless stream of criticism. I stared into his sunken eyes, now closed to all but their own inner light, the same eyes that once were all-seeing, all-knowing, and also, I had little doubt, witness to the most repulsive crimes of man. It was improbable, it was implausible, but it was only then that I was certain I had always loved him and that I loved him now.

Slowly, carefully, I slipped my hand into my pocket—the pocket of my linen sports coat—and reached for the hypo. In the dark corner of the hall, I had already loaded it with its colorless potion of justice. He would not have a natural death. That was what I had promised myself.

He seemed suddenly to move his head and look at me—his eyes just at that moment opened.

"Israel?" he said.

"No," I said. "It's me. It's Michael. It's your son."

"Oh Michael, I'm so glad it's you!"

My hand was still in my pocket, searching. But the hypo wasn't there. I must have put it in my other pocket. Instead, I felt something thin, a little sticky, like rubber, bending beneath my fingers. I lifted it out. It was my sister's hospital bracelet. The bracelet Karen had worn the day she died.

"Oh dear God!" I cried, and fell upon him, weeping, my heart breaking into pieces upon his tiny, frail breast.

From some deep unconscious place, he found the strength to wrap his arms around me and hold me tight.

CHAPTER 29

Everyone thought I was still at school, but I used to sneak back to see her all the time, almost every day. I couldn't help myself. I don't know why I didn't tell my father and mother. I came early before they showed up. Or late after they went home.

"How's it going?" I said.

Her lips curled into a fine note of sarcasm. "Nathan was by this morning. He was cheery, too. He brought me this."

She pointed to a pile of vacation brochures for places like Barbados and Tuscany.

"He thinks I'll be fine by summer. We'll bicycle through Provence."

"Mom would never let you go off to Europe with a guy. You're not old enough."

"Nor will I ever be. And thank you for not contradicting me. Do you have any cigarettes?"

I gave her one. In those days you could smoke anywhere.

"Thank God I don't have lung cancer," she said. "Can you imagine what a drag *that* would be?" She laughed, sucking a thick, fragrant plume up through her nostrils. "Mom and Dad aren't around, are they?"

"Not that I know of. Dad's at the store, I guess. I don't know where she is."

"Probably looking in the broom closet for The Cure. She's certain they have one somewhere and for some reason they just won't give it to me."

"It's hard on her," I said.

"You would think she's the one who's dying," she replied.

I did not know how to take these glib moods. She wanted me to be glib right back, but I suddenly felt I no longer knew how. Maybe it was just that she couldn't see herself. She couldn't see how thin she had grown, how green-gray and scabrous her face had become. She knew she'd lost a few teeth, but probably forgot about it as people do when they get used to something, and didn't realize that when she smiled it radiated hopelessness rather than joy. She was once such a beautiful girl.

But she surprised me again.

"Mikey, I need to tell you something. I've been thinking of how to tell you for a few days now. We all know I am going to die; it's not about that. I'm okay with that. No, I am. As much as I can be. But something else." She took my hand. "I'm in a lot of pain, Michael. Look at me, please. Look at my face. They want to dope me up all the time, but I don't let them. I don't want to not *be here*. You know what I mean? And even when I let them dope me up, I hurt anyway, terribly, horribly, badly. So why should I be a zombie, too? It hurts like nothing I ever thought could hurt. I want to tear my insides out of me. It's not just one place, like my side or my back. It's everywhere. Everywhere hurts. They want to do more chemo, but I don't want more chemo. It's almost worse than the pain. You get so sick, you never dreamed you could get so sick, but you go through it because you think it's worth it, because you think maybe they can fix you and you can go home. But it's not going to work, Michael."

"Sure it will."

"So why should I? Why should I go through it?"

"But maybe it will work this time," I said.

"Michael."

I looked away.

"You have to help me," she said.

"Sure!" I said. That was more like it. "Whatever you need."

"I can't do it by myself."

"Do what?"

"Michael," she said, "are you listening to me?"

"Of course I'm listening to you."

She stopped for minute and took a deep, vexed breath, but then she looked up at me with bright, gay eyes; and with her mouth closed, I almost could believe she was the lovely girl I had grown up with—the urchin, the funny little troublemaker, the A student.

"I want to end it," she said. "I want you to help me."

"End what?"

As if I were the younger one she patted my hand and stroked my face. "Me," she said. "End me. I want to die on my own terms. I want to die now, before it gets worse, and before I lose my mind. I want to die while I'm still me."

I could not feel my legs, only a strange beating in my chest and stomach, as if a creature had materialized inside me and was thrashing to get out. I must have grown faint and wobbly because she ordered me to sit down, and then just laughed out loud—at me, I realized—and when she did, the gaps in her mouth—where once the snowy white teeth of perfect girlhood had been—poured black emptiness into the room, and decay and the aroma of gall, and her face sank beneath her bones.

"I just need a lot of morphine," she said.

I had no idea how to get morphine. I watched around the hospital for a while and carefully followed the nurses until I found the room where they kept the narcotics. The room itself was not locked, and there was a window in the door through which I could see the cabinet where the drugs were kept. Each nurse seemed to have her own key. They carefully logged every withdrawal on a clipboard that dangled from the side of the cabinet. I did not want to arouse suspicion, so I took Karen with me on these scouting expeditions, pushing her along in her wheelchair, her arm attached to a tube of some sort of solution, and lately, an oxygen mask in her hand, with which she could grab a little air when her lungs failed her. She was brave and happy on these jaunts, even though she had barely enough energy to speak. From time to time though, she perked up.

"You're going to need to steal a key," she said, "and sneak in in the middle of the night. You'll have to have a white coat or something."

"Can't you just take a bottle of aspirin?" I said.

The plan was patently ridiculous, and I told her so. But it took on the form of a game for us.

"You could make love to . . . that one." She pointed to a particularly unattractive nurse—pencil thin, knobby knees, screechy voice, no breasts, black wig, and old, too. "And while she's in ecstasy, you slip the key off the ring."

"While she's in ecstasy?"

"Or you could wait till she goes into the bathroom, and then make a mold of the key with a bit of clay."

We were two spies in a James Bond movie.

"We need some underworld connections," she said once. "Do you know any drug dealers?"

As a matter of fact, I did. But I told her I didn't.

"A drug dealer could get us anything we wanted," she said.

It went on this way for two days or so, that's all, really. In my memory, it seemed like it was an extended adventure, something we did for weeks and weeks, like a summer vacation about which you tell so many stories for years and years to come—but not at all. It was only two days. She was going. Not dying yet. But going. Her pain got worse and worse almost with each hour, and I knew she was terrified that her brain would go. I didn't know which was worse. Because if her brain did go, she wouldn't really be aware of the pain, except in an animal kind of way—but she would have lost everything and still have to suffer on. And sometimes even now she'd do funny things—talking about her shoes as if they were alive, recalling things that never happened, asking for an apple and then when she got it asking for an apple. But then I thought, if her brain does somehow remain whole enough, what then? She'd have herself, but what would she be? Just pain. Just a circle of pain closing her off from everything except the pain.

On the second day, in the evening, she said to me, "Hurry."

Visiting hours, in those days, were pretty strictly enforced, and I had to sneak onto the floor, which I managed without too much trouble. The night nurses were at their station, chatting quietly, occasionally glancing up at the monitors. An orderly was napping in a chair near the bathroom, not far from the dispensary. The walls were heavy with many layers of paint—recently they decided pale green was more comforting and less frightening than white. But I was frightened anyway. The floors had been recently Lysoled and I heard my shoes squeak on the linoleum. I stopped in my tracks and hugged the wall. Nothing else moved. A radio was playing at the nurses' station. "Night Fever" by the Bee Gees. I took a breath and crept along the wall towards the chamber. The orderly stirred in his chair and cracked one eye open. I froze. He yawned and stretched his arms wide, looked around and stopped when he faced my direction. But then miraculously he shut his eyes again and reclined into his chair emitting an easy-going sigh. Quickly, I darted into the drug room.

It was just a metal cabinet with a simple lock, like on a file drawer—not even a padlock. I had planned to jimmy it with my penknife. What I had not planned on was running into the skinny nurse with the black wig who was organizing bandages on a shelf and noting the inventory in a big black book.

She looked up at me slowly.

"May I help you?"

"Oh," I said. "This is the wrong room! I got confused. I thought—"

"You can't be in here," she said.

"Oh," I said.

"Your sister's room is in the opposite hall. Pass the nurses' station, make a right, then proceed down that hall."

"Oh," I said.

She gestured toward the door.

"Everything looks the same on this floor," I said. "It's easy to get lost."

She waited for me to turn around and leave, which I did, my heart not only pounding in my chest, but breaking. What was I going to do? What was I going to do? How could I help her, my sister? For I had made up my mind to do it, and it was a terrible decision. But I was only going to go this far anyway—get her the morphine. I would never have administered it. Never would I have done that, and I didn't believe for a minute that Karen would either. It was part of some fantasy we had, that's all. I walked casually past the nurses' station. Oddly, they did not question me. I now know if you act with authority you seldom are questioned, but on that day everything was a surprise to me. I opened Karen's door. She had a private, and in the dark I could make out her bed and her slight, almost cloudlike figure upon it. On tiptoe I edged closer to her. A bit of streetlamp knifed through the window, and delineated the now terribly sharp features of her face in the half light of a studio portrait. Her flesh was patchy and almost liquid, her lips blue like fountain pen ink, her few long strands of hair sticking out of her bare head like electrical wire, now gray, now white.

Suddenly she unbolted her eyes—shockingly, like a blast. I jumped back.

And then a broad and half-crazy, delirious smile. "You got it! You got it!" She was mad with joy. She grasped my wrist and shook it with glee. "Tonight!" she said. "Tonight!"

"Karen—"

"Tonight! Promise me!"

I held her hand too.

"I will always be grateful to you, Michael," she whispered. "You will always, always be my prince, my savior."

I looked at her for a long time.

"When you're asleep," I said.

She took a fine, deep breath and, delicately, smiled at me. "Thank you," she said. Tears formed in her little eyes, like honey dripping sweetly off the edge of the jar, and with my finger I lapped them up and brought them to my lips.

I waited a long time, until I knew she was asleep.

Then I took the pillow and sent her to her rest.

My father's arms had released their hold on me as he sank back into his sad, empty slumber, and now I sat in my little chair keeping watch the way people do when death is near, by not looking. Instead, I listened to the heartbeat of the floor and ceiling, the pulse of the nurses' shoes as they padded down the hallway, the breathing of the clock and the monitor and the air itself as it settled around my father's deathbed. Beneath all this life, my father's own breath grew thinner and more wooden with every heartbeat. Nothing stirred in the long night, but morning came at last, on strands of pretty, amber light filtering through the Levolors.

What a strange, strange time, I thought. My father finally was allowed to forget, while I was forced to remember. As if there were not enough room in this world for both of us to carry that burden.

As always, in the breast pocket of my linen jacket I had a volume of his journals. This was the last one. #24. I caressed the flaky, soft leather in my hand as if it were an old dog I'd grown to love, and smelled the must rising from its pages as if it were steam from my mother's soup, fragrant and tempting, ripe with anticipation. I looked over at my father. He was still sleeping peacefully.

CHAPTER 30

From this point on, the chaos of battle overwhelmed him, and yet never in his life had he felt so free. He had run back to his post to find his men—Dovid, Ari, Pinchas, Lev—firing wildly at anything that moved. He cautioned them to conserve their ammunition and shoot only when they had a clear shot. The first wave came through the burned-out alfalfa, just as he had predicted—three tanks covering an infantry assault that moved slowly and relentlessly toward the perimeter. Some of his mines exploded, killing or maiming a few foot soldiers, but the tanks advanced steadily, firing directly at them, shredding their pathetic concrete bunker and leaving them exposed. Yet he experienced an almost divine sense of calm and a clarity of vision and mind such as he had only had in dreams. He could see every corner of the battlefield as if it were a painting he might be studying in a museum, noting every highlight and brushstroke. He felt no fear. Instantly he understood the battle was desperate, but his men could not have known he thought so. His leadership was easy and precise, and his demeanor tranquil and confident.

As the tanks progressed, Dovid cried out over the din of cannon and rifle fire, "Where's the goddamned PIAT?"

They stuck their heads up and saw Moskovitz crawling toward the barbed wire, pushing the PIAT before her. They immediately began to give her cover. Heshel yearned to be there with her, but he kept his post, firing with precision on anything that looked like it might endanger her. Finally, she set the rocket launcher on her shoulder and fired. She missed, cursing, pounding the earth with her fist.

"She needs help," he said.

Without a second thought, Dovid was over the side and running toward her. Heshel watched as Dovid slid down beside her, calming her with some witty remark. She laughed, in fact. Dovid! he thought, the happiest man on Earth! His heart pounded as the two of them now edged dangerously close to the forward-most tank. Dovid steadied the PIAT on Moskovitz's shoulder. Again she fired. This time there was a huge explosion and the tank erupted in flame. The terrified crew leapt out, screaming, their shirts blazing, their skin scorched black upon their arms and neck, with hairless scalps that continued to blister white and green as they ran. Dovid turned and waved triumphantly at Heshel, but Moskovitz covered her face in horror. In any case, their victory was short-lived. The tanks continued their lumbering, deadly advance, and behind them the Bren carriers rolled forward, spewing a relentless barrage of fire. Moments later the Arabs had cut through the barbed wire. Soon after that another threesome of tanks broke through from the north, and were headed straight into the center of the kibbutz. Post 7 had fallen. Post 6 had fallen as well. Heshel watched the blood-soaked survivors running, helter-skelter, towards the ruins of the Bet Am, falling over dead bodies, or being hit themselves and collapsing in a pile of their own exploded organs.

Suddenly, Ari was pulling at his sleeve. A runner had come up from the rear.

"The retreat has been ordered," he cried. "We've got to move back."

Heshel signaled wildly to Moskovitz and Dovid. Their joyful expressions gone, they were now desperately trying to adjust the firing mechanism—the PIAT had jammed. Dovid was beating it with his pistol, and Moskovitz, tears flowing in rage, was frantically pressing the spring back into its track. Heshel pulled himself out of the foxhole and rushed over to them.

"You two . . . get back. Retreat."

"But the tanks!" she cried.

"Don't worry," he told her, "we'll set up another perimeter."

He calmly handed Dovid one of his two German grenades, and told him to throw it at anything that came near them.

"As soon as you get to the trench line, I'll follow," he said.

He took her hand, to give her courage. Then he turned from them, and began firing at the Arab line.

But he was not really interested in killing anyone. He did not want to hurt the poor foot soldiers of the great Egyptian army or even blow up their tanks. He did not hate them, or even blame them for what they were doing. He knew they were filled with ideas that were not their own and that they were convinced of the rightness of a cause which had nothing to do with them. He knew that when they were victorious they would feel happy and powerful for once in their lives, pleased that they had followed orders so well and stood firm in the face of death. He knew this because he had been one of them and now he was no longer one of them. In the blindness and smoke of war, he could finally see for himself what mattered and what did not matter. They—the advancing armies with their bloodcurdling battle cries and their deafening cannon—were not in the slightest important to him. His drama was being played out on some other field, and now, at long last, he had had a glimpse of it.

From the back of his head he saw his beloved Fradl and Dovid disappear behind some rubble close to the trench. They would be safe. He reached for the remaining grenade on his belt. He did not want to waste it.

Running forward a few yards, priming it as he ran, he bent one knee, arched his back, and with a great circular motion, tossed the grenade at the nearest tank. It hit with a clunk, and didn't explode. He fell flat on his face, laughing. It was wonderfully, wonderfully poetic. Even in smallest detail, German technology had but one ambition: to kill Jews.

Then he got up and ran for his life.

=========

They rallied in a fortified trench near the ruins of the Bet Am. There were now only thirty-odd people, plus several dozen wounded. They had lost almost two-thirds of their number.

In a panic, Heshel realized that Moskovitz and Dovid were not there. No one had seen them. Well maybe someone had. There were some wounded down in the trenches, and maybe they were helping them. Someone else said no, they weren't there. Everyone was out of the trenches. All the wounded were here. Anyone who was not here was . . . he didn't need to finish the sentence.

The tanks had now broken in on all flanks and were rapidly advancing toward them. Some of the Jews still fired back. They tossed Molotov cocktails, threw stones, anything to keep the tanks at bay. In the meantime, Tuli, the Haganah commander, quickly laid it out for them. The only avenue of escape was through the Arab village, which did not seem possible. They could, on the other hand, make a last stand on a hill above the village—in the old, abandoned house that commanded the road below—but, he said, they could never get the wounded up there.

"But we can't leave the wounded alone," someone said.

Silence fell among them.

"No," someone else finally said, "we can't leave the wounded alone."

=========

But it wasn't really a question of making it to the abandoned house with or without the wounded. They were already surrounded. The injured desperately needed the attention of a doctor—the kibbutz doctor had been killed in the early morning. Ammunition was down to a few rounds per person. There were no grenades, no PIAT. The Bren had been knocked out hours ago. No one had had a sip of water since daybreak.

"The Egyptians fight well," someone remarked quietly, meaning, or at least hoping, that there might be no massacre if they surrendered.

Tuli called for a vote. Some wanted to make a run for it, take their chances among the villagers, or skirt the village somehow, through the wadi that ran along the eastern edge of the town, but no one had a plan that gave any hope of breaking through the enemy lines. A few others thought they might be able to fight on a little longer, but no one could say what the point of that would be. There had been no contact with headquarters for hours. There would be no reinforcements, no salvation.

Someone suggested suicide. Kill the wounded, then kill themselves.

But suddenly the Egyptian guns fell silent. The tanks stopped grinding their way up the hill, and the soldiers ceased their incessant battle cry. A voice, in thickly accented English, called out through a bullhorn: "He that walks in peace is blessèd of Allah! Put down your arms! Surrender and live!"

Light as air, made of nothing but sound, it pierced their hearts. Even the strongest, Avigdor, the sabra, began to weep. Without speaking, one of the women fashioned a white flag from a bloodied bedsheet and tied it to a wooden spoon.

Heshel Rosenheim stood up and peered over the sandbags.

The desolate land was stretched out before him, the broken buildings, the burned-out fields, the smoldering trees, the bodies of men and women scattered like grim confetti in colors of red, brown, and gray on the hardened, merciless sand. One of those could be his Moskovitz, he thought, another his Dovid. He suddenly understood how much time had passed, for the sun had moved far across the fine blue sky—why, it was late afternoon! He had flown through this day almost as if it had never happened—and it was the one day in which everything had happened. He saw that there was movement among the corpses—some were alive! Moskovitz could be alive. She was smart, she was swift. Perhaps she was hiding beneath some rock or slab of concrete or in some hole, or had escaped through the runoff canal down into the wadi, skirted the village, made her way to the next outpost, or was lying right in front of him, flat on her stomach, only pretending to be dead, waiting for him to come and get her, drag her back to safety, so that they could slip like earthworms through the enemy lines in the black of night, and make their way up the coastal highway to the fortified Tel Aviv, or she had dug a little tunnel for herself and made it all the way to the orange grove where she refreshed herself with fruit, then snaked her way from tree to tree, stump to stump, and out onto the dunes that led to the sea, where perhaps she had disguised herself as an Arab woman—she was dark, was she not? dark eyes, dark hair—and so perhaps she walked among the Egyptians exchanging pleasant glances, until she walked right through them and found a little village where they might feed and bathe her, comb her hair, take her silence for shock or infirmity, keep her safe until one night she might escape and find her way home. She could have done that, any of that, she could be lying under a dead cow, or under the boards of the fallen watchtower, she could be holding Dovid in her arms, soothing him, pressing his wounds closed with her strong hands, whispering to him, Courage! Courage! *and he would be smiling back, saying,* No, I am the happiest man on Earth!

"I see them out there," he suddenly said. "Moskovitz! I see you! Dovid! I see you! There they are. I can't leave them there, can I? What would we be," he cried, "if we left them there?"

Out of the corner of his eye he saw Tuli rushing up to restrain him, but he cocked his gun and ran out into the face of the Egyptian army.

CHAPTER 31

When he awoke he was lost in whiteness. Sunlight washed over him in one great wave, too bright for his eyes. A woman was near him, also in white, but dark eyes, dark hair, and the scent of dried flowers. "Fradl," he said. And then he went dark again.

=========

But the one in the next cot over turned out to be Avigdor.

"We're in Cairo," he explained, rather jovially.

"Very funny."

"No, we are. We're prisoners. This is the prison hospital.

Actually it's not a prison. It's the general hospital. They're treating us quite well, as a matter of fact."

"We were captured?"

"We surrendered."

"I didn't surrender."

"You did."

It was like this, he told him. Tuli had shot him. Yes! You were running out like a crazy man, mumbling, screaming. He meant to shoot you in the leg, but in the commotion shot you in the chest. He was very upset about it. But after all, was he supposed to sacrifice all of us because you had lost your head? They would have shelled us to pieces. Anyway, he shot you. You went down hard, and we thought you were dead. But we had to act quickly, I guess, and Tuli ran out with the flag, the white flag on the spoon. It was kind of humorous in a way, in retrospect. But at the time we didn't know if they would shoot him or not. He walked out there with a sheet tied to a spoon. They could have mowed him down. We were all concentrated on that. We'd forgotten about you, to be honest. An officer came forward to meet him. They exchanged words, and they seemed to be arguing, which scared the hell out of us, but then Tuli waved, and one by one we each came out, laying down our guns so they could see them. Then someone, I think it was Tamara, you know, the cook, she said "Hey! He's alive." She meant you. So we dragged you out with us.

Avigdor shrugged, "And now we're all here." He was referring not to the hospital but the prison compound, which, he explained, was basically an army barracks. "Nothing terrible," he said. "In the meantime, there's a cease-fire. They never made it to Tel Aviv. We stopped them!"

Heshel laughed. "A prisoner of war?"

"Yeah," said Avigdor, "the war is over for us."

==========

Heshel studied the ceiling, which was cracked in many places and thick with a long history of paint. He had finally made it to Egypt. He was finally out of the mess he'd gotten himself into. His plan had worked in spite of everything.

The sun was warm, and the windows were open, letting in the flies. A radio was playing Arabic music, and down in the kitchen dinner was being prepared and the aroma of cumin seeped up through the floorboards. It was a large ward with many beds, and families were visiting their sick, so the air was filled with chatter. It was lovely, actually.

Obviously, they weren't worried about anyone escaping. The two guards near the doors were playing an amiable game of cribbage and smoking cigarettes, and the nurse was sitting at her desk writing reports, content to let the day pass without her assistance. Heshel's head was beginning to clear, and he was beginning to remember—the battle, and before that the confrontation with Levin, and before that laying the mines, and before that the drive through the desert, the days in the watchtower, the evening in the orange grove, the revelation of her kisses, and before all that, the trip across the sea, the D.P. camp, the British soldier offering him Spam . . . all the way back he flew, and all the way forward.

Her voice came to him now, and the scent of her skin. And then, as if a film were projected onto the ceiling, he saw her pounding the dirt when the PIAT wouldn't fire, and running with Dovid toward the safety of the trench. What had happened then? The screen went blank. Yet perhaps he had seen something. Perhaps out of the corner of his eye, those eyes which had been so unearthly clear-sighted—but nothing came to him.

There was a pitcher of water nearby. He tried to pour himself a glass, but found he could move only with great difficulty. His chest was bandaged all around, and when he twisted his torso he cried out in pain. The nurse and guards looked up. She said something that Heshel could not understand, and she left the ward.

"I'll help you, Yekkeh," said Avigdor. "I'm only in with a little dysentery."

Heshel looked at him. "What happened to Moskovitz?"

"Who?" he said.

"Yael."

"Ah," said Avigdor, "Yael."

=========

Avigdor poured the water into the glass and set the pitcher down with care. He was a large man with large hands and a boisterous disposition, and it was difficult for him to be delicate. He laid himself down on his cot and cradled his head in his arms, thinking how to begin.

"After the surrender," he said quietly, "a few of the Jewish commanders—Tuli, Gabriel, maybe someone else—were allowed to walk through the battlefield and count our dead and collect our wounded. Already the Arab villagers, or some of them, anyway, were scavenging whatever they could get their hands on—you know, pulling clothes off corpses, wedding rings, shoes—whatever they could steal. Someone ran off with our sewing machine. They took the typewriter. The milk pails. The kids' pencil boxes. Anything. Everything. We saw them floating parts of the piano down the drainage canal. And they were whooping and singing and having a good time. We couldn't understand it. They were our friends. I tell you this not to upset you, but because it's what happened. The Egyptian officer told

Tuli he regretted this, but what could he do? That's what he said, anyway. What can I do? So Tuli and the officer walked through that graveyard as these vultures picked at our dead—and there were many dead, Heshel, many. I can't help but get very emotional, I'm sorry, I'm sorry I'm crying, but when I think of our heroes, when I think of Lev and Shlomo and Dodi . . . I knew them all my life, some of them. You and your friends were new, since the war, so you can't understand. Or maybe you can, I don't know. Not that we didn't love you, too. For sure we did. When we called you Yekkeh, the German, it was with affection. I hope you know that."

"I know that," said Heshel. "But tell me about Moskovitz."

"I can only tell you what Tuli saw. It was not very far from Post 5. They had been trapped between some debris and the trench, got caught out in the open. During the worst part of the battle, I guess. It looked like your soldier—I don't remember his name, the Frenchman—Dovid, right?—Dovid—he must have been hit first, because . . . well, because she was cradling him in her arms, on her lap. He was dead, though apparently she didn't know he was dead because she was crying for them to help him. They came up to her—Tuli and the Egyptian officer. But don't jump to conclusions, because, because . . ." He sighed deeply. "Well, as soon as he saw her, he knew it was bad, really bad. These things are so hard to talk about. But here it is. Her belly had been ripped open. Her guts were pouring out on the ground beside her—it was obvious, it was obvious what happened—she had stayed with the Frenchman to help him. She could have run for it, but she didn't. She was going to help him, you know, to hang on, and maybe she thought that when the shooting stopped she'd pull him to safety or something, or maybe she'd just surrender so he could get some help—I don't know what was in her mind. Heshel, she was gutted like a fish. Her insides

were all on the ground beside her. Tuli begged the Egyptian officer for a doctor, but the guy told him she was too far gone and he had too many of his own wounded, but Tuli made him promise, made him promise to bring a stretcher and take her to the field hospital, but the officer said to him, 'Maybe you should shoot her.' But Tuli said back to him, 'You did this! You shoot her!' but neither of them could do it. Tuli said she was beautiful then, like an angel—her face, radiant like a bride, he said. I don't know what he meant by that, she must have looked terrible, but that's how he described it. Anyway, he tried to calm her, but all she said was, 'Take care of Dovid first.' So the Egyptian promised he'd send the stretcher. Tuli said he made him promise twice. And then they left her there, to find more wounded, and count more dead."

"But then she's alive!" he cried.

Avigdor shook his head. "I don't think so. She didn't make it here with us. We haven't heard a word about her." He paused and said with great difficulty, "And there were stories."

"What stories?"

"In the Arab village. The one we thought of as our friends."

"What about them?"

"They cut off heads, put them on poles. Two heads. Ran around all night celebrating, then threw them to the dogs. One of the heads . . . was a woman."

"It can't be."

"It's only a story, I don't know."

"It can't be," he said again.

Avigdor closed his eyes and said no more.

=========

None of this seemed possible. He'd seen them so close to the trench. They were inches from safety. Up on the ceiling above his bed he could see them all three huddled together, then he watched as they'd left him, saw them scurrying up the field toward the trench, slipping beneath some blown-out concrete. Then he had turned to throw his grenade.

And then he knew what had happened.

=========

"They weren't shot," he said. "And she wasn't bayoneted, if that's what you think. It wasn't a mortar either."

"Sure it was. Or she was stabbed and gutted."

"No," he said. " No *one was that near them."*

"What then?"

"Grenade," he said.

=========

He understood it all now.

He understood why he had been granted such clarity of vision. Why every nuance of the field was at his command. Why he had become so fearless and reckless and full of hope. Why he was allowed his one moment of supreme happiness.

No, *she had not stayed behind to save* Dovid. *She was killed with him, by the same explosion. The* German *grenade had misfired.* He *had seen that kind of wound before, it was so common it even happened in training.* And *yes, somewhere in the back of his head, he had heard it go off, hadn't he?* He *must have.* And *one of his secret eyes must have seen* Dovid's *arms fly from his body like rockets, spewing fuel of blood, and his other eye must have seen* Moskovitz *thrown into the air, her stomach splitting open like a tin can, terror and surprise on her face.* He *had given them the instrument of their own deaths.* He *must have known what would happen. Had to know. Killer of Jews. Heinrich Mueller, SS-Obersturmführer.*

Now he understood the meaning of divine retribution. Even if there were no God, now, for him, there was. A God that would never set him free. Never undo what had been done. Never absolve him of his crimes.

It had been the grenade.

=========

Avigdor watched him. After a while he took a deep breath and spoke again.

"There is something else I should probably tell you."

Heshel lay still as a stone.

"She was pregnant," he said. "They could see the child."

Wincing in pain, the wounded man turned on his side so that Avigdor could not see his face.

"Six months pregnant at least. She was hiding it. Can you imagine? If anyone had known," he added, "she would never have been allowed to stay."

=========

In a little while the nurse came strutting down the floor, followed by the doctor, a small man wearing a fez and a vested tweed suit. He had a jolly smile, and spoke a beautiful, richly textured English.

"Ah," the doctor said pleasantly, "he seems to be awake!"

He picked up the charts.

"Heshel Rosenheim . . . is that right?"

Heshel looked at him.

"Your name? Do we have it correctly? Heshel Rosenheim?"

When the prisoner did not respond, the nurse eyed the doctor with concern and said something to him in Arabic. He shrugged and then bent down and spoke directly into his patient's ear, as if he might have lost his hearing, perhaps due to shell shock.

"Your name. What is it? Who are you? Can you hear me? Who exactly are you?"

"My name? Who am I?" he said in Hebrew.

"What is he saying?" asked the doctor.

This time it was the nurse's turn to shrug.

The man in the bed stared past the doctor, up to the white-painted ceiling. He tried to see what he had seen before—the movie of his life—he tried to see his boyhood days in Berlin, his mother and his father, he tried to smell the mothballs of his mother's cedar chest, or taste the schnitzel she prepared on Thursdays, he tried to feel the comfort of sitting at his father's knee, studying his grammar and listening to his father's stories in French and Italian, he tried to see himself in his new SS uniform, and feel the oil that he used on his dagger as he rubbed it between his fingers, and he tried to see himself sitting in his dark office with his precious accounting books, ordering the little men in striped suits to do his bidding, he tried to feel the pleasure of that, he tried to see the long march back to Bergen-Belsen, and the last days of starvation and fear, and how he hid among the corpses and how he avoided the lice and how he carved the numbers in his flesh and how he fooled the British and how he laughed when the starving Jews died from eating too much too soon, and how he fooled the Jews in their D.P. camp and how he slogged onto the shores of this strange land, and how he plotted his escape and how he was ambushed by the Arabs who he thought could save him, and how he came to be a soldier in the army of his enemy, and how he fell in love with the woman of a hated race, and how he fathered a child who would never know its father, and how he was shot by his own captain at the very moment he had grasped his own salvation—but none of it came to him. All he saw was the blank, white, broken plaster of the bare ceiling, bright with nothing.

He looked at the doctor. Finally, he could be anyone he wanted to be.

"My name is Heshel Rosenheim," he said.

CHAPTER 32

I was startled when I heard him cry out.

He was looking straight ahead, as if someone were standing at the foot of his bed.

He reached out his hand. "Please!" He was speaking in some mix of Yiddish and German, his voice almost inaudible, shattered, like glass. "Come closer so I can see you."

Even though he wasn't speaking to me, it was I who came closer.

"Dad," I said, touching his shoulder gently.

He suddenly looked at me as if waking from a dream.

"Your brother was just here," he announced.

"I don't have a brother," I said.

"Oh no, that's right, you don't."

"Do you know who I am?"

"No," he said simply.

"I'm Michael," I said. "I'm your son." When there was no response, I asked him, "Do you remember your name?"

"My name?" He thought for a while. "No," he finally admitted. He began to cry. "Isn't that awful? I can't remember my name. Can you tell me?"

But before I could answer, his eyes lit up. He suddenly seemed to recognize me. "Israel! You've come! You've come!"

"I'm not Israel, Dad. I'm Michael. I don't even know anyone named Israel."

"Don't lie," he said, stroking my hand. "It's all right. You don't have to hide from me anymore."

"Who is Israel?" I said.

"Who is Israel? What a question!" He tried to squeeze my hand, but all his strength had finally abandoned him. And yet somehow he found the strength to smile. "After all this time! Have you read everything?"

"Yes, I think so. I think I've read the whole thing."

"Then you understand?"

"I'm trying," I said honestly.

His words were like falling leaves slowly drifting down, long spaces in between, alighting almost in silence upon my ears.

"Do you see I meant him no harm, your father?" he said. "Do you see that I didn't know then . . . who I really was, or who he was? How could I see? I had no eyes. It was only later I was given eyes. But I did everything I could to make it up to you, didn't I? Didn't I? I knew I could never make it up to you. But what can a man do? Only what is allowed him, and no more. Such is the mercy of God! The money I gave you, the clothing, the education, all of it is nothing. I know. I know. Oh my boy! Every single thing I did with every moment of my life was for you, and I know that it was nothing, nothing, nothing. . . ."

He clutched my hand.

"Israel!" he begged, his gluey eyes filling with tears, "I only ask one thing. Say me Kaddish." He meant the prayer for the dead, the prayer of remembrance, that only a son can say for a father, only a father for his son. "Please! Please!" he went on feverishly. "Say me Kaddish!"

"Daddy," I said to him. "It's Michael."

"Michael?"

"Michael. Your son."

"Who?"

He closed his eyes, sank back, darkness seemed to spread over him.

"Dad!" I cried. "Don't go!"

Suddenly he shot straight up in bed.

"Forgive me!" he wailed. "God in heaven, forgive me!"

And then he fell back like a stone.

He let out one long, hoarse exhalation—one could not call it a breath—and then there was no sound at all.

I stared down at his body. His arm, disfigured by the concentration camp tattoo, was splayed out over the side of the bed as if his last wish were to keep it as far from him as possible. I studied the grim numbers that had become the algebra of both our lives. I saw the endless procession of locomotives depositing their freight of human suffering—day after day, night after night—into the gates of Majdanek, Auschwitz, Treblinka, Sobibor, Ravensbrück. I imagined the little bookkeeper in his grim little office, his account books opened upon his well-organized desk, the pen in his hand, the ink stains on his fingers, as he counted the eyeglasses and shoes, the gold fillings and braids of human hair.

And yet I stood there amazed. In spite of every horror, every cruelty, every act of despair, when I looked upon his face I could not help but see light, and, as when I had read the words of his journal, I could not help but feel hope, like an ice pick to my frozen heart.

Yet I found it so hard to believe any of it really happened. How could a person change from one thing to its direct opposite, as if becoming someone else is as easy as changing your tie? And yet, what if it were true? What if he had been in the SS and on kibbutz and served in the Palmach and was a hero of the War of Independence and through pain and loss finally achieved some sort of capacity for love?

I remembered how once he tried to explain to me the meaning of repentance. I was playing with the fringes of his long, elegant tallis. He smiled down at me.

"In Hebrew," he said, "it means *turning*. Better, it means *re*-turning. It means to come back, Mikey, to come back to your *true* self." And then he laughed and pinched my nose. "And what could be easier than that?"

"So why do we have to do it every year?" I asked him.

"Because, my dear little one, there is no one true self. And that is why repentance can never end."

I'm not saying he was saved. I'm not saying any of us can be saved, or that in the celestial balance all those commemorative plaques, all those rescued orphans, all those wildly extravagant donations would outweigh a single death in the gas chambers of Majdanek. But when I consider the things he had done in the second half of his life, what acts of mercy he showed the world, even if no mercy was shown him, and what joys he must have felt, just to have my mother, my sister, and me—three people to love!—even if they could never love him for the person he actually was—Oh! I thought—in atonement—what power!

But forgiveness?

Only when he met the ghosts of those who perished under the

weight of his ledgers could he be absolved, and only if they saw fit. And surely, surely they would. For tempered by the gas and the crematoria, the starvation, humiliation, pain and filth, they would surely have become angels. What else was left to them? Forged in such a crucible of unimaginable suffering, how could they bear the suffering of even a single molecule of God's creation, let alone a whole man? They could be his judges.

He had called out for Israel. Israel! Let Israel be his judge!

And then suddenly I understood.

Who was it who asked Kaufman for the Memorial Book of Durnik? Who was it who brought my father the Cheez Whiz box of journals from wherever it was long hidden? Who was it who visited him in secret, long into the night? And why was my father the one who saved April from the orphanage or the D.P. camp or wherever she was? Why would he be the one who knew how to find children? Why would he be the one to search them out himself? What was he after?

There could only be one conclusion: there had been a child.

Not Moskovitz's child, but Heshel Rosenheim's child. The real Heshel Rosenheim, the Jewish Heshel Rosenheim, the one in the lice-infested uniform and torturous wooden shoes. And the name of that child was Israel.

Perhaps he had been secretly born in the camps and hidden from the guards, or perhaps he was born in the time before the Nazi roundups and saved by some kindly Lithuanian peasant. Perhaps they had once spoken of it. . . .

"Just tell me about your little Jewish life!"

"But about what? About what in particular?"

"Just talk! Is that too hard for you? Should I find someone else?"

"No, no! I'm happy to talk."

Or, overcome with guilt, my father had scoured the records for any shred of evidence, any hint of a life before, during, after . . . sought out a survivor, a relative, a friend . . . and found that, God be praised! there *was* someone—a child. And he must have been searching for him all those years, bringing child after child back to America—as he had April—hoping that one day, one of these children would be Heshel Rosenheim's. Heshel Rosenheim's Israel.

And perhaps—perhaps he had found him. Yes! And then he secretly sent him money, clothing, paid for his school. Perhaps he brought him to New Jersey and settled him with some family and quietly watched over him as he grew. Yes, this was the Rosenheim who wrote to Kaufman. Israel Rosenheim! He had finally figured it all out and decided to expose my father—of course! of course!—but then—then—he read the journals. Just like me. He read the journals and relented. His heart cracked open, his anger slid away, he allowed himself to hope, and then he decided to offer this hope to me. And why to me? So that I might stand by my father when he could not. So that I might say the Kaddish that he could not.

It was not likely I would ever meet him. It was not likely that I would ever be sure of his existence. (For who could prove that it was not my father who wrote to Kaufman, produced the Cheez Whiz box, and visited himself each night, to comfort himself with the dream of forgiveness.) But of Israel Rosenheim's power I was certain.

The man in the bed beside my chair may have been a monster, a criminal, a fugitive. And yet, as I looked upon his pale, distorted face, emaciated beyond recognition and only barely human, I wept tears of love. I knew I was not alone in this. I knew that Israel Rosenheim felt as I felt. I knew that the entire Jewish community felt as I felt. They would soon come out to honor him. They would sing eulogies of praise to him. His name would be in the papers, not just here in West Palm Beach County, but in Miami, and in New York, and in New Jersey, and even, without a doubt, in Israel, where he would be honored in the Holocaust Memorial for his good works. His would be an example of the exemplary life, and the blessings of his deeds would live on for generations.

No, I would not be his judge. I would be his son.

I bent down and kissed his hand.

CHAPTER 33

It was with great trepidation that I stepped out of the car.

People were streaming by me. They were mostly old people, groups of women, couples, a few men by themselves. They moved slowly, as old people do, but with expectation, as if something great were about to happen to them. Interspersed among them were a few younger families, the women holding their daughters' hands, the men their sons'. They marched across the asphalt as if drawn by some call, a sound I could not hear. Even in the open air I could smell the mixed multitude of perfumes and colognes rising like an offering of incense, sweet and pungent, familiar and suffocating. They laughed and chatted, gesticulated broadly, stopped occasionally to tie a shoe or make sure they had their eyeglasses, then rejoined the stream as easily as water rejoins water.

I stood behind my open car door and watched them. In my right hand was my father's tallis bag. In my breast pocket his little prayer book.

I had spent the rest of that morning signing papers. Not many really. Dad had long ago made all his own arrangements, paid for everything, and left complete instructions about the funeral, including the plain pine coffin, the small graveside ceremony, and no viewing. He was to be interred next to Mom. He even preordered a stone. The thought of them sweltering forever beneath the relentless Florida sun made me uneasy, and I thought briefly about taking them back with me to California or returning them to New Jersey and burying them next to poor Karen. I was quite certain I didn't want to come back here again, and I thought, when will I ever visit them? But then again, when did I ever visit Karen? The answer was never. I had never visited Karen. Ever. Not once.

I now knew that I would have to do that. I would have to look her grave in the face, so to speak. It was a sobering thought.

All this occurred to me as I was sitting there filling out those papers. I also realized that I had never in my life been to a funeral. Yes. I had not been to Karen's funeral. That had proved impossible for me. And I had not been to my mother's funeral either, though I was less certain why.

I had always told myself that I didn't go to Karen's because I was taking final exams—as if you couldn't get your exams delayed if your sister just died—but that is exactly what I had been telling myself for years, and that's even how I actually remembered it—pounding out those exams, tears flowing from my eyes. But there were no exams that day or even that week. I had been hiding in my dorm room, sleeping. I slept for several days, maybe longer. I roused myself only to stumble to the bathroom or to take a drink of water or stuff some Cheerios in my mouth. Then I'd fall back into a stupor. When my mother died, it was the same.

Only that time, I was on the road and I told my father I couldn't break my engagements, they'd sue me. But I did break my engagements, and stayed in my motel room watching television and drinking beer and tequila and ordering in pizza and Chinese food, until Ella, on her way back from the funeral, found me and dragged me home. I also recalled that when I told my father that I would not be coming to Mom's funeral, he did not even berate me. Maybe he despised me then, or maybe he pitied me, or maybe he just loved me.

I remembered all this while I was signing papers and watching the morticians slide my father's body onto their gurney. They lifted him together with the sheet and slid him off. He hit the gurney like a bag of cement, banging his head on the stainless steel frame. I winced. He, of course, did not.

I watched them wheel him out. At least they had not put him in a body bag. They had a special exit in the rear, to keep him out of sight of the other patients. It was in the dark space, at the end of the hall. I thought that was a good idea. So they quietly wheeled him away and when they reached the end of the hall, I understood it was the last time I would see him. I couldn't help myself. I waved good-bye.

For all that I had learned, with all my clues and evidence, all my questions and reading, I still was certain of very little. I would never know with absolute certainty if the iconography of my youth—those six blue-black numbers on my father's arm—had been burned into his skin by torturers, or cut into it by his own tortured hand—but I did know this: those numbers were the very equation of our lives, yet they added up to nothing, explained nothing, and never would, and now their mystery had doubled, tripled, quadrupled, expanded in an exponential curve out into infinite space, where they would hover over every deed and every thought and every step I would ever take.

I signed the papers they put in front of me. I nodded when the morticians told me what my father had decided upon. I shook my head when they asked me if I wanted to change anything, if I wanted a nicer casket, or a viewing, or a ceremony inside their beautiful air-conditioned chapel. They told me they would deliver the little benches for sitting shivah, and the laminated cards with the prayers on them, and they suggested a good caterer I might call, and they handed me a little box filled with funeral announcements that I could fill out "when I was feeling a little better," and a glossy how-to kit to help me through this troubled time (how to write an obituary, how to tell family and friends, how to contact a rabbi of one's preferred denomination), and finally they told me that the burial could not happen till after Yom Kippur, for religious reasons, but not to worry because it would still be within three days of his passing, as they put it, so it would be kosher. Then they shook my hand and went away. I looked at the hospice nurse who had been called in earlier in the day. She smiled sympathetically and told me it was time to go home.

I passed Nurse Clara at her station. I knew it would also be the last time I would ever see her. That struck me as somehow poignant.

Suddenly she hugged me.

"You be good, now!" she said.

Driving down the same roads my father used to drive, in the same car, sitting in the same overpadded seat, listening to the same stupid radio station—he always wanted big band, I always changed it to classical—I found myself slinking down as low as I could so my head was barely visible above his fuzzy-covered steering wheel. I wanted to know what it felt like to be him, but all I noticed was that I couldn't see over the steering wheel.

I pulled into a gas station and threw away the hypo. Actually I squeezed it out into the toilet, and bent the needle till it snapped. Walking back to the car, I felt that familiar heaviness against my chest—his journal in my breast pocket, the final volume that I had finished reading just moments before he died. The story had abruptly ended with the words "My name is Heshel Rosenheim." No mention of how he got to America, how he met my mother, how his past tied to my past. If he had just connected his story to my story, to the world I had known, to my mother, my sister, me, the house in New Jersey, the wallpaper store, anything—I might have been able to make more sense of it. I might have been able to break through the *secret*—

With a sigh, I tossed it onto the car seat.

Just then, a bit of yellow paper, tightly folded and neatly creased, slipped out from between its pages. It must have been stuck to the back cover, and the force of my throw dislodged it. Stained with little spots of mold, and brittle as old newspaper, bits of it fell off in my hand as I unfolded it. I was surprised to see it was in English, written hastily, and with an unsteady hand, as if the police were about to knock down the door.

My Darling Dear Michael,
It is not likely you will see these notebooks while I am living. Only if I should be suddenly crazy, or if someone else gets hold of them, or if for some reason you really need to see them, if they will somehow help you at a desperate hour in your own life, then maybe.

The man in this story could not erase the past. He did not want to erase it. He did not want to forget it. How could he forget it? He wanted merely to transform the past into something else. He wanted to turn the shadow into light. He wanted to believe that some part of him was still good and life-giving. He did not ask to be forgiven, nor did he seek punishment. He sought redemption.

The man in this story made a choice. He chose, as we Jews love to say, Life.

God might continue to torment him—as God had every right to do—but what was required of this man was to simply live his choice. What else could he do?

As for me, I, too, thought all was lost. I thought no help would come, and all would remain in darkness. But one day something happened. It was the day you were born. On that day, I held you in my arms and I knew there was holiness in this world. I looked at your face and saw for the first time the face of Mercy.

Now I must stop my writing. Enough is enough. But I praise God that you are my son, and my love for you is eternal and full of gratitude.

I pray that when it is time for you to make your choice, you too can recall the past, and embrace the future.

Your loving father,

Heshel Rosenheim

I sat in the car a long time, holding the letter in my hands, and reading it over again and again.

I got home close to four. There was a note on the door from April. It was a condolence card. How she knew he was dead, I didn't know, but I'd stopped asking such questions. I went in and collapsed on the sofa, exhausted.

Voices outside my door awakened me.

"Jonathan! Jonathan! Are you there? It's Rose Gitlin! Time to go!" Her voice was as warm as honey, not the slightest impatient or upset. "Are you in there, sweetie?" she called. "Listen, we have to go. But if you change your mind, we'll wait downstairs a few minutes. And if not, we'll save a seat for you."

"This is Harry," another voice said, "the husband. If you're late, no big deal. Just come!"

I heard their footsteps move away, and then I heard one of them shuffle back.

"We're all thinking of you," Rose Gitlin called through the closed door.

And then she ran off to join the others.

I sat alone in my father's apartment thinking. Around me were piles of loss, missed opportunity, lies, secrets, resentments, and also smiles, pleasures, joys, a whole history of a family that was no more.

Finally I got up and stood in front of my wall. All the items I had so carefully posted did, in fact, tell a story, but not the whole story. They could never penetrate to the core. I reached for the map of Berlin. I took it down and folded it up. Then I reached for the pictures of German soldiers cut from magazines, and then the wedding invitation, the photo of my grandparents, the train ticket marked GvH. As I was setting them down, I noticed one item lying on the floor that I had never gotten around to putting up—my mother's straw hat, the very one that had floated across the surface of the swimming pool the day she collapsed playing mahjongg. Kept all these years in the dark of the closet shelf, the creamy orange straw was bright and cheerful, as was the floral band and floppy brim. It even still smelled of suntan lotion. Without thinking, I put in on my head. Instantly I realized I had found the final clue. I reached for a Post-it. On it I wrote: *She knew.*

I returned in my mind to the scene of the German argument, as it came to be known in our house. My father had just stormed from the room, the dishes rattling on the table and the screen door slamming behind him. His volume of the *International Military Tribunal at Nuremberg* was still sitting like a mammoth hunk of bad cheese right in front of my nose.

"That wasn't nice," my mother had said to me about my behavior toward my father. I had told him German was just a language, and that obviously he was still reading it, too, and there was no harm in it, and then he called me a Nazi.

"Well, he wasn't nice to me, either," I told her.

"He's your father," she said. And it seemed like that was the end of the matter. But now as I stood there with my mother's Creamsicle-colored bonnet on my head, I recalled how she had walked around the table, and hands trembling—those delicate nurse's hands that were always so stoic and fearless when we had gashes on our heads or blood pouring from our knees—with those hands now in a vortex of trembling, she hefted the huge volume to her breast, and swayed side to side, almost as if praying. Tears welled up in her eyes.

Perhaps at the time I told myself she was just upset that we had argued, but I knew even then that these were not those kinds of tears. Finally she ran into the bedroom and put the book away in some secret place. And that is what I now understood was the key, remembering it as if for the first time. For I never saw that book, or any of its other twenty-three volumes, again. Nor, I now realized, had I ever actually seen them before. No. I assumed I had, but I hadn't. They had never been out on the shelves. They were held in a private, secret place. And my mother knew exactly where.

"He's your father," she said again when she returned to the dining room. She seemed to be herself once more.

But her hands were red, as if from wringing. And around the edge of her wedding band was a deep purple line, as if she had ground it into her skin over and over and over again.

=

I stood there with my mother's hat on my head. There was yet another story. My mother's story. A young girl's story, a young wife's. A love story.

I recalled that there was a storage locker in the basement. I found her ancient vanity case at the bottom of a pile of junk—an aluminum ice chest, stacks of magazines, dusty folding chairs, wooden tennis rackets. The case was made of cardboard, upholstered in pretty fabric with a bone handle and a little brass latch. When opened, the mirror dangled sadly from the lid on a few dabs of dried glue. For her sake, I pressed it back in place. But my attention was soon drawn to several tightly bound stacks of letters tied with faded ribbon. They were all still in their slit envelopes and addressed to my mother in my father's tight, precise script. But as I fanned through them, I came across one that was in another hand. It had no stamp on it and had never been mailed. In fact, it was still sealed. I examined it in the dim light of the single lightbulb that hung from the storage room ceiling on a long, shredded cord. I brought the letter to my nose—it smelled of basement, but also of the last, mauve vestiges of Shalimar, my mother's scent, the scent that idled behind her as she passed in her evening dress and filled my head with dreams whenever I entered her closet to fetch her a scarf from the top shelf. Holding the letter in my hand, I saw my mother as a young woman who wore Shalimar not merely on special occasions, but every evening, for her own pleasure, as she sat at her desk or upon her bed, reading love letters from my father, and writing one she never mailed. A letter addressed simply to "Heshel."

Heshel:
The days, the weeks, are all darkness, and my heart can stand no more. When you left, I tried to wash you off me. I bathed, and

bathed again, because the very thought of your touch repulsed me. I had to wash all my clothes. I burned our photographs. I burned the wedding dress. I burned the garter and the stockings and the nightgown. I burned them all in the fireplace, and then I ran out of that apartment to go home to Mama and Papa. I ran out of there and I stood on the street in front of the apartment. It was daylight already, and the super was there sweeping, and he said, Good morning, Mrs. Rosenheim, and I cannot tell you how my heart stopped in my chest and how horrified I was to hear those words, the very first time anyone called me that. Do you know how I had dreamt of it? How I practiced hearing it, and like a stupid little girl sang it to myself and (so stupid!) with Hilda and Betty—Mrs. Rosenheim, Mrs. Rosenheim—*but when I heard the super say it, I had to hold my stomach, I was so sick. But then I realized I couldn't go to my parents' because I knew I just couldn't tell them. So I stood there on the street and Mr. Devivo looked at me like I was crazy. I ran back into the building and ran up the stairs, and I didn't even wait for the elevator. Oh yes, I started crying again, even though I had been crying all night.*

I thought about Papa, because Papa never liked you. He said you drank too much. He pointed to the bottle of schnapps on the buffet and said he had that bottle four years. And now it was empty. He said he didn't like a man who felt sorry for himself. And I hated him for this! I told him he was ignorant and unfeeling. I told him how much you had been through and how people don't just heal overnight. I even screamed at him. I screamed at my own father for you.

Anyway, I stayed in the apartment as long as I could stand it. I didn't eat anything all day. I thought I should call the FBI. I thought about calling Senator McCarthy. I would call Washington and ask for the Un-American Committee or whatever they call it. I did not know how to do that. Do you call the operator and ask for the Un-American Committee? I was glad we don't have a phone, because I knew I'd never go downstairs to Mrs. Warshaw. I could just see myself calling the FBI to report my own husband while she's standing there counting the minutes. But I had to do something. So I decided to go down to the pay phone on Milford Avenue. There was Mr. Devivo again with his Hello, Mrs. Rosenheim! I must have been pale as a ghost. He asked me if everything was copasetic. Copasetic! I said, Sure! I smiled at him. Can you imagine? Before this I always thought you could know what a person was feeling by their face. Now I see how secret life really is.

I went down to Milford Avenue, but my hands were shaking like a leaf, and the change kept slipping from my fingers, and I couldn't even find the slot. I put the nickel in the dime slot and it got stuck and I had a hard time getting it out. I finally got the operator, but when she said what number please I just couldn't. I couldn't say FBI. I just couldn't do it. I just hung up and there were some kids waiting for the phone and they said, Lady are you done? So I took off. I ran down Springfield Avenue and then up Avon Avenue and I think I was on Clinton Place when I realized I was due at the hospital in half an hour. I was so confused I got on a bus and went to work. It was probably a good thing. I was so busy I couldn't think about anything except what was right in front of me.

Anyway, I got off at about 5:30 in the morning, and I went for coffee over at Toddle House and I don't know why I just walked past and found myself standing in front of a little synagogue, a shul. It must have been 7 A.M. *already. I just wanted to sit there and think. It was Orthodox, and I could hear the men finishing up the morning prayers. They were mostly old, and I don't think they saw me. I tiptoed around to the women's side and found a seat right near the partition—it was like a lattice made of brass—and I sat down. I guess I fell asleep. I'd been up already for twenty-four hours at least, probably more. And when I opened my eyes the men were already done with their prayers, and they were folding up their prayer shawls and unwrapping the tefillin from their arms and putting them in their little bags.*

But there was one man, sitting on the bench in the corner. He was still wrapped in his tallis and his tefillin, and his book was still in his hands, and he was still davening, weaving the way they do, back and forth, right and left, left and right, and he just wouldn't stop. Even though he was speaking so very softly, you could make out that he was actually trying to say every word, and also that he really didn't know the words very well at all. I tiptoed toward him and from behind the partition I watched him. I was as close to him as I am now to the paper I am writing this on, but to him I was invisible. I don't even know why I cared so much to watch him, but I couldn't help myself. I just did what I did.

I watched him and listened. He prayed from the book, and as I said, he pronounced every word, every blessing, with the utmost precision, but whispering it as if he were speaking directly into God's ear. When he said "Adonai, Lord God," he bowed his knees and lowered his head, and his body quivered under his tallis. I thought this was very beautiful for some reason. The others had sped through their prayers, had skipped over the words, maybe didn't even know what they were saying half of the time, and they were very happy with themselves. But this one remained in his place and said every syllable and struggled through every sentence because he didn't know it by heart. Some people would say he was calling attention to himself, but I was drawn to him anyway. So I stayed and watched him.

Finally, though, one of the old men came up to him, and I heard him say, "It's time to go. Come back tomorrow. One day at a time—you'll see—God will be here tomorrow too!" That's the way they talk, isn't it?

So this one, the one still praying, stood up, and even standing he was all bent over like an old man, even though he obviously wasn't—and with great sadness he removed the tallis from over his head so that I could see his face at last, and he folded it and placed it over the back of the bench, because it wasn't his—it was one of those you can borrow if you don't have one, one of those for the stranger, or the boys who forget theirs.

All I could do was stare at you in wonder. I thought I would scream. It was you! But being silent then was the most important thing in my whole life, and I knew it. So somehow I kept it down, somehow nothing came out, not even a peep. Secretly, I made myself inch closer until I could smell your skin and feel your breath. I had to be sure it was you.

The old man patted you on the back and began making his way up the aisle. You waved at him. And then, when he was gone, and you were all alone in the synagogue, you picked up your tallis and draped it over your head again, and began to pray some more. I watched you pray until every word was spoken, and every prayer was prayed. And when you finally were done, you said not another word. You just turned and walked out, as if you did this every day.

I left that place and I went home. I slept for the first time since all this started, and now I am awake again. I've been sitting here on the bed writing this for I don't know how long. It must be long because I'm out of cigarettes, and out of coffee, too. I have to think, and I don't know how to think about this. I have to go to the Acme for a can of coffee and I have to go to Nate's for a pack of Herbert Tareytons, but I don't know how to do that either. That's what it actually feels like. It feels like when you have a choice like this to make, the whole world is just a jigsaw puzzle that doesn't fit together, and until you make that choice you don't know where any of the pieces fit. You don't know how to go shopping anymore. You don't know what the world will look like when you go out the door, and you're too afraid to step out the door to find out.

To tell you the truth, what I wish is that right now the door would open and you would be there and you'd have a can of Maxwell House in one hand and a pack of Tareytons in the other, and you'd perk some coffee and we'd light up, and the whole world would be clear to me once more, and that the dream you told me about—because that's what I've decided to call it—has evaporated into thin air, mysteriously, just like the schnapps in my father's bottle, which I happen to know you never ever touched.

Lily

I folded the letter. I put it back in the envelope. I slipped it under the package of letters. I closed the case. I put the case back under its pile of junk, the ice chest, the magazines, the folding chairs, the tennis rackets.

I went upstairs. I dialed the phone.

"Hello?"

"Josh?" I said.

"Hey, Dad. What's up?"

I don't know how, but the words rushed out of me.

"Josh," I said, "you know that thing about Frau Hellman? You remember?"

"Sure," he said.

"I thought maybe I had it figured out, but I realize I don't. I haven't figured it out at all."

"That's okay," he said. "Me neither."

"The thing is," I said, "I don't think I can do it alone. Josh, will you get on a plane? Will you come out here and help me?"

"Me?"

"Oh God, I'm so sorry for being such an ass. I'm so sorry I hurt you."

"You didn't hurt me, Dad. I was just worried about you. You're going through stuff, remember?"

"I'll buy you a ticket right now," I said. "You can come out tomorrow."

"I don't know, Dad. It's Yom Kippur tomorrow. I don't know if I'm allowed to fly."

"Then the day after tomorrow. Josh, listen"—I found myself just telling him—"Grandpa is dead. He died today, a few hours ago. Quietly, in his sleep, as it should be. Nothing terrible. Nothing out of the ordinary. Just as life is supposed to be. But the only thing that's not as it's supposed to be, is that you are not here with me. I love you, Josh. It's time for us to do our thing—together."

I thought, Oh!—*do our thing*—what a stupid expression. What a way to try to tell him what I was trying to tell him.

But I could hear his little funny bone working, "Well, guess what?" he said in his wonderful smart-ass way, "I'd much rather be bored by you than be bored by some stupid rabbi."

My heart stopped, and tears welled up in my eyes, and I could not think of a joke or a bon mot or a clever riposte, or anything.

And that is what brought me to here, standing beside the car door watching the people flow into the synagogue like rays of light returning to the sun. I had Mrs. Gitlin's ticket in my pocket. The tallis bag in my right hand. My father's little prayer book by my heart. Somewhere inside that building, near the front, the Gitlins were seated near the Futernicks and the Mosemans, and beside them an empty seat. In another row, probably farther back, would be April and her mother, a woman of gratitude and a daughter of poetry. On the bimah the cantor would soon rise and begin the chanting of Kol Nidre—releasing us from our vows to God, so that we might forgive our failures to ourselves. His voice would rise with the ancient melody, heartrending and bittersweet, solemn and purifying. People would close their eyes and sway to the music, desperately seeking some truth within themselves.

I stood by my open car door, thinking, should I go in?

I knew there was no truth to find inside or out. And yet here I was.

Already on the horizon I could see the dark clouds of a hurricane slowly moving toward us. No one wore a raincoat or carried an umbrella. None of them seemed to know they were under siege and the enemy was about to storm the gates, kill the men, rape the women, steal the children. Or perhaps they just knew it wouldn't rain today. Yes, they knew things I did not know. Perhaps they even knew the secret of Heshel Rosenheim.

I looked out past them to where the sea would be, past the synagogue, past the shopping malls, the condo complexes, the Denny's and Einstein's Bagels and Red Lobsters, the nursing homes and hospitals, the golf courses and dog tracks. A storm was coming, no doubt about it. But then again, so was Josh.

And I said to myself, you know, the old man wanted me to say Kaddish for him. So what the hell.

And that's when I took my first step.

ACKNOWLEDGMENTS

Heartfelt thanks to Michael Carlisle, who for some reason had faith, to his father, Henry Carlisle, who had faith even earlier, to my excellent editors at Random House, Dan Menaker and Adam Korn, who worked so hard on this book's behalf, to Cecile Moochneck, who opened the door, to Jennifer Futernick, for an excellent reading, to Emmy Smith, for telling me to write about something Jewish, to Rifka Postrell, for help with the Hebrew and for telling me stories of the early days, to Susanne Stolzenberg, for correcting my German, and most of all to two people without whom this book would never have been written: Sam Lavigne, my son, whose editorial acumen made all the difference, and my dear wife, Gayle Geary, whose insight into the nature of secrets and the possibility of transcendence forms the spiritual core of this book.

In the course of my research, I used many texts and websites, but I would like to single out a few without which this novel would have been much the poorer: *Genesis 1948: The First Arab-Israeli War* by Dan Kurtzman, Abba Eban's *An Autobiography,* David Ben-Gurion's *Israel: A Personal History,* Menachem Begin's *The Revolt,* Konnilyn G. Feig's *Hitler's Death Camps: The Sanity of Madness,* particularly her account of events at Majdanek, including her translation of the list of goods shipped from that camp (which I amended and abridged), Raul Hilberg's *The Destruction of the European Jews,* Yaffa Eliach's *There Once Was a World,* and *The Holocaust Chronicle,* Louis Weber, publisher. And most of all, I am indebted to two heroic writers, Primo Levi and Elie Wiesel, whose every word informs this work.

not me

MICHAEL LAVIGNE

A READER'S GUIDE

A CONVERSATION WITH MICHAEL LAVIGNE

Michael Lavigne discusses *Not Me* with Binnie Kirshenbaum, author of *An Almost Perfect Moment* and *Hester Among the Ruins*. (Editor's note: The emotional and philosophical depth of this discussion reflects the poignant, cerebral, and often controversial elements found in *Not Me*, a novel that thoroughly explores the essence of humanity and is embedded in an authentic, and often disturbing, Holocaust history.)

Binnie Kirshenbaum: Is there such a thing as true redemption? And if so, what of forgiveness? To forgive, to forgive entirely without reservation, is that a kind of redemption, too?

Michael Lavigne: I do not know if redemption is possible. I do know that we must live as if it were. That means not only within ourselves but also in our relationships with those who have tormented us. I suppose the essence of the redemptive stance is empathy—this is the origin of ethical behavior in general. If we live with empathy, we also live with hope. Forgiveness is another matter. Is it possible to forgive without reservation? I suppose that depends on the offense. Frequently in myself I have found that a shadow of distrust seems to lurk beneath the surface of forgiveness.

BK: No doubt there are others, but *The Great Gatsby* and *The Human Stain* come to mind as novels with protagonists who reinvent themselves. How do you see Heshel Rosenheim's reinvention of himself in light of the lies lived by Fitzgerald's and Roth's characters?

ML: You've put Heshel in much too fine a company. But I do see, in both Gatsby and Colman Silk, American types—for all their individuality, they have archetypal qualities that speak to American racism and classism, a critique of American values. Both are stories of America's reinvention of self. And while Heshel certainly reinvents himself, his is a more existential voyage, an accidental one that sends him on a long and reluctant journey. On the other hand, I think of Gunter Grass, who after all these years finally admits his Nazi past—Waffen SS, by the way—so perhaps Heshel is an archetype after all.

BK: It is my own contention that comedy is tragedy taken to its conclusion. To make Michael Rosenheim a comic by profession was, I think, exactly the right choice, but an unexpected one. Why a comic and not a carpenter or lawyer or salesman?

ML: It just happened. I actually tried to change it. I tried to write him as a psychologist, and also as a rabbi; it didn't work. But a comic does seem emblematic. When I was in graduate school it was common to say that the contemporary novel could be only comic. This reflected how ill-at-ease we felt, and still feel, in speaking of ourselves as if we really had a right to a point of view, as if meaning was not merely self-imposed. Seriousness was seen as sentimentality (the worst of all possible crimes!). I never quite got that. I don't see what's wrong with sentiment, as long as you are not just whitewashing the truth. Perhaps I chose "comedian" precisely because a comedian is the least sentimental of creatures, and yet the most covetous of simple things, like love, family, and home. One of my very best friends was a comedian, quite a good one. He died of cancer. I guess I wanted to write something for him. For a time, in college, I was his straight man. What I learned was, as a comedian, you see everything around you very clearly—actually, you see way too much—but then the trick is to avoid engaging with it. As my friend used to say, "You have to see the funny." And that's Michael's MO.

BK: When Heinrich Mueller refers to himself as a "pencil pusher," Adolf Eichmann is echoed. And later in the novel, Michael notes seeing Eichmann's eyes in Heshel's eyes. How deliberate is this parallel, and does it further the conversation on the banality of evil?

ML: It is deliberate, of course. We are all insiders when it comes to evil, all part of the machine that causes human suffering. It becomes clear to us only if our field of vision is pierced from the outside, when some object that has been out of range, or vaguely in the periphery, forces itself into focus. In *Not Me,* Heshel's line of sight is interrupted by Moskovitz, but also (perhaps not unusually) by his own sense of superiority, which forces him to engage in various acts of kindness that ultimately explode his illusions. In a general sense, the banality of evil does not describe a merely personal moral blindness: it is societal. In this sense, the Nazism of *Not Me* and Heshel Rosenheim is a marker not only for fanatical movements in our own time, but for our failure as ordinary, decent people in the West to come to terms with even the most basic issues of human welfare: health, poverty, race. For me personally, writing this book required a willingness at least to try to explore my own blindness, and examine how my own illusions of moral certainty have hurt those around me.

By the way, I was also thinking of Milton. For him, the source of evil is injured pride. This sense of injury as a source of identity is at the heart of *Not Me,* and also, it would seem, of so many of the world's woes.

BK: If we live a lie, do we at some point come to believe it to be true, or to be a greater truth than the facts may show?

ML: The lie is the greater truth. The identities we construct to fool everyone but ourselves in fact fool us the most. Mythology is much stronger than fact. Ask any Israeli or Palestinian.

BK: Early on, before he has any idea what those journals contain, Michael wants no part of them. Does he harbor a suspicion that something is not as it seems with his family? Is it foreboding or is he simply not very interested in his father's life and history?

ML: Two things here. First, I think children fear certain kinds of knowledge about their parents, just as parents fear certain kinds of knowledge about their children. Braving that frontier is one of the tasks I assign Michael.

As for secrets, there are none. They roam about the house and everyone knows they are there—it is merely the specifics that elude us. My wife, Gayle, grew up in such a house. All throughout her childhood she was riddled with doubt about her mother—like the kids in *Not Me,* she imagined all kinds of scenarios—her mother was a secret communist, her mother was a spy, her mother was . . . on and on. So many things seemed somehow out of whack. Naturally, this raised great doubts in Gayle's mind about who she herself was, about what she could trust to be real. It was only when she was seventeen that she learned the truth. This, by the way, was one of my starting points in writing *Not Me*.

BK: Is it love that awakens the humanity in Heinrich Mueller? Is love his salvation? Or was it not love at all, but a redirection of hatred? And what role does love play in his newfound compassion?

ML: It is actually conversation—his ability to have one. Love comes at the end of that conversation, not at the beginning. What emerges first is empathy—and this only slowly. Empathy arises from contiguity, I suppose; from rubbing shoulders, but not in the same old way. Heinrich had plenty of contact with Jews in the camps, yet he never saw them as anything but Other. That's the issue of blindness coming up again. The Jews were always right there, he just couldn't see them. Somehow, as Heshel, he allows them to enter his field of vision. I don't think I can explain it more than that. It's a mystery. And like everything mysterious, it is always present, just invisible. Call it the string theory of the soul. There are all these dimensions, alternative universes, all around us, all the time. Then suddenly, for no reason, two of these collide and bang! A new universe is born. For Heshel, it is not about love or hate, but about reconfiguring his universe of perception so that he actually can love and hate; then there is this wholeness in him that transcends categories.

BK: A disturbing effect is created with the details of uniforms. Heinrich/Heshel is so pointedly unimpressed with his lack of a uniform as a soldier in Israel (such a lovely note is hit with his being pleased with the Eisenhower jacket he gets). Later Moskovitz tells him he looks good in his uniform. This reflects the intent of SS uniforms, the elegance of them, and how attractive the men looked in uniform. Is there something inherently fascist and/or sexually exciting about all uniforms? Or were you getting at something else with these parallels?

ML: No one else has mentioned this business of the Eisenhower jacket, which seemed so important to me when I wrote it. It does completely encapsulate Heinrich and at the same time point to the Heshel he is one day to become. However, I myself never drew the connection with Moskovitz's remark—I was merely thinking about her feelings—her love and anger and her inability or refusal to express them at that moment. The uniform is both distancing and intimate. It romanticizes. The object recedes, and the space is filled up with feeling; all men look good in uniform. Heinrich's vanity separates him from those around him, but in the end he becomes the uniform, doesn't he? It is while wearing it, finally embracing what it seems to stand for, that he kills the two people he most cherishes.

BK: How does Michael's distance from his own son mirror his relationship with his father? Is the distance between both sets of fathers and sons the by-product of secrets kept for too long?

ML: Michael's distance from Josh is a reflection of his distance from himself. Memory and love are connected, just as are memory and ethics. In this regard I always think of E. M. Forster's "only connect." Michael lives in a world of entropy—nothing holds together. Michael actually has no secrets, only holes. Perhaps these are caused by Heshel's secrets, but I rather think it is his horror at his own past that torments him. If his love for his sister destroyed her, even with the kindest of intentions, what might it do to his son? Certainly he had to ask himself that question. Beyond this, though, I think I was asking myself—how do we hold our lives together when we truly have no clear sense of identity? How can we love if we are disconnected from ourselves? It's not just Michael's problem. It's the condition of our lives.

BK: There are moments when there seems to be something of Raskolnikov in Heshel, when it seems to be guilt and guilt alone that is driving him. Or on some level does Heshel continue to believe that as Heinrich, he never did anything very wrong?

ML: I think on every level he thinks he did something wrong. But he pities himself enough not to punish himself or turn himself in. Even though he spends the rest of his life atoning for, and even absorbing the identity of, his victims, he does it in secret. What does that say about him? Like Raskolnikov, it is not merely guilt that drives him, but a sense of inherent superiority. This is also what he has to break through. Does he succeed? The reader can judge. In general our problem is not that we don't see that we've done wrong, but what we do with that information. How do we repress it, transform it? How does it debilitate us, innervate us?

BK: I know a woman who, as an adult, learned that her adored and beloved grandfather had been an SS officer and served time in prison for war crimes. How does someone—can someone—reconcile these opposing forces of revulsion and hatred with filial love?

ML: I am curious to know how she dealt with it. I think filial love is very complex, as it is wrapped up in one's own identity to such a great extent. It is rarely without its compliment of resentments and anger, yet its pull can be irresistible, even when parents and children no longer speak to one another, or speak only in generalities. But I do think that a child, however grown, cannot be whole unless he or she reconciles with his or her parents, regardless of their crimes. In Michael's case, love wins. It is important, not only for his own well-being, but for that of his son. But even greater than that is the role of love in holding off the strong forces of chaos and cruelty that wish to, and often do, rule the world. The power of family love is to bind us together against these forces. The more we extend that family, the safer we will be.

BK: During his time in Israel, Heinrich's anti-Semitism periodically revealed itself in his thoughts and to the reader. This struck me as absolutely true. Does he really never again harbor these thoughts? Is it possible to entirely eradicate our own prejudices and bigotry? Or must a bit of it always linger?

ML: I don't know. I really don't. To what extent do we ever fully slough off the prejudices of our youth? To what extent does immersion in the other eradicate the old self? Years ago, I lived with a non-Jewish woman. Everything was fine until one day when we got into a huge fight about something, I can't remember what, and she called me a dirty Jew. She immediately retracted it, of course, but there it was. I have many residual prejudices of my own. They don't guide my life, or my behavior, but they lurk, and every so often come into consciousness. By the way, the woman I spoke of—long after we broke up, she converted to Judaism. Strange, but I hadn't remembered that until just now. In that way, I am like my character, Michael. So many things are repressed; you never know what is really driving you.

BK: If we are to assume that Heinrich the Terrible indeed transformed into Heshel the Good, hope is offered. Why is such a transformation so slow in coming to our collective human nature? Why after it is proclaimed "never again" has genocide happened not only again and again, but the world has consistently turned a blind eye? Have we not learned anything from history?

ML: The only way for the world to change is for people to actually listen to each other's stories. This is not so easy. At heart, I don't believe human nature can change. However, I have seen, and I know it to be true, that individual people can change in quite astounding ways. But to do so, one must constantly struggle against one's own instinct and will. It requires a very high level of self-awareness and motivation.

But let's face it, people enjoy conflict; we cannot learn from history because we are always rewriting it. It's fine and good to say "Hey, you guys, stop shooting at each other." But when somebody crosses our own turf, it's a different matter.

So much of conflict is in the realm of imagination. You get a Muslim and a Hindi in the same room. They sit down to dinner, share jokes, and have a nice time. But you take the idea of Islam, and the idea of Hinduism—and then all the sudden you have Kashmir, and everyone is killing each other. How is that possible? As it happens, that seems to be the subject of my next book—not Kashmir, but the tragedy that while conflict is largely imaginary, it is at the same time absolutely inescapable.

BK: What elements of *Not Me,* if any, are autobiographical?

ML: When I wrote *Not Me,* I was convinced nothing in it was autobiographical. And indeed, there are no Nazis in my family, and no Holocaust survivors, either. No terrible family secrets, no journals, no horrible parenting. My real father was born in Newark, New Jersey. I don't think fiction should be autobiographical—it's so much more interesting and pleasant to make things up. But of course, much of me did intrude into the story on slippered feet, so to speak. At first it was the use of familiar locations, which helped in creating a sense of reality for my characters. The father's apartment is my parent's apartment, much exaggerated. Kibbutz Naor looks very much like the one I lived on for a short time when I was seventeen. But then I noticed that little events, memories of which I was only partially conscious, crept into the story. The violin in the closet (I had forgotten entirely that my real sister did play the violin as a child), the business with the magic act for show-and-tell (in real life, it was playing the saxophone—I stood up to play and realized I had forgotten how—but I got so many laughs, everyone thought I was being awful on purpose: a great life lesson)—things like that. And of course, I must have been dealing with my own father's death, though I was only vaguely aware of it as I was writing. But no, the novel itself is not autobiographical!

BK: Please tell us a little about your writing process and perhaps you can use that to segue into a brief mention about the contents of your next project.

ML: I don't like to talk about what I'm working on, because, who knows, I may just tear the whole thing up and start on something else. But mainly, if I talk about it, it loses some of its energy, and becomes harder to write. My process, though, is to begin with a premise—a "what if"—and go from there. I don't know who will inhabit the book, and certainly I don't know what will happen except in the vaguest outline. I do write notes from time to time, but they are also in the form of "what ifs." I like to set up road blocks for myself, allow things to happen for reasons I have not yet understood. I sometimes create histories of characters, timelines, relationship schematics, things like that. I also do an enormous amount of research, mostly as I'm writing. But basically, I just sit down and write at least three pages a day, five days a week, and see what happens. In *Not Me,* the premise was "What if my father were a Nazi?" In the new book the premise is something like: "What if someone frees himself from tyranny, only to become the victim of something even worse?" I'm trying to be unclear. I hope I've succeeded.

QUESTIONS AND TOPICS FOR DISCUSSION

1. How does the nature of memory play an important part in this story? What traps and opportunities does memory create for Michael and for the people around him?

2. Discuss the role of place setting in this novel and in fiction in general. How, and why, are places "characters," and how does place affect you personally?

3. What kind of person is Heinrich? Do you know any people like him? Could you be such a person?

4. What feelings are aroused in you by the descriptions of the concentration camps and by Heinrich/Heshel's role in the murder of thousands?

5. Why do you think the author opted to make Heinrich a bookkeeper as opposed to a Nazi soldier?

6. Hannah Arendt created the phrase "the banality of evil," referring to Adolph Eichmann, the architect of the Nazi death camp system, and those like Eichmann who commit unspeakable acts under the guise of "just doing their job." Does Heinrich fit that description?

7. Do you think it plausible for a person to change as dramatically as Heinrich/Heshel did? Is it plausible that someone like Heinrich could find salvation by embodying the nature of his enemy?

8. What is the role of God in this novel?

9. Everyone tells lies. Why do we lie to ourselves and others? What secret knowledge do we all carry with us? Consider a time in your life when you have been unsure whether to reveal or to conceal an important truth, and had to choose between "the truth shall set you free" and "what they don't know won't hurt them." How did you resolve it?

10. Every family has secrets. What are the effects of family secrets and how do they affect Michael's life? How have they affected yours? What happens when they are uncovered?

11. Part of the plot structure of this novel is in the form of a mystery or detective story. Is it successful in sustaining an aura of suspense until the novel's conclusion? Do you feel the mystery of Heshel's identity has been solved? Why or why not?

12. Is guilt what drives Heshel Rosenheim? If so, what is the true nature of that guilt? If not, what is it that drives him? Do you think guilt itself can be a conduit to redemption?

13. If Heshel Rosenheim is indeed Heinrich Mueller, do you think his son should be able to forgive him? Could you forgive him? Can the good that Heshel/Heinrich has done in his life make up for the bad? What is the role of good works in the balance sheet of redemption?

14. Michael's relationship with his sister is unique within the novel for its purity and wholesomeness—yet it is this relationship that pushes Michael to commit a terrible crime, and become, in

essence, like the man in the journals. What are the moral implications for Michael, for causing destruction in the name of love?

15. The relationships between fathers and sons in this novel are ambiguous and complex. In what ways do they disagree on how to live their lives? Which of the generational disagreements would you attribute to historical change, and which to individual character differences?

16. April Love is a mysterious woman who keeps popping up in the oddest places, including in bed with a man ten years her junior. What does she represent to you? Why did the author bring her into the story?

MICHAEL LAVIGNE was born in Newark, New Jersey. He began seriously writing fiction only at midlife and was a participant in the Squaw Valley Community of Writers. *Not Me* is his first novel, and he is currently working on his second, set in Moscow, where he once lived. He lives in San Francisco with his wife, Gayle.

ABOUT THE TYPE

This book was set in Sabon, a typeface designed by the well-known German typographer Jan Tschichold (1902–74). Sabon's design is based on the original letterforms of Claude Garamond and was created specifically to be used for three sources: foundry type for hand composition, Linotype, and Monotype. Tschichold named his typeface for the famous Frankfurt typefounder Jacques Sabon, who died in 1580.